Peonies FOR Paige

Peonies for Paige

In Bloom Series Book 1

KASEY KENNEDY

*For my mom, Sarah Kathern Walters,
the most avid reader I've ever known.
I miss you every day.*

CHAPTER ONE

PAIGE PULLED A handful of light pink peonies from the bucket in the sink. Her hands were cold from the water, and the silver ring with a carved Celtic design, a high school graduation gift from her grandmother Rosie, slid around as she gently shook the flowers. She turned towards the worktable and put the flowers into a bucket where her coworkers–Lauren, her closest friend at In Bloom, and Tilly, a fun-loving college sopho-more–could reach them.

Paige picked up her empty spray bottle and took it to the sink. She twisted the cold tap and was surprised to see a small trickle come out–the pressure had been fine a few moments before. She turned the handle off and on again. This time there was no trickle, only a gurgling noise. She called to Anna Lee, the owner of the flower shop, "Something's wrong with the water pressure."

Anna Lee came over and twisted the handles. She was a strik-ing, albeit petite, figure. She wore a floor-length, prairie-style dress covered with bold pink hibiscus flowers on a bright purple background. Her shiny, silver-gray hair had chunky layers falling past her shoulders and soft strands framing her face. She wore a chunky pink beaded necklace with matching earrings.

"That's not good. I better call the plumber and nip this in the bud," Anna Lee said, raising her left eyebrow. "Luckily, my plumber is top-notch. Trained by the best–his father. And he's not hard on the eyes either." She chuckled. "The pleasure of owning an antique building."

The In Bloom flower shop of Bloomington, IL was in a historic Standard Oil building, a former gas station and full-service garage. Its retail shop and consultation area took up the old station and one of the garage bays. The other bay was the workspace where they currently sat working on bouquets and boutonnieres for today's wedding.

The building always made Paige smile when she pulled into the parking lot. The garage doors were painted with a mural of flowers–roses, tulips, lilies, dahlias, and her favorite, peonies. It reminded her of her grandmother's garden, which she missed deeply. As a child, whenever her three brothers got together and started picking on her, she would hop on her bike and pedal the mile to her grandma Rosie's house. A needed refuge where a cookie and a hug were always waiting.

"How old is the building?" Paige asked.

"Around ninety years. They built it to last, but it needs routine maintenance, like most of us." Anna Lee smiled and patted Paige on the arm before returning to the worktable.

Paige stubbornly gave the handle one more turn. This time, there was no gurgle, but she felt the pipes shimmy like they were being shaken from below. There was a loud popping noise, and the faucet shot into the air, rising with the force of water that shook the pipes. "Oh, no!" she shouted, as the water hit her.

The cold water drenched her hair and *The Big Bang Theory* t-shirt she wore, and she shrieked as the water ran down her jeans and splashed upon her pink tennis shoes. *Oh bother, klutzy me did it again.*

Anna Lee dove under the sink, turning off the water supply with the grace of a synchronized swimmer. A retired synchronized swimmer.

Tilly and Lauren jumped off their stools and hurried over. Lauren grabbed dry hand towels off the counter. "Oh boy, Paige," she said, smiling and obviously trying to hold back a laugh.

"Go ahead and laugh! I know I look ridiculous." Paige giggled. She grabbed an offered towel and began drying her long, auburn hair.

Tilly helped Anna Lee stand up. "Are you okay?" she asked.

Anna Lee pulled a leaf off her dress. "I'm fine. Working in my garden keeps me in shape."

"Your reflexes are amazing," Paige said as she dabbed the water on her shirt. "I was so shocked by the water spraying all over me, I couldn't even think about a turn-off valve."

"I'm calling the plumber right now," Anna Lee said, leaving the workroom. "There are clean work shirts in the office. Grab a dry one and change."

It took a few minutes for Paige to dry herself off as best she could, change her shirt, and for the excitement to die down. Anna Lee returned and roamed around the worktable, advising and teasing the team.

Paige put one earbud in so she could listen to Anna Lee or her coworkers if needed while also listening to *The Hitchhiker's Guide to the Galaxy*, one of her favorite sci-fi novels. She'd fallen in love with it as a teenager when she'd discovered it in her oldest brother Jack's room.

Paige missed something Lauren said and came back to the conversation when Lauren nudged her on the arm. "What are you listening to today, Paige?" Lauren teased.

She squirmed on her stool. "An audiobook." She hoped Lauren wouldn't ask for the name of it. As an English literature major, she felt a little silly confessing her love of sci-fi to her friends. She already felt like an odd bird around her coworkers. They were both from the Chicago suburbs, had attended enormous high schools and seemed like exotic, colorful parrots where she was more like a sparrow.

"Well, how many more days until you leave for New York to take the publishing world by storm?" Lauren wrapped the bouquet she was working on with a navy silk ribbon.

Paige stopped the audiobook app on her phone before responding. "Eight! Can you believe it? I've been talking about the internship for months and it's finally almost here." As Paige picked up a rose stripper to remove the prickly thorns and unwanted stems from the rose in her hand, a twinge of nervousness bubbled up. She had not heard from her contact at the publishing company in months, and she hoped everything was on track for her start date. She made a mental note to follow up ASAP.

"Time has a funny way of always moving forward. I'll be glad when finals are over and summer break starts. But I will be sad when you leave." Lauren frowned at Paige, but it didn't cover the sparkle in her denim blue eyes.

Paige scoffed. "You're leaving for Europe! You won't be sad."

Lauren smiled. "Maybe you're right, but I'll be a tiny bit sad."

Anna Lee stopped behind them. "I'll be sad when both of you are gone. Don't forget the sendoff party for Paige next Friday. I'll bring in a cake. Even if you're not working, stop by and get a piece so I don't take any leftovers home. Neither I nor Salty need the calories." Salty, her orange tabby cat, jumped up on the worktable to see what was going on when he heard his name. He probably thought it was time to jump in his backpack for the ride home on Anna Lee's purple scooter.

The front doorbell jingled, and Anna Lee left the garage bay to check on the customer.

As Lauren and Tilly talked about their weekend plans, Paige thought about her growing to-do list. It seemed for every task she marked off, three more were added. This weekend she had to study for finals, which meant putting off final moving preparation tasks until Wednesday, after exams. She'd be in the library tonight, preparing for her Shakespeare final on Monday.

Returning from the retail side, Anna Lee called out, "Lunchtime, ladies. I'll keep an eye on the storefront while you eat. We have a lot of work to do before we take these flowers to the venue. Try to keep your break to thirty minutes."

"Is the plumber coming soon, Anna Lee?" Lauren asked.

"No, he can't make it until tomorrow. It'll be all right. The water is working in the bathroom. We just can't use this sink until he comes."

Lauren nodded. "Glad we have another option."

They went to the tiny office behind the retail counter to grab their lunches. Paige pulled her lunch and a book from her backpack.

Sitting at the picnic table behind the building, the three young women ate lunch and talked about finals and boyfriends. Paige brought out her book when the topic of boyfriends came up. She didn't want to think about her ex-fiancé, Caleb. Though it had been five months since he called off their engagement, the pain was fresh and sharp, stinging like a paper cut.

After break, they gathered around the worktable and turned their focus to the wedding centerpieces. Anna Lee's model arrangement had a twelve-inch, round tree slice. On top of it were three mason jars filled with sprigs of baby's breath and the light pink peonies. Lying between the jars, on the tree slice, were two pale pink roses. Paige thought they were almost perfect. *If only they had some dark pink peonies, they would be perfect.* As much as she didn't want to talk about boyfriends with the other women, she couldn't help feeling sentimental around wedding flowers.

After they finished the centerpieces, Anna Lee asked for a volunteer to help deliver them. Everyone knew the ask was coming, as Anna Lee always asked for a volunteer to drive the van. She said she didn't mind driving it, but everyone knew she'd rather not. Over lunch, they'd discussed it and Paige had drawn the short straw since she didn't have a date waiting–other than the library and *Macbeth*.

"I'll drive, Anna Lee," she said.

"Thank you, Paige. Lauren, will you watch the front while we load up the arrangements?"

They loaded the van in ten minutes. Paige checked her watch. If all went well, she could grab dinner in her apartment and be at the library by six p.m.

"Want to meet for coffee tomorrow?" Lauren asked as she wiped the clippings and other debris off the worktable. "It may be our last chance to get together before we each take off for the summer."

Paige swept up the leaves and clippings that had fallen on the floor. "I love that idea. I plan to spend the day in the library, studying for finals. All right if we meet on campus?" Paige walked the dustpan over to the garbage can.

"Certainly. I work in the morning. How about two?"

"Perfect. I'll be ready for a break by then. Text me when you get to campus, and I'll meet you in the student center."

PAIGE AND ANNA Lee delivered the flowers to the venue and had ample time to set up the tables. When they finished, they stood back to admire their work. The overhead lights in the reception hall were on low and strings of battery-operated fairy lights circled around the centerpieces, giving the space a dreamy quality.

Anna Lee took the boutonnières to the men's dressing room and Paige carried the box of bouquets to the room where the bride and bridesmaids were getting ready. She offered her congratulations to the bride and left quickly.

Back in the reception hall, Paige found Anna Lee talking to the wedding coordinator. Paige joined the women in conversation, hoping it would not take long. Her stomach growled and Anna Lee laughed.

"I think that's our cue to leave. Ms. Smithfield, it was a pleasure talking to you. Let me introduce you to my assistant, Paige Bell. Paige, this is Ms. Smithfield."

"It's nice to meet you, Ms. Smithfield," Paige said, extending her hand to shake, a smile on her face.

"Likewise. I love your uniform!" Ms. Smithfield eyed the logo on Paige's purple polo shirt with "In Bloom" stitched in white lettering, pink daisies replacing the o's.

"Thanks! Is there anything left to do, Anna Lee?" Paige hoped she didn't sound anxious, but she had a lot of tasks on her list.

"No, we're all wrapped up. Let's go."

In the van, Anna Lee sang along to the Janis Joplin song, "Me and Bobby McGee" on the radio. Paige appreciated the lack of conversation as she ran through her evening's schedule.

Back at In Bloom, they removed the containers that had carried the arrangements from the van. As they unloaded, Anna Lee asked Paige if she would drive the van to her house on Thursday morning to bring several pieces of rehabbed furniture that Anna Lee had repaired and repainted to sell in the flower shop. She would also have flowers from her garden to pick and bring in. Paige agreed and marveled that she only had two more days of work at In Bloom. She would miss Anna Lee and her friends, but she was excited to move to New York and start her internship.

CHAPTER TWO

ENTERING HER APARTMENT, Paige took a few moments to survey the mess. There were open boxes for items that would be stored at her parents' house while she was in New York for the summer. On the blue loveseat were two suitcases that she would fill with clothes, beauty supplies, and accessories to take with her. She had a chart that mapped out her outfits for the ten weeks she'd be in New York–ensuring she was taking pieces that would serve multiple outfits. She took a deep breath, grabbed her planner, and flipped to her current "to-do" list and scanned the tasks listed. "Call Mom" was the easiest one to knock off.

She picked up her phone and dialed her mom's number. While the phone rang, she slid a frozen pizza into the small oven in her kitchen and set the egg timer on the counter for twelve minutes. When her mom answered, Paige thought about setting a separate timer to limit her time on the phone. If she wasn't careful, they could talk for an hour.

Paige asked how things were going at home and listened to her mom's updates. Sue Bell was a yoga instructor. It amazed Paige that her mother had built a yoga community in rural central Illinois. Paige and her brothers were thankful when their mom grew her practice. Her dad was a painter, and they'd had to learn about tightening belts growing up; it could be months between art sales.

Now adults, Paige and her brothers were averse to small business or commissioned careers. Her older brothers, Jack and Brian, were accountants at separate firms in Chicago and her younger brother, Logan, was planning to go to law school once he finished high school and college.

The timer went off and Paige grabbed an oven mitt. She adjusted the phone on her shoulder and said "uh huh" for the twentieth time. Placing the pizza on top of the stove, she took a plate out of the drainer.

"Honey," Sue asked, "when do we need to come get your things?"

"Friday. I have finals through Wednesday and will need more time to pack. Plus, I work Thursday and Friday. I've got a hotel reservation for Friday night since my flight is early Saturday. Someone will need to come back and get my car from the airport. Don't forget that." Paige took the pizza cutter from a drawer and began cutting.

"Ah, then your dad and Logan will come. I have three group classes and two private sessions. Friday's my busiest day of the week." Sue said she wanted to start dinner soon herself. Paige looked at the digital clock on the counter. It was almost six-thirty. If her mom was starting dinner now, they wouldn't eat until late.

"Well, I won't keep you mom, if you need to start dinner. I need to eat and then go to the library to study for my Shakespeare final." Paige picked up a slice of pizza and took a bite.

"Oh, I almost forgot, honey. I heard today that Caleb got engaged to Moria Banks. I don't know how long ago or if you've heard."

Paige slumped down into the hard chair at her small kitchen table with a thud. "What? Really? No, I didn't hear that. Wow."

Images of Caleb flashed through her mind. Their first date, the day they got engaged, the engagement pictures in the hayfield at the "golden hour." He'd called off their engagement on Christmas Eve. She'd thought they were exchanging gifts and had his wrapped gift in her lap when they had stopped at the gas station. When he'd gotten back in the car after pumping gas, he'd said, "Look, Paige. I've decided I'm not ready to get married. I'm telling my parents tonight but wanted to tell you first."

Wait, what did he say? Paige had been shocked, which was beneficial because it had kept her from crying in front of him. At least she'd managed that dignity. Once she'd gotten home and had her mom's gentle arms wrapped around her, she'd bawled until she dry-heaved.

Her mom was talking but Paige had no idea what she'd said in the last sixty seconds. "Um, mom I gotta run. I have a date with ol' Willie, you know."

She hung up the phone without waiting for a reply. There was too much to do to worry about what Caleb was doing with his life. He wasn't going to NYC in a week to work on his career. It was fine. Paige planned to stay single until she was thirty, anyway.

PAIGE ALMOST BACKED out of meeting Lauren for coffee on Saturday. She pondered whether an extra hour of studying would serve her better. But when she walked into the student center and saw Lauren's bright smile, she was glad that she came.

She grabbed a latte and joined Lauren at the bar-like ledge that ran along the front window where it would be easy to people watch.

Lauren looked up from her "German for Dummies" book and gave Paige a lopsided grin. "Hello! Glad you could join me."

"Hi! German for Dummies? Don't you know you're supposed to write "learners" on a piece of paper and tape the paper over the "Dummies" part of the title? A teacher suggested that once. I'd rather consider myself a learner over a dummy any day of the week." She sat on the stool and tucked her backpack under her feet, one foot on the strap so no one could grab it.

"That's a cool idea. Not surprised to hear that come out of your mouth. Classic Paige."

"Boring classic Paige, right?" Paige smirked.

"No. Classic, smart Paige. Well, are you ready for finals?" Lauren took the top of her coffee cup off and blew on the contents.

"Not yet, but I will be. It's hard concentrating when I haven't heard from the publishing company since the original acceptance. I'm a little nervous–feels like I've been ghosted."

"You haven't heard from them? You're supposed to go in a week! That's *verrückt*!"

"Um, bless you?"

Lauren laughed. "*Verrückt* is German for crazy. At least," she paused and tilted her head, "I think it is."

"I hope you aren't required to use that word while you're there! But it's the right word for my situation. After their offer in February, nothing. I am getting worried. I leave next Saturday! You'd be freaked out too, right?" Paige lifted her coffee cup and wrapped both hands around it, breathing in the delicious cinnamon and vanilla aroma.

"Yes, I would. I've triple-checked all of my transportation and hotel reservations this week. Ten weeks in Europe is going to fly by and I am hoping for no hiccups! Have you thought about reaching out to them?"

"Yes, it's on my to-do list. I need to concentrate on finals first. I'm sure it's fine. I'll follow up mid-week if I still haven't heard anything. You're lucky to spend the summer in Europe. Well, I shouldn't say lucky, you didn't win a sweepstakes or anything. You are focused and determined, and this was a dream of yours that you made happen. You are going to accomplish great things in your life. I'm so grateful to have a friend like you. Meeting you at In Bloom last year was a blessing." Paige leaned towards Lauren and put her arm around Lauren's back, with a squeeze. She rested her head on Lauren's shoulder for a few seconds.

"Aw, thanks friend." Lauren leaned her head on Paige's. "I'm glad we met too! You have a calming grace about you, you have been so supportive of me this past year as I've switched majors and changed my summer plans, all against my parents' wishes."

"You switched from pre-law to a business major and you're still planning to pursue an MBA, I don't know why they aren't supportive of that."

"I told you," she sighed. "They're both lawyers and they wanted me to become one too. I thought that's what I wanted as well, until I got into college and had my eyes opened to other opportunities."

"Oh Lauren, your parents will come around." Paige took a sip of her coffee. "They have to! You're brilliant and you're going to be super successful! I know it. They will be very proud of you. I'm sure they are now but they're not sure how to show you."

Lauren smiled, but there was hurt in her eyes. "I hope so. Enough about those open wounds. I'm taking the two books you gave me on my trip. I can't wait to read them, but I hope I'm just reading while actually traveling, on a bus, plane or train. There is so much sightseeing to do while I'm in each location! I'll post on my vlog often so keep an eye on it."

"Oh, I will, believe me," Paige said. "What are you going to do if you meet your soulmate on your trip?"

"Well, that wouldn't be so bad, would it? My dream is to live abroad after school. It'd be great to fall in love and have a reason to go back."

"But you have a few more years of school first to get both your bachelor's degree and your MBA."

"Oh, you're too practical," Lauren said, rolling her eyes and shaking her head back and forth. "And you're probably right. I won't look for love while I'm traveling. But if it finds me, then *c'est la vie*! Speaking of love lives, when are you going to get back out there?"

"Nope. Not it. I'm not dating! I must stay focused. Besides, I'm not ready to get my heart trampled on again." Paige remembered the pain of the breakup and shuddered.

"Just because you date someone, it doesn't mean you'll get your heart trampled. Let's make a pact. If you don't fall in love with anyone before I get back from Europe, I get to set you up with someone, a blind date. And if I don't meet anyone on my trip, you set me up on a blind date. Deal?" Lauren's blue eyes took on a mischievous sparkle.

Paige hesitated. Dating at all was a terrible idea. A blind date was even worse. But maybe Lauren would forget "the pact" before she came back from Europe. "Deal," she said, gulping down the last of her coffee. "I need to get to the library and continue studying. See you next week!"

CHAPTER THREE

$\mathcal{F}$INALS WERE TOUGH, but they provided a needed distraction from thoughts of Caleb and his new engagement. Thursday morning, Paige drove to In Bloom to pick up the van, she grabbed the keys from the office, and then drove to Anna Lee's house. She parked in the brick driveway and smiled at the house. It was a pink two-story Victorian, with purple window trim and doors, and Paige's favorite feature–a turret. She dreamed of spending an afternoon in the room, reading. She hopped out of the van and walked to the back gate. Everyone knew that if there was sunlight outside, Anna Lee was probably in the garden, and that's where Paige found her.

Anna Lee was in a long dress that was tied up on one side with a piece of twine, exposing black rubber boots that rose above her knees.

"Good morning, Anna Lee!" called Paige as she walked through the black metal gate.

"Mornin'," Anna Lee said, turning towards Paige. She stood beside the tiny garage that served as a garden shed and scooter storage, holding a pair of snips in her hand. "The furniture that needs to go to the store is on the back porch. You can move it all yourself. Load it up first, then grab another bucket from the shed, will you? There are more peonies to cut than I expected."

14

Paige walked up the wooden steps to the back door. Inside the screened in porch, she easily identified the furniture that needed to go to In Bloom—they had Anna Lee's custom leaf-shaped price stickers on them. There were three wooden chairs that had circles cut into the seats to hold planters. Anna Lee had painted them in bright pastel colors and added whimsical details like vines running up the legs. These were a hot seller; they rarely sat in the store for more than a few days before they were sold.

After loading the chairs into the van, Paige walked into the garage and located the stack of plastic buckets in the corner. She looked around and marveled at the amount of garden paraphernalia in the small space. There had to be three rakes, at least four shovels, and several garden hoes along the walls and no less than six worktables covered with pots and small hand tools. Anna Lee sold starts of flowers from her garden in the flower shop. Paige could see that she was filling small pots with seeds on two of the tables.

Outside, Paige asked if she should add water to the bucket. Anna Lee nodded as she reached for another peony flower.

"Those peonies are taller than the ones we have at home," Paige said as she brought over the bucket with water.

"These are tree peonies." The way Anna Lee said peonies, it sounded like pine-ys. "You're used to herbaceous peonies that die back after the first frost. These lose their leaves but don't die back so they grow taller. The pink ones with the pale, white patches are called Multicolored Butterfly and the white peonies with the purple and golden yellow in the middle are called Do-Jean. The DoJean plant was cultivated by Sir Peter Smithers, a British spy and botanist." Anna Lee cut two more flowers and handed them to Paige.

Paige marveled at Anna Lee's knowledge of plants as she took a deep whiff of the flowers in her hand, enjoying the sweet smell before putting them in the bucket. She looked at the small tree

Anna Lee was cutting from and noticed a green canvas cloth that attached to the garage on one side and to several poles in the yard that covered the row of peonies. Looking down the row of peonies, she saw several shades of pink and white flowers.

"I love these, Anna Lee! They're beautiful!" she exclaimed. "Are these being used in a wedding this weekend?"

"We will use some of them for a wedding," she replied. "We'll make the arrangements tomorrow. Some of them will be dried for wreaths; we'll hang those up in the office. Whelp," Anna Lee changed the subject. "You ready for New York?"

Paige felt as though she would grow wings and fly thinking about the trip. "Absolutely! Can't believe it's finally here. A mere forty-eight hours until my flight. I'll have a little time to settle in before I start on Monday. I sent an email this morning asking what time I should be there. It's strange that I haven't heard from them since the initial offer letter in February. Oh well, it's a big company, I'm sure they have a plan for me. I hope things go well this summer and they offer me a permanent job for when I graduate next spring. That's my dream, you know."

Anna Lee harrumphed. "I don't know why you gotta run off to New York to fulfill your dreams. Plants should just bloom where they're planted."

Paige smiled. "The big publishing houses are in New York, Anna Lee, and I want to make an impact on books. I want to be an editor so I can help writers bring their stories to the market. Maybe someday I can move back here and still be in the industry, but to get started, I need to go."

"Yeah, yeah. I know. Everyone has to go *out there*," she waved her hand dismissively, "to find themselves. Find something. That's just hogwash! Let's get these buckets in the van and head to the store. Salty!" she called, and the fat orange cat came running from the back of the yard. Paige hadn't noticed him.

"That's the best cat. I've never seen one come when called and we had lots of cats on the farm. Well, we were pretty loose with their names. That probably didn't help." Paige lifted two buckets and started for the van.

"Salty is my buddy. He's special," Anna Lee agreed. "Oh, this is your first day in the shop this week. The water issue you noticed was worse than I originally thought. The plumber started yesterday–he has to replace all the pipes. It's a big ol' mess. Might have to close the store a couple days next week, but I hope not."

"Yikes. I'm sorry to hear that. Besides the disruption, sounds like an expensive fix." Paige closed the back doors of the van.

"Yes, that's why we save for a rainy day. And this one is pouring!" Anna Lee laughed and scooped Salty up. He'd been winding himself around her legs. "I'll grab Salty's backpack and jump on the scooter. See you at the store. Drive safe."

Paige climbed into the van and wondered how the workday would go if there was a plumber in the shop. It might be a needed diversion from thinking about all the things she needed to complete before her flight on Saturday.

CHAPTER FOUR

PAIGE BEAT ANNA Lee to the store and waited in the van, checking the to-do list in her planner. Lauren pulled in and parked next to the van, so Paige threw the planner into her tote bag and jumped out. Tilly pulled up just as Paige's feet hit the ground.

Paige walked to the back of the van and opened the doors, waving the others over to help unload the furniture and buckets of flowers. "Aren't these gorgeous?" she asked as Lauren and Tilly approached.

"Scrumptious!" Tilly made a smacking sound with her lips.

"Hey, they're not to eat, silly," Lauren smirked.

"Guess I'm hungry," Tilly replied.

Everyone grabbed a painted chair and a bucket of flowers and carried them to the back door. Paige dropped her tote bag and went back to the van for the last bucket. As she locked the doors, Anna Lee rode her scooter into the parking lot. She was an amusing sight with her purple helmet, long dress still tied with twine, and gray backpack, which had a clear plastic bubble from which Salty peered out.

Inside the building, Anna Lee let Salty out of the backpack. He ran to the front and climbed up on a shelf to lie in a patch of sunlight streaming through the window. He licked his paw three times and curled up to take a nap.

"Paige!" exclaimed Tilly. "You haven't seen the plumber yet! Just wait–he is truly scrumptious!"

Paige pictured a middle-aged man with a beer belly, figuring Tilly was pulling her leg. "Oh really? Are you going to ask him out?"

"I can't do that; you know I'm dating Kyle. But the plumber may be your type–he's tall, quiet, and handsome. The strong, silent type, you could say. Don't you agree, Lauren?" Tilly asked.

"Oh yes, definitely handsome," Lauren answered. "I think he's everyone's type. Even Paige's. You'll regret that you're leaving when you see him, Paige."

Tilly nodded her head. "What time will he be here today, Anna Lee?" Tilly was tying her apron on, and Paige experienced a twinge of jealousy. Tilly was always well put-together. She wore the cutest fashion trends, and today her medium brown hair with professionally enhanced caramel highlights was in a French braid that rested on her left shoulder. Paige's own hair was in a messy bun on top of her head.

"He'll be here this afternoon," Anna Lee replied. "He had some personal business to take care of this morning. And, we have a new person starting this afternoon. Her name is Dominica, but she goes by Nica. With Lauren and Paige leaving, we needed another team member. Please welcome her and help me show her the ropes. Things will be crazier than normal with a new gal and the plumber. And ladies, I heard your fawning over the plumber, please keep your hands to yourselves if you can."

They all laughed at Anna Lee's remark. Lauren brought two boxes of merchandise out of the storage room. "Paige, one for you. One for me. Let's get these out before the store opens."

The rest of the morning passed quickly. Tilly and Anna Lee went to the garage bay to work on the arrangement design for the weekend wedding that would use the beautiful peonies from Anna Lee's garden. Lauren and Paige took care of shoppers in the store while discussing how finals went and talking about their summer plans.

After noon, a petite brunette with a smile that would make a beauty contestant jealous came into the store asking for Anna Lee. Paige assumed she was the new hire and introduced herself.

"Anna Lee is working in the back. I'll take you to her. Are you a student at ISU?" Paige wondered if Nica was in high school. She looked young.

"Yes," Nica said excitedly. "Finished my sophomore year. What about you?"

"Finished my junior year. I'm leaving Saturday for a summer internship."

"Neat. Where are you going?" Nica asked.

"New York City. A publishing internship." Paige pushed open the door that led into the garage bay.

"Wow!" Nica responded with a lift of her shoulders and her beautiful smile. She was enthusiastic and seemed kind. Paige thought she would fit in well with the team at In Bloom.

Anna Lee looked up from her sketch pad. "Wonderful to see you, Nica! Let's go to the office to fill out paperwork. But first meet Tilly. Did you meet Lauren out front?"

"Yes, I did. It's great to meet everyone. I can't wait to get started," Nica beamed.

PAIGE WAS AT the cash register when the front door opened with its usual squeak and bell ring. She looked up, expecting to greet a customer. The man that walked in was obviously the plumber that the girls had been drooling over earlier. He was tall, with black hair that needed a trim; the front of it draped over his left eye. Her gaze swept down the length of him. She took in his broad shoulders, slim waist, and long legs. He carried a red toolbox, wore tan work boots, and appeared to be sucking on a sucker.

She looked at his face and noticed his crooked grin, almost a smirk. Paige's cheeks lit up like a firecracker. Busted. She was caught checking him out. She cursed her fair skin tone; it didn't take much for embarrassment to show on her face.

"Cool t-shirt," he said, glancing down at her chest.

Paige's eyes popped. Was he making fun of her? She had been told so many times that her clothing choices were "too much" or "odd." She wore what she liked. She was wearing a dark blue t-shirt that was designed by her dad. Across the front, a white eagle was carrying a pen in one talon and a megaphone in the other. Anna Lee liked her employees to express themselves and wear what they wanted. She just asked that they wore the In Bloom-branded shirts when they delivered flowers.

"Thank you," she said with a hint of hesitation. "My dad designed it."

"Wow, your dad, huh? It's awesome. Free speech, right? That's the message?"

"Yes," she smiled, proud of her dad's design. It had come out of a lengthy ideological conversation between the two of them. "Free speech and 'the pen is mightier than the sword.' Now, how can I help you?"

"I'm here to replace the pipes. Miss Anna Lee is expecting me." His lopsided grin curved up and filled in completely. Paige understood why Tilly called him scrumptious. She had a flash of regret that she'd be leaving in two days.

"Right," Paige replied. "We were expecting you."

Nica returned and put a register tape on the counter.

Paige could not tear her eyes away from the handsome plumber. "Nica," she said, "will you let Anna Lee know the plumber is here?"

"Sure. Be right back."

As soon as Nica left, Paige kicked herself for not going after Anna Lee instead of asking Nica. If she had, she wouldn't be in this awkward situation. She was still flushed from her earlier embarrassment. Darn her Northern European ancestry. She shuffled a stack of receipts on the counter. There was no reason for doing this, but it kept her from having to make small talk with the stranger.

Said stranger approached the counter and placed his toolbox on the floor. He leaned on the counter and cleared his throat.

"Can I help you?" Paige could not ignore his presence. She looked up and found him gazing at her. His brown eyes reminded her of her favorite brand of toffee.

"I think we started off on the wrong foot. My name is Trevor. What's yours?" He stood up straight and held out his hand for her to shake.

"Paige. I wasn't trying to ogle you when you came in."

"It's all good. I'm used to it."

Paige laughed; it was apparent he was mocking himself. "Conceited much?"

"Not conceited. Self-assured." He took the empty sucker stick out of his mouth and asked her for a place to throw it away. She leaned down, picked up the trash can under the counter, and held it out for him.

He tossed the stick in the trash and started to say something when his eyes widened and his shoulders hunched up. A second later, Salty appeared on his shoulder. The cat must have climbed up his back.

"Oh, no!" Paige exclaimed. "I've never seen that before. Are you okay?"

Trevor grimaced. "Um, is there a parrot sitting on my shoulder?"

Paige laughed. "No, that's the shop cat." She stepped around the counter to coax the cat down. "Come here, Salty." She held out her arms and Salty leaped into them. She gently lowered him to the floor.

"That was unexpected." Trevor turned to look over his shoulder. "I didn't even see it when I came in."

"Oh no, you're bleeding." Paige said, stepping closer. "Salty got you on the neck. Come around here and I'll clean it and get you a bandage." She gestured for him to sit on the stool behind the counter. Her early embarrassment was gone now that she had a task to complete. She pulled a small first aid kit out from under the register and turned to Trevor, sitting behind her. Her body tingled with the nearness of him. She could smell his aftershave, with its aromatic notes of juniper and musk.

"Well, I can't wait to tell my nephews about a cat climbing up me like a tree," Trevor said, watching Paige open the antiseptic towelette.

"Nephews? How old?" Paige asked, dabbing the towelette on his neck, wiping up the dripping blood before resting it on the scratch.

"Ye-ow! That burns. They're four and two. Best little dudes around."

"Well, yes, they'll get a kick out of your story. Hold on. Let me get a Band-Aid." She tossed the towelette in the trash and turned back to the counter for a bandage. The wrapper did not want to tear open, and she fiddled with it for several seconds.

"Here, let me help with that." Trevor put his hand lightly on her arm and she turned to him.

"It's being stubborn," she said.

"Looks like they've been around for a while." He ripped off the end of the wrapper. "I remember being here when I was little. My dad was repairing something, and Miss Anna Lee asked if I wanted to help put loose roses out in a display cart that she used to have in here. There were buckets on the cart for the different colors of roses–pink, white, purple, etc. She warned me about the thorns, but I forgot and grabbed onto a stem that cut my finger. It bled like crazy. She grabbed that same first aid kit and doctored me up. I think I fell in love with Anna Lee that day. She slid into the role of cherished aunt quickly."

"You don't listen to directions. Noted." Paige applied the bandage to his neck and smoothed it down.

"Hey, I was a kid. I'm better at listening now."

"You're all set. Watch the area around the scratch for streaks. Could get an infection."

"Yes, doctor," he teased, leaning forward. "I'm coming to you for further treatment if needed."

Paige smiled as she shook her head. "Not a smart idea; I'm not a med student."

Trevor stood and it seemed like the space behind the counter shrunk in half. He was way too close. The logo on his shirt was just inches in front of her face. If she leaned forward a few inches, without even moving her feet, she could rest her forehead on the logo and his chest. Where did that idea come from? She leaned back, hoping he would realize that he was in her personal space.

"Well, thanks. Even if you're not a med student, I feel like I've been taken care of," he said. "I hope I'll be seeing you often. I estimate this job is will take a couple of weeks."

"Sounds like a big job. Tomorrow's my last day, though. For the summer, at least. I'll be back in time for fall semester." Paige wondered why she clarified that she would be back. Dating was *not* on her near-term agenda, so it didn't matter.

"Going home for the summer?" he asked, walking back to the front of the counter.

"No, I'm leaving for an internship in New York."

"That's cool. Where's home, by the way? College students are rarely from here." He pulled another sucker from a pocket on his tool belt.

"Near Pontiac."

"What do you mean by near? Is the address Pontiac or something else?" He pulled the wrapper off the sucker and Paige picked up the trash can again.

"Yes, a Pontiac address, but my home is in the country."

"Ah, got it." He popped the sucker in his mouth as Anna Lee came through the door.

"Hello Trevor," she called as she walked into the showroom. "I'm glad to see you again! Sorry for the delay. I was working on an arrangement and didn't want to stop, or I would forget where I left off."

"Not a problem, Miss Anna Lee. Paige was taking care of me."

Anna Lee smiled, and Paige blushed again. Why did his statement feel like it implied more than what had occurred?

Anna Lee took Trevor to the back and Paige was relieved he was gone. Out of sight, out of mind. Well, that's what she tried telling herself, anyway.

CHAPTER FIVE

P AIGE RESISTED THE temptation to check for email on her mobile phone. If she peeked once, she'd peek every five minutes, and that would not be appropriate while she was on the clock at work. She decided she would wait until she got home so she could concentrate on the anticipated response from her contact at the publishing company. She had already memorized the subway and bus schedules and knew the route from her apartment to the office building. Depending on what time they wanted her in, she'd know which route she had to take.

After leaving work, she stopped at the university library, returned the last three books she had checked out, and proceeded on to her almost empty apartment. After dinner, she wanted to pack all the boxes that her family would take with them on Friday and reorganize the suitcases that would go with her to NYC on Saturday.

In her apartment, she turned on her favorite cleaning play-list and cranked the volume on the speaker when Gavin DeGraw's "She Sets the City on Fire" started playing. She thought about the coming summer in New York. She hoped she would set that city on fire. Well, at least the publishing company where she'd be working. She packed up everything she could and began cleaning. She cleaned until she was satisfied that her efforts would get her deposit money back, and then made a salad using all the remaining veggies in the fridge.

She called her longest and closest friend Macey and caught up on their respective weeks; it was their usual Thursday night phone call. All through high school, it had been a nightly call. Once they each left for college, it turned into a weekly call. Of course, there were a lot of 'emergency' check-ins when needed.

After hanging up the call, she arranged dinner on the table, pulled out her laptop and booted it. She took a bite of salad and entered her password. She smoothed the curling edge of the "Don't Panic!" sticker to the left of the laptop's touchpad. She smiled remembering her brother Jack giving it to her on his first trip home from college. He'd found it in an independent bookstore near his campus and knew Paige would appreciate *The Hitchhiker's Guide to the Galaxy* reference. While she waited for her email application to launch, she stood to grab a flavored water drink from the fridge.

Sitting in front of the laptop again, scanning all of the emails and deleting the junk ones, she was happy to see the email reply from Leslie, her contact at the publishing house. Until she read it.

Dear Ms. Bell,

I am very sorry to inform you that there was a terrible mistake. We accidentally offered two students our summer Editorial Assistant internship. We cannot take you on as an intern this summer because we do not have the resources to train and oversee two interns properly.

Again, my deepest apologies. We would like to ask that you apply for next summer's program or if your schedule allows, you could apply for the spring semester internship. Please keep in mind the deadline to apply for the spring semester

*internship is May 25th. We will make our selection for
spring by June 1st.*

*I know this is not what you expected or wanted to hear. I
apologize for the disruption this will cause to your summer.*

*Sincerely,
Leslie Maron, Director of H.R.
Garland Wilson Publishing*

Paige lost her appetite. How could this have happened? How could a company do this? Why wasn't *she* the one they picked out of the two? She closed her eyes and took a deep breath. She recalled her mom's soothing voice when leading a yoga session–"Deep breath in, smell the roses." She would then pause. "Slow breath out, blow out the candles." Paige followed the advice in her head five times. Then she stood up and shook her whole body like a rag doll being shaken by an energetic three-year-old.

She felt sick to her stomach thinking about the financial impact. She'd spent months planning her budget around the internship, saving enough money for all of the extra expenses. She hated the feeling of financial insecurity that this news brought. She'd worked so hard for so long to avoid this particular feeling of helplessness.

She grabbed her budget binder and sifted through the cash envelopes, moving money from envelopes marked "NY Transportation", "NY Food", and "NY Misc." to the "normal" envelopes for transportation, food and misc. She then opened her budget tracking spreadsheet on her laptop, made a few notes about rent and utilities and sat back, twisting the ring on her right hand.

Putting her fight-or-flight response on pause, she pulled out her planner and started a new list.

Call mom
Call Ms. Maron
Cancel flight-refund?
Cancel apartment-refund?
New place to live-home is last resort
Summer job(s)-talk to Anna Lee about In Bloom-2nd job
somewhere else?
Call adviser-spring internship-would postpone grad?
Apply for spring internship ASAP

Looking at the urgent items on the list, she felt calmer. A setback, not a failure, she told herself.

CHAPTER SIX

OH NO! AS Paige pulled into the parking lot Friday morning, she remembered that Anna Lee was going to bake a cake for her last day in the flower shop. She should have called her Thursday night to tell her that the plans had changed. She could have saved Anna Lee from the time and effort of baking a cake.

She dreaded telling Anna Lee and her friends that she wouldn't be going to New York for her internship after all. They would probably groan and regret all the times they'd had to listen to Paige talk about her excitement for the opportunity.

She opened the back door and tripped over a large wrench that was lying past the threshold. She would have landed flat on her face if the person who left the wrench on the floor hadn't caught her. Paige's arms crossed at the wrists and rested against Trevor's chest; his hands gripped her upper arms tightly.

"Uff," she said at the impact of her body crashing into his.

Trevor grunted as he absorbed the impact of her body. "Whoops! I should have moved that wrench. You came through that door like a person on a mission." He chuckled.

Paige pulled herself upright, feeling a flush creep across her face. She pushed her long hair back over her shoulder and straightened her pale green t-shirt. "Wow, that was close. I'm glad I didn't go flying across the floor. Thanks for the catch."

"It's all right. I'll expect payback later. I'll think about the best way for you to repay me." He smiled at her and Paige wondered why his hands continued to be on her arms. Though, the feel of his warm, firm hands on her arms was thrilling. It had been a long time since she was this close to a handsome guy. And truthfully, Trevor was a hundred times more handsome than Caleb.

"I'm all right now. You can let go." She wanted to take back the words when he released her. "Repay?"

"For saving your life!" He raised his hands and shrugged his shoulders. "Surely my kind deed should be reciprocated."

"I don't know about saving my life, preventing a broken wrist, maybe." Paige looked at the surrounding mess. There was a jack-hammer leaning against the wall behind her, and the fact that he had used it was apparent with the broken concrete path that ran along the floor behind Trevor. "Wow, you've been productive this morning."

"Yeah, I've had to dig a trench to get down to the old, corroded pipes. They must have built these garage bays after the original building. They poured this concrete right on top of the main water pipes. Like I said yesterday, this is a big job. I'm sorry you won't be here to see it finished."

"Well, that. I need to talk to Anna Lee about that. I may be here after all. We'll see. Wish me luck." Paige looked around but didn't see anyone else in the garage bay.

"Why might you be here longer? Could this be my lucky day? I thought you said you were leaving for an internship."

"Well, let me talk to Anna Lee first."

Anna Lee entered the garage bay and gave Paige a big smile. "Ready for your last day, Paige?"

"Can I talk to you Anna Lee? Privately?" Paige wasn't ready to share the news with Trevor yet.

"Surely. Let's go plant ourselves in my office. I could use a cup of tea right about now, anyway." Anna Lee turned, and Paige followed her to the office behind the register.

When they got to the tiny office, Anna Lee gestured Paige forward and closed the door behind them. "Cup of tea, dear?"

"No, I had a coffee already this morning and too much caffeine gives me the shakes. Anna Lee," she forged ahead. "I lost my internship. I found out last night. They said they 'accidentally' made offers to two people and can only take one. I know this is a big ask and I know you hired Dominica since I was leaving. I don't want to take anyone else's hours, but if it's an option, I would love to continue to work for you this summer. I still need to find a place to live, but if I can work here and pick up another job, then I wouldn't need to go home for the summer. Going home is an option, but I don't really want to do that."

"Well, poo! That's an enormous pile of manure! I'm sorry to hear that, Paige. I know you were looking forward to it." Anna Lee picked up the electric kettle and poured hot water into a cup. She opened a drawer and searched for a tea bag in the ancient wooden desk that appeared to have been left by the original gas station owner. Finding one she wanted, she opened the pouch and plopped the bag in the hot water, holding the submerged tea bag down with a pair of snips.

"I was! I'm still shocked. Spent the morning making phone calls to back out of my flight and my apartment in New York." Paige shuffled her feet and remembered Trevor's warm hands on her arms. She wished she had time to think about that encounter in private. She knew there were some juicy daydreams to be fleshed out.

"That's very practical. But how are you *feeling*?" Anna Lee emphasized the last word.

Paige sighed. "Lots of things. I'm a bit angry and very sad. A tad bit embarrassed. I've spoken about this to everyone I know. I should have known better than to get my hopes up again."

"Again?"

"Never mind. Long story." Paige didn't want to share her broken engagement with Anna Lee.

"Well, you'll weather this storm, Paige. And to answer your question, yes, I can keep you on for the summer. I can't promise a lot of hours, but I'll see what I can do. We have a big wedding tomorrow, and I could use your help. Might be a pleasant distraction since you won't be going to New York. Come in at eight. Why don't you go on and open the register? Things are going to be a little topsy-turvy here while Trevor is replacing all the pipes," Anna Lee sighed.

"Is he old enough to do all that plumbing on his own, Anna Lee?" Paige knew she should mind her own business but didn't want to see anyone taking advantage of Anna Lee.

"Oh, he's old enough. And he was trained by the best. I've hired his father countless times over the last thirty years. Trevor is great. I've known him since he was just a little sprout. He used to come with his dad when he was big enough to carry a wrench. He was the cutest kid. I think he grew into a very handsome young man. Don't you?" Anna Lee's eyes crinkled when she smiled.

"I suppose. But I'm not interested in dating right now." Paige stood quickly and put her hand on the door. "Thanks for letting me stay on for the summer. Now I need to find a place to live. If you have any ideas on that front, I'm all ears."

"A place to live, huh? Talk to Nica. She said something about a roommate yesterday. She'll be in tomorrow. Not sure if she is looking for one or if she has a thorny one. I was trying not to eavesdrop."

"I will, thanks!" Paige walked out of the office with a lighter step, one problem solved. She had one job for the summer, it would be good to find another one to keep her busy and to make rent, once she found a place to live.

LAUREN HAD THE day off, but even she came into In Bloom for cake. Anna Lee's chocolate sheet cake with chocolate icing was not to be missed.

They cleaned off one end of the long worktable to make room for the cake and plates. Anna Lee knocked on a tall metal vase with a pair of gardening shears to get their attention. Paige was still amazed how loud four people could be in the large space.

"Well, this isn't the send-off we expected today," Anna Lee began. "Luckily for us, Paige is staying here for the summer. It's lucky for us, because we will continue to be amazed by her knowledge of any book ever written, her immediate recall of music lyrics, and her all around charming personality. Anyway, we'll celebrate *our* good fortune and commiserate with her disappointment in not getting to live her dream this summer. I know this is not what you wanted, Paige, but I believe there is a magic in the universe and sometimes the universe brings us what we need, not what we want."

"Hear, hear," Trevor said, placing a hand on Paige's shoulder and causing her to jump. The others laughed–they had watched him come up behind her.

Paige turned towards Trevor and smiled politely. All eyes were on her and she didn't want the others to see her discomfort. It was bad enough Trevor could see the pink color spreading across her face.

Anna Lee broke the unusual silence that had fallen on the group. "Let's have cake!" She lifted a knife and cut into the decadent dessert.

Paige received the first piece of cake and turned to hand it to Trevor. The others were talking, and Paige hoped they wouldn't hear her ask Trevor, "What did you mean by that?"

"I think Miss Anna Lee is right," he answered, "sometimes things happen for a reason that we don't always see." His eyebrows pinched together but loosened quickly. "It's disappointing, but we roll with it. I'm sorry to hear you aren't going to your internship. What happened?" He cut off a small piece of cake and Paige watched the plastic fork and chocolate goodness move towards his full lips. Tilly's word "scrumptious" came to mind, and she wasn't sure if the thought was regarding the cake or his lips.

"Long story." Paige looked at the slice of cake on her plate. "I don't want to bore you."

"You couldn't bore me," he replied. "Tell me what happened."

He appeared genuinely interested, so Paige told him about the mix-up and added, "I'm stuck here for the summer as long as I can find a place to live. If I don't, then I'll go home for the summer and try not to sulk."

"You need a place to live, huh?" he asked. "I've got an extra bedroom. Rent's cheap."

Paige stammered. "Thanks, but that won't work. I don't even know you. You could be a murderer or serial killer for all I know." Paige took a bite of cake, hoping to distract herself from his comforting eyes.

He leaned in close. She had no choice but to look him in the eye. "I'm not a murderer. But I would kill to lick that chocolate off your lip."

Paige groaned. "You are—" She lost the insult as he put his thumb on her lip and rubbed gently. Her toes lifted in her sneakers.

"There, I got it," he put the thumb that had brushed her lip into his mouth. Paige saw a dab of chocolate on his thumb. "That icing is delicious."

"You're a brute," she said once she caught her breath. His touch sent a bolt of electricity through her body. Paige had never felt such a strong physical reaction to a man's touch. It was like the final scene in a movie when the music intensified and the picture faded to black.

Trevor chuckled. "My friends say I'm a pretty good guy. You can decide for yourself when you get to know me better."

Paige wasn't sure if she wanted to know him better. There was something about him that intrigued her. Perhaps it was his confidence, or maybe it was the way he made her feel: excited, like she'd finished a fantastic book that made her feel lit up from the inside. Glowing in the aftermath of a satisfying ending when she could take comfort that the characters were where they needed to be, and their futures were looking better than they had at the beginning. But whatever it was about him that caused her toes to curl and made her a little nervous, she had to protect her heart. Plus, dating could impede pursuing her career.

Paige put her plate down on the worktable and sighed. "Look, if you couldn't tell by what I said earlier, my life is in shambles right now. My career has been derailed, and if I can't find a place to live, I will be driving my disappointed self home to mom and dad's. I don't think there will be a chance to get to know you better."

"Hey, it'll be all right," he said. He reached out and gave her shoulder a light, quick squeeze. "Remember what Anna Lee said, there's magic in the universe. I get the feeling you're a smart lady who always bounces back up. You're chasing your dreams and making it happen for yourself. There was a mix-up, but I didn't hear 'the end' in your story. Only hurdles and hiccups. They happen in life. That's what life is. It's how we prove we're capable of picking ourselves back up. Most of the time. Yes, sometimes it's unbelievably hard and then we ask for help." He paused, looked down, and ran his hand through the shaggy hair on top of his head. He raised his eyes to her and held her gaze intently before shifting the conversation. "Well, I should get back to work. Miss Anna Lee is not paying me to flirt with the help." Trevor winked and turned away.

Paige stared after him and let his words sink in. He was right; as far as bad news went this wasn't that bad. It wasn't like a broken engagement or a terrible medical diagnosis. She wished she had his wisdom all the time. She could even see herself falling for someone with that wisdom, someone to be a sounding board when things were difficult, someone to lean on and take comfort in. But she reminded herself that she was not ready to date. The breakup with Caleb had hurt too much. For now, she would focus on finishing college and getting a sensible job at a New York publishing house where she could help develop beloved books. To be a part of the industry she loved. Where she could surround herself with romance and drama, where it was safe–on the pages of a book.

CHAPTER SEVEN

P AIGE'S DAD, FRANK, and her brother were waiting in the parking lot when she got home. She parked next to her parents' van and smiled. The back doors of the aging van were open, and her dad and brother were sitting on the bumper. Even with the disappointment of losing the internship, there was nothing like spending time with her family.

Logan threw his lanky, six-foot-tall body on to the hood of her car and Paige pushed on the horn and held her hand in place for five seconds, long enough to get under her skin, but not long enough to get Logan off the hood.

As she climbed out of her car, her dad wrapped her in a tight hug. She smelled the familiar scent of paint and paint thinner on his denim button-down shirt.

"I'm sorry about the internship, pumpkin," he said. "I know how much you were looking forward to it. But it's just a setback. It's time to throw white paint on your canvas and start again."

She sighed. "I know, dad, but I was counting on this internship to lead to a job after graduation. It's important to have experience in this field, it's pretty competitive!"

Her dad nodded, listening. "You know I wish you would get back to creative writing. You've written some wonderful stories. I would love to see you devote more time to it."

"Dad," she said, feeling exasperated, "maybe in the future. But it isn't a financially stable career. I will have student loans to pay back on top of living expenses once I graduate. That's not a great time to rely on creative writing. Besides, I haven't felt like writing in a long time."

"Sometimes," Frank leaned back against the van, "you have to just put your butt in the seat and put in the time. You won't always feel like it or be hit with inspiration."

"I know. I know," Paige said, "but you're stressing me out. It's been a disappointing week and on top of everything else, I don't have a place to live after today. There's a new tenant moving into my apartment. I explained what happened to my landlord, and he was extremely sympathetic, but there's a contract."

Logan punched her in the arm. "You can't come home, sis. I'm using your bedroom as my game room. Sorry, not sorry." Paige wanted him to be more than just an annoying younger brother, and she hoped that in a couple more years, he would mature and they would be close. She felt the two of them were the most alike out of the four siblings.

Paige punched him back. "If I can't find a place to live, I will be home and you *will* vacate my room. But I'm hopeful. Anna Lee said that the new girl may need a roommate. I'll see her tomorrow and find out. Well, should we load the van and then go to dinner or dinner first?"

Logan jumped in. "Dinner first! I'm hungry! I'm a growing boy!"

Frank laughed. "I hope you don't grow anymore, Logan. But I agree, let's go to dinner first. Is that all right with you, Paige?"

"Absolutely."

After dinner, Frank and Logan moved her furniture and boxes to the van and left.

Paige loaded the two suitcases in her car and went back to the empty apartment to see if she'd left anything. Like checking out of a hotel room, she wanted to look in all the drawers and closets one more time to make sure everything was out. Satisfied that the apartment was empty, she shouldered her backpack and picked up her purse. She locked the door and dropped off the keys at the apartment manager's office.

CHAPTER EIGHT

EAVING THE HOTEL Saturday morning, Paige gave herself a pep talk on the drive to In Bloom, her dad's words from the night before echoed in her head as she told herself, "This is just a setback. Thomas Edison didn't invent the light bulb on his first try. If he hadn't persisted, we might be reading by oil lamp. I will have a great summer, even if I have to go back home. I just don't want to go home. I don't want to risk running into Caleb or Moria."

She was thankful for this morning's shift at In Bloom. Keeping busy was the best thing for her to do right now. Obviously, the hours and money were a plus.

It surprised her when a picture of Trevor flashed across her mind. He'd flustered her yesterday, flirting with her–his words, not hers. For a moment, she thought if she had more healing under her belt, then she would consider dating him. But he was probably entrenched in Bloomington. Would he even be interested in coming to New York to live? Would he be able to get a plumbing license in New York? Why was she thinking about this?

She wanted to call Macey, who always gave the best advice when it came to guys. She had spent countless hours talking Paige down after the broken engagement with Caleb. Macey would help Paige gain perspective on Trevor. Paige grabbed a pen and the small pad of paper that was always in the car cup holder and jotted a note to call her.

Another driver honked when she didn't see the light turn green. She dropped the pen and paper in her lap, shook her head, and drove the last few miles to In Bloom.

Anna Lee said Trevor had offered to work seven days a week until the repairs were done. Paige hoped he wouldn't be in the shop today. She needed to find a place to live pronto, and he was such a distraction, a handsome distraction with a quick wit. If she didn't find an apartment soon, she would be commuting the fifty minutes from her parents' house to work. And it would be harder to find a second job for extra money.

Since Trevor had removed the pipes coming in from the main water line, the flower shop had no running water. Anna Lee asked Paige and Nica to fill gallon jugs with water from the beauty salon on the other side of the street.

They each grabbed two jugs and walked across the parking lot. While they waited for cars to pass, Paige asked Nica if she was still looking for a roommate.

Nica beamed. "Yes! We could use another roomie. Would love to split rent three ways instead of two, and we have an extra bedroom! It would be great if you moved in with us. It's me and my cousin Izzy. She's a wild child, super outgoing. You'll love her!"

"More outgoing than you?" Paige asked with a smile as they crossed the street.

"Oh yes, she's a riot. You know the type—an instant friend to everyone she meets."

"I'm a little nervous about living with two extroverts, but I turned in my apartment keys last night and I'm desperate. I'm sure it will be wonderful! I don't mean to sound like it won't work or I'm not appreciative. Do you have a lot of parties?" Paige wondered what she was getting into.

"Not exactly. It's a conservative building. We'd get in trouble. But Izzy loves to throw dinner parties that wrap up early. She's a fabulous cook. You won't starve." Nica pushed open the salon door.

They filled the jugs with water and returned to In Bloom. Paige wanted to call her mom right away to tell her she might have a place to live. She asked Anna Lee if she could take a quick break. She went outside to the picnic table, sat on top with her feet on the bench, and called.

Paige was saying goodbye to her mom when she saw Trevor's truck pull into the lot. They locked eyes, and she thought she could rush inside before he approached her, but he jumped from the truck and walked straight toward her, a sucker sticking out of his mouth and a box of Krispy Kreme donuts in his hand.

She hung up the phone and started to stand, but Trevor stopped directly in front of her, giving her no room to stand without bumping into him.

"Hello there," he said, pulling the sucker from his mouth. It and his tongue were bright red.

"Hi, I was finishing my break." She gestured past him, hoping he'd let her pass.

"I was curious if you found a place to live." He shifted on his feet but did not move aside.

"Maybe. Nica has an extra room. I'm going after work to check it out. But I can't imagine saying no. I don't want to move back home."

"Rough home life?"

"Not at all. It's great. As long as you don't count my younger brother. He's a pain in the...never mind." Paige shifted.

"Ha! My sister probably says the same thing about me." He smiled and the corners of his eyes crinkled.

"I believe she does. I don't actually know you and I already think you're a pain." Paige waved at him to step aside.

He stepped back enough for her to stand, but he continued to block her path. Paige would not be intimidated; she had enough experience putting up with three brothers.

"Why don't you go out with me so you can get to know me?"

Paige shook her head before he even finished. "Can't. I'm too busy." She started walking towards the building.

"I don't buy that. You're no longer leaving for an internship; I can't believe Anna Lee has enough work to keep you that busy. What else are you doing?" He strode past her and blocked her way to the back door. The exterior door was propped open, and Paige could see inside through the screen. Lauren, Tilly, and Nica were sitting around the worktable and could likely hear the conversation.

She lowered her voice. "Look, I think everyone can hear us. Can we take this up another time?"

Trevor turned and looked through the screen door. "Good morning, ladies. We'll be in shortly. Here, I brought donuts!" He opened the door and put the box of donuts on the counter by the sink. Turning back to Paige, he said, "Let's step back over to the picnic table."

She turned away and walked towards the picnic table, hoping they were out of listening range. "Well?" She stood with her arms crossed and knew she looked childish.

"I'm not trying to be a jerk. I want an honest answer. Why won't you go out with me? I don't buy that you're too busy. Are you not attracted to me?"

Her cheeks warmed, and she looked away from him. She noticed that the side of his truck said, "Peter Morrison and Son Plumbing." She remembered that Anna Lee said his dad had passed.

"That cute blush answers that question," he said with a smile. If it wasn't for the warmth in his voice, Paige would think he was making fun of her. "Would you be embarrassed to date a plumber? You probably only date upperclassmen. Men studying to be lawyers or executives."

"No!" she blurted. "I'm not like that." Though, she secretly worried she was. Professional, white-collar jobs meant not worrying about paying for necessities and emergencies.

"All right," he said. "Then you must be in a relationship already. Why didn't you just say that?" Trevor took the stick from his mouth and dropped it in the garbage can next to the picnic table.

"I'm not in a relationship, but I don't want to date right now." Paige looked at her watch. Her break was going on ten minutes now and she didn't want to make Anna Lee or the others mad. "I should get back inside."

"Ah, you're mending a broken heart. How long?"

"What?"

"How long since your breakup?"

"Almost five months. It happened on Christmas Eve."

Trevor shook his head. "Dang. Boyfriend or fiancé?"

"Fiancé." Paige started for the door. "I'm not ready to date. Can we drop it?"

"Sure. Sure. I understand. You simply need a little more convincing. I get it and I'm up to the challenge."

Paige turned back towards him. He raised his arms up to flex his biceps. Paige noticed that his navy-blue t-shirt rose and exposed his waist. She shook her head as her gaze stuck on his stomach. Trevor belted out a hearty laugh. "This is going to be easier than I thought!" he shouted as she entered the building. She let the screen door slam behind her.

TREVOR WALKED TO his truck with a grin on his face. He hoisted the toolbox from the truck bed and sat it on the ground. He opened the door to grab his tool belt off the seat, along with a handful of suckers which he stuffed into the tool belt.

He chuckled, thinking about the interaction with Paige. The words out of her mouth said she wasn't interested in dating, but her eyes betrayed her. He knew he was coming on strong, but she intrigued him. Certainly, she was beautiful, with her auburn hair, green eyes, and fair skin. She didn't seem overly fixated on her appearance. She wore makeup in soft, natural tones that accentuated her features. But it wasn't only her appearance; there was a strength and a challenge behind her eyes that spoke to him.

Strapping on his tool belt, he thought about his dad. The tool belt had belonged to him. Trevor had his own, but when his dad passed, he traded his for his dad's. It was a source of comfort and a sharp reminder of the loss. "I wish you could meet her, Pop," he whispered quietly.

He remembered meeting Paige for the first time. She'd had on a shirt that she said her dad designed. He could hear the pride and love that she felt for her father in her voice. They had that in common. And she was unique. She didn't seem concerned with fitting in with an Instagram crowd. She seemed real, down-to-earth. That was a huge plus in his mind. He had trouble picturing her in New York, she seemed more Midwesterner than a Manhattanite.

Trevor could not remember the last time a girl turned him down. He wasn't used to the chase, but if Paige required chasing, he was going to chase. He was confident that she would be worth the effort. Knowing that she was hurt because of a breakup with a fiancé gave him a brief pause. He would have to consider this in his pursuit, but he was thankful that the guy was out of her life.

As he walked in the back door, he scanned the workshop for Paige but didn't see her. He greeted the ladies again before heading to Anna Lee's office, where he could access the crawl space.

Anna Lee stood up from her desk as Trevor approached. "Mornin', Trevor. Thank you again for coming in on a Saturday. I appreciate that you're trying to get done as fast as possible. I don't suppose it has anything to do with the pretty girls in my employ." She raised an eyebrow and grinned.

"Miss Anna Lee, I told you I want to get this done as fast as I can, so your business isn't disrupted. Dad always talked highly of you, and he would've kicked my a-, um, butt if I dawdled on this job." Trevor looked away, not wanting Miss Anna Lee to see the flash of pain in his eyes.

"Your dad was wonderful, and he raised an outstanding son." She gave him a quick sideways hug. "All right then. Get to work! Stop dawdling."

"Yes, ma'am." He shook his head as he made his way to the trapdoor that led to the crawl. She was as perceptive as anyone he'd ever met. Though he'd only met her a few times growing up, she always made him feel special. So important for a child without a mother at home.

CHAPTER NINE

PAIGE STRADDLED HER stool and looked at the sample arrangement for today's wedding on the table. It had two white, wooden crates that were stacked offset, so the bottom crate had room for a few flowers to flow over the sides. The top crate was filled with flowers–soft pink and purple roses, with dark purple wisteria draping over the edges.

"Wow, this is a gorgeous arrangement," Paige said as she pulled a bucket of roses closer to her. "Anna Lee never ceases to amaze me."

"Oh, no you don't!" exclaimed Tilly. Her brown ponytail with the perfect curl, swayed back and forth. "Spill it. What the heck happened outside with the hot plumber? We are all so jeal'y right now!"

Lauren jumped up and closed the door that separated the work bays from the retail store and office area, where they could hear Trevor talking to Anna Lee. She came back and gave Paige a nudge with her shoulder. "Agree. Spill. You say you don't date, so what was that all about?"

Paige shook her head. "I didn't say I *don't* date. I said I'm not dating. Oh, never mind."

"Did he ask you out?" Tilly questioned. "Don't hold out on us."

"Yes, I guess he did."

"You guess? Or he did?" Tilly was bouncing on her toes in cute ballerina flats.

"Yes, he did. I said no." Paige busied herself, concentrating on filling a wooden crate with recycled floral foam.

"If there is anyone to get you ready to date, it's him. I agree with Tilly–he is scrumptious!" Lauren winked at Paige. Paige would miss Lauren when she left for Europe.

"Nica," Paige said. "Help me out, please. Get these hens off of me." She smiled to let the others know she was teasing.

"I'm with them, *Chica*. He is hot!" Nica shimmied her shoulders, like she was dancing on her stool.

Paige rolled her eyes. "Fine. Fine. I agree, he's very good looking, but there are other things in life, you know."

"Yes, we know, Paige," Lauren slid a deep purple rose into her arrangement. "But sometimes, it's okay to go on a date, have fun. You weren't even supposed to be here this summer. Maybe this is the universe's magic working in your favor, like Anna Lee said yesterday. Let loose, have some fun. We want to live vicariously through you. Don't we, ladies?"

Nica and Tilly shouted their agreement as Anna Lee and Trevor walked into the workshop.

"Sounds like y'all are having fun," Anna Lee said. "How are the arrangements coming along?"

Paige was trying to figure out what Anna Lee was feeling when the southern dialect came out–was she teasing or stressed?

Lauren was the unofficial supervisor of the group. "We will be done in plenty of time, Anna Lee."

"Good to hear," Anna Lee said. "Let me know if you need me to jump in. I want to get the van loaded by two. Any volunteers to drive today?"

Paige was eager to get to Nica's place to look over the available room and apartment but wouldn't pass up the extra time on the clock, and therefore extra money on the paycheck, to deliver the arrangements. "I will, Anna Lee, if no one else wants to." She looked at the others. Everyone shrugged.

Trevor smiled broadly as he held open the screen door for Anna Lee. Paige wondered why. It occurred to her that no one was watching the store front. "Do you need someone to cover the front, Anna Lee?" she asked.

"Yes, we should only be a couple of minutes, but it would be great if you could cover." Anna Lee stepped outside, followed closely by Trevor.

"I'll go if no one else wants to." Paige hoped for a moment alone to settle her nerves and splash some water on her warm wrists.

"Go for it." Lauren smiled at her and Paige had a feeling that Lauren could read her better than even her mother could.

She stopped by the restroom before remembering that it was out of service. She grabbed her plastic water bottle from the refrigerator and poured some over her wrists in the restroom sink before proceeding to the front.

At the cash register, she tidied a display of handmade greeting cards. Besides her own up-cycled creations, Anna Lee let several local artists display their wares in her store. They sold birdhouses and fairy gardens made by a local Vietnam Veteran; witty, wooden signs made by a mother-daughter duo; and vibrant, stained-glass sunlight catchers to hang in a window made by a group from the Adults with Developmental Disabilities center.

Paige twisted the ring on her right hand, a nervous habit. She didn't even realize she was doing it. A customer walked in, and Paige greeted her with a comment about the warm weather and asked if she needed help. When the customer declined, Paige straightened a display of dried floral arrangements that they'd made under Anna Lee's watchful eye in the workshop. The customer picked out a birdhouse as a gift and Paige rang up the sale.

Anna Lee walked into the retail space as the customer was leaving. Anna Lee called out a greeting, recognizing the customer, and they chatted amicably. Paige gave Anna Lee a wave and headed back to the workshop. She braced herself for the teasing that would continue from the others.

She climbed back onto her stool and picked up where she'd left off on her first arrangement, counting the finished arrangements on the side table and calculating that the others had made, on average, two each. She'd hurry to finish her first. It wasn't a competition, but she treated it like a competition. Everything was a competition with three brothers. Paige learned to be tenacious growing up with them and it had served her well. She'd sold the most Girl Scout cookies five years in a row.

"Paige," Tilly singsonged, "your boyfriend left. He got a call and rushed out; told Anna Lee he'd try to get back later but couldn't promise he would. He looked shook up. Maybe a dire plumbing emergency."

"First of all, he's not my boyfriend," Paige said, trying not to sound as exasperated as she felt, "and second of all, I'm not going out with him. I've got too much going on." Paige concentrated on the flowers in her hand. She was having a difficult time maneuvering a spray of wisteria into the corner of a lower crate.

Tilly laughed. "I think you're going to eat those words, girly. Just wait."

CHAPTER TEN

PAIGE DROVE TO Nica's apartment after work. The apartment was on the top floor of an old house that was subdivided into apartments. Nica and Izzy's apartment took up the entire third floor. There were two apartments on each of the first and second floors. The staircase to their apartment ran up the outside of the house and Paige wondered if it would get icy in winter.

"This must count as a workout," she thought as she trekked up the twenty-five steps to the apartment door. She knocked on the door and looked around her feet. There was a metal milk delivery box and a one-person bench on the small landing.

A tall brunette opened the door in a glittery pink sweatsuit and pink Converse high-top sneakers. "Hi!" she called, "you must be Paige! Nica is changing and will be right out. I'm Izzy–it's great to meet you!" Izzy held out her hand and Paige marveled at how her long fingernails were the same shade of pink—with glitter, matching her sweatsuit.

"Hi, it's a pleasure to meet you too. I'm excited to see the apartment. Did Nica tell you I moved out of my apartment last night? I'll drive to my parents' house tonight–it's an hour away." Paige followed Izzy into the cozy and efficient kitchen.

"No, she didn't. Wow! Where are your parents? Would you like a glass of tea? It's sun tea–I brew it on the landing outside the door." Izzy grabbed two glasses from the cabinet before Paige even responded.

"Tea would be great! My parents live outside of Pontiac, about an hour North on I-55." Paige took a sip of tea and smacked her lips. It was tart! "Lemons?"

"Oh, yes. Sorry, I should have warned you! And I remember the Pontiac exit–Nica and I are from Chicago. We take I-55 home." Izzy added another slice of lemon to her own glass.

Nica joined them in the tiny kitchen. "Hi, Paige. I see you've met my cousin Isabel. Let's show you the apartment and the available bedroom."

Paige followed the cousins through the apartment. There was a cozy kitchen, a large, combined living and dining room, and a small office besides the three bedrooms. It was fun to see their bedrooms; it told a lot about their personalities. Izzy's room was romantic and feminine, pink on pink. Nica's bedroom was an interesting mix. On one hand, it was sporty–two posters of the Chicago Bears hung on the wall, and a rack of more tennis shoes than Paige had ever owned next to the bed. On the other hand, there were two cork boards filled with cutouts of home decor. They looked to be inspiration or vision boards. Paige asked and Nica explained her dream was to flip houses. She was getting a degree in Physical Education to appease her parents, but she hoped to flip houses full-time eventually.

Leaving Nica's room, Paige said, "I think you two are exact opposites. How is that possible?"

"Although we're cousins," Nica answered, "we grew up to-gether. Izzy's dad died when she was young, and her family came to live with us. I think since we're the same age, we had to dis-tinguish ourselves. Whatever I liked, she hated and vice versa."

Izzy agreed, "We kept getting lumped together. Our parents acted like if one liked something, the other must too."

"Do you have other siblings or is it just the two of you?" Paige asked.

"Are you kidding? We come from Latino Catholic families!" Nica laughed. "I'm one of five and Izzy is one of six!"

"And you all lived in one house?" Paige asked incredibly.

"Yep. *Loco*, right?" Nica explained. "Our parents bought a large house, five bedrooms and a huge basement that they turned into the boys' bunkhouse. We made it work."

They showed Paige the extra bedroom. It was big enough for her but lacked furniture, so she couldn't stay the night. Once they talked about rent, utilities, and some basic house rules, she agreed to rent the spare bedroom.

Paige gave her dad a call to tell him about the apartment and asked if he could bring the bed and a desk tomorrow so she could settle in right away. He agreed and Paige told him she'd be home in a couple of hours.

"Izzy is making enchiladas for dinner; you have to stay, Paige," Nica said as soon as Paige hung up the phone. "Remember I told you Izzy is a fabulous cook?"

Izzy gave a shrug. "A house of fourteen! Our mamas needed help in the kitchen. Not that Dominica cared! She was always outside roughhousing with the boys."

"Hey!" Nica replied, "I may not have learned to cook, but I can wash dishes. And with your fancy manicure, you don't want to do it so it works."

Paige thought wistfully about what it would have been like to have grown up with a sister instead of three brothers. Nica and Izzy seemed close and at ease with each other. Paige didn't have an easy time with her female roommate her freshman year of college and convinced her parents to let her live off campus the last two years so she could concentrate on her studies without a roommate. It helped that her older brother Brian had done the same thing before her.

"Do you have a boyfriend, Paige?" Izzy asked as they sat down to eat.

"No, I'm not interested in dating," Paige responded. "I'm focusing on my education."

"Boring!" Izzy rolled her eyes. "Isn't the point of college to find a husband?"

"Pay her no mind, Paige!" Nica responded. "That is not the point of college. Unless you're Izzy, who's majoring in 'How to be a Mrs.' But Izzy, I think Paige is holding out on us. You would not believe the handsome plumber that is working at In Bloom–he has his eye on Paige and the rest of us think it'll be just a matter of time until she falls under his spell. Did I mention he is handsome, with great hair and a muscular physique?"

"Tell me more." Izzy raised an eyebrow, and Paige thought about the qualities that Nica called out. Besides those physical characteristics, he was also funny, confident, and friendly. If only he wasn't a plumber and if only she wasn't leaving for New York…her mind drifted away when Izzy tapped her foot, pulling Paige back from her reverie.

"He's okay, I guess," Paige started. "But like I said, I don't have time…" her voice trailed off.

"You were going to go to New York this summer, and that just got canceled yesterday, so how are you so busy?" Nica took a bit of her enchilada.

Wow, Nica was direct! "Well, because I need to come up with a new plan. I'll need a second job this summer because Anna Lee won't be able to give me a lot of hours. She hired you thinking I'd be gone. I don't want to take anyone else's hours away or feel like Anna Lee's summer charity case. So, a second job, maybe a third. I can probably pick up an online class. I'll make an appointment with my advisor right away and talk about options.

Losing this summer internship is setting my career goals back and I want to get back on track. See, there's no time for dating." Paige took a deep breath.

"Slow down, *chica*," Nica said. "There's more to life than career goals or finding a husband." She gave Izzy a stern look. "Life is in the balance."

Paige thought about Nica's words. Yes, life should have balance. Work was important but so was love. And family. She didn't have to rush into these things. There was time. Maybe seeing Trevor would help her get past the hurt left by Caleb's abrupt breakup. She didn't have to commit to a relationship or anything. But a date or two might be a good distraction. Maybe she could take that risk.

"Oh boy, you sound like my yoga-teaching mom!" Paige shook her head, imagining her mom saying the same thing.

"I think your mom is brilliant then!"

"Maybe you'll get to meet her tomorrow when my dad brings my things." Paige smiled. She was going to love living with this pair of cousins.

CHAPTER ELEVEN

AFTER DINNER WITH Nica and Izzy, Paige drove home to her parents' house. Her mom, Sue, was waiting for her on the front porch swing when she arrived.

Paige grabbed her backpack and joined her mom on the swing, tossing her bag on a wicker chair.

"How was the drive?" her mom asked.

"Uneventful." Paige looked out at the huge front yard. The oak and maple trees stood strong, warding off danger. She always took comfort looking at them at night from the living room or her upstairs bedroom. She listened to the chirps, trills, and whistles of the birds, busy with final socializing before settling down for the night.

"The apartment was all right? Your dad told me you asked if he could bring furniture tomorrow, so I am guessing it is."

"It's great! It'll be fun living with Nica and her cousin Izzy. I'm excited about having roommates again." Paige yawned. "Wow, it was a long day at the end of an up and down week. Finals, the disappointment of losing the internship, and… oh, never mind."

"And?"

"I met a guy at work. He's not working there. I mean, he is working there. Temporarily. He's a plumber, and some pipes, or all the pipes, need to be replaced."

"A guy."

"Yes, a guy that's handsome and seems to be into me. But I don't know. I don't want to date right now. There's my career to worry about. In order to get established, I'll need to go to New York. Why start a relationship when there's so much up in the air?"

"I see," Sue replied.

"You agree with me, right?"

"I didn't say that." Sue sipped from the mug in her hand. Paige could smell the sweet apple scent of chamomile tea, her mom's favorite. "There's more to life than a career. I think I did something wrong in raising you kids. You are all career focused. I thought we would raise artists, free spirits, cippies..."

"Cippies?"

"Yes, cippies," Sue repeated. "Hippies, only cooler."

"You made that up," Paige said. She thought Sue's words were similar to Nica's. Life was more than a career; it needed balance.

"Hmm, maybe I did. But the point is, there's more to life than your career. Falling in love, exploring, adventures, getting married, giving me beautiful, artistic grandbabies."

"Mom, I'm only twenty-one! Can't I wait to get married and have babies? Geesh. Jack's married. When will he and Becca give you grandkids?" Paige stopped the swing with her foot and her mom continued forward awkwardly, lifting her mug up before it spilled.

"We'll see. Nice deflection, hon. Now, back to this guy at work. What's his name? What does he look like? Has he treated you well? Has he asked you out?" Sue kicked Paige's foot forward to get the swing moving again.

"Trevor. Tall. Dark hair. Brown eyes. I suppose so. And I suppose so. Did I answer all the questions?" Paige leaned back in the swing and closed her eyes.

"On the surface, yes. How do you feel when you talk to him?"

Paige again wondered if her mom had a psychology degree

that she hid from them. "Nervous. Like I could like him if I'm not careful."

"That's not a bad thing, hon. Why don't you go on a date and see what happens? What harm could come of it?" Sue had turned in the swing so she could watch Paige. Paige could tell by the sound of her voice.

"Mom, I'm scared. After Caleb…" she trailed off.

"I know that was an awful breakup, but it's been a while. Maybe it's time to try again. Maybe dating someone new will take some of the sting of the breakup away."

"It's only been four months and three weeks! When you said Caleb was engaged again, it threw me. How could he be engaged already? Do you think they were dating while we were engaged? Do you think she's pregnant?"

The sound of the chain creaking put Paige on edge. She considered running to the garage to get a can of WD-40. Her mom would call her out for avoiding the conversation though, so she clenched her jaw instead.

"Don't speculate. Try to put him out of your mind."

Paige grunted.

"I know it's difficult," Sue continued. "But you can. And I think the best remedy for getting your mind off of Caleb is to go on a date with this Trevor, the plumber. A plumber!" It sounded like Sue squealed. "A tradesman! I can't wait to meet him."

"Mom, I haven't even agreed to go out with him. Aren't you getting ahead of yourself?"

"Honey, I feel something magical in the air tonight. I have a good feeling about this! Let's head inside. Mosquitoes are biting."

Magical. The universe. Good feelings. Like the fantasy books she read as a child. Why was she surrounded by these universe-reading, tree-hugging, magic-believing, canvas-painting adults? Maybe she should call her brother Jack, the accountant, and get his perspective.

AFTER KICKING LOGAN out of her bedroom, she shut the door and sank into her oversized reading chair. She picked up her phone and looked at the time. It was only nine p.m. She wondered if Macey was on a date or able to talk. She sent a text instead of calling.

PAIGE: hey, can u talk?

Waiting for a response, Paige leaned over to the bookcase and grabbed a well-loved copy of *A Wrinkle in Time* by Madeleine L'Engle. She thumbed through the pages, looking for and reading highlighted passages. Ten minutes later, her phone rang. It was Macey.

"Hey, sorry for bugging you so late," Paige said, answering.

"Not a problem," Macey responded. "I was just playing backgammon with my mom."

"Do you wish you could stay in Dekalb over break? Wouldn't it be more exciting than hanging out with your parents over the summer?"

"No. I enjoy coming home and laying low for the summer. If I stayed there, I would have to work a lot more to afford an apartment. At least here, rent and food is free." She yawned. "You know all about that. But you're the independent type and choose to stay in Bloomington versus coming home."

"Hey, if you had a younger brother like Logan, you would stay away too."

Macey laughed. "True. What's up?"

"Well," Paige tried to organize her thoughts before jumping in. "I need you as a sounding board. Got a lot on my mind and can't think clearly."

"That's not like you," Macey responded. Paige nodded, knowing Macey couldn't see her.

"Right. Well, I met someone."

"Yes?" Macey sounded intrigued. And like she was eating something. "Tell me more."

"His name is Trevor, he's the plumber that Anna Lee hired to fix the plumbing issue at In Bloom. Well, not just fix, but also replace a bunch of the pipes."

"You met a plumber? Does he have a butt crack?" Macey laughed.

Paige groaned. "You had to go there, didn't you? So far, no. I think his pants fit well. Very well actually." She pictured Trevor's full physique and smiled. "He's quite handsome. He's several inches taller than me, probably six foot. He's got dark brown, almost black, hair, light brown eyes. He's funny, charming, flirty—"

"With everyone or just you?" Macey cut her off.

"Good question. I think just me. He teases the other girls but doesn't seem to flirt with them. I don't know. I've never been a great judge of flirting. It's so awkward."

"Yes, you prefer to have it scripted. I'm not sure what help I can give you. Sounds like there is a handsome guy that's into you. What's the problem?"

"I'm not ready to date. You know. After Caleb…."

"Come on now. It's been five months. Do you think there is a proper amount of hibernation needed after a breakup? You should have gotten back on the dating horse a week after Caleb so cowardly walked away from the best woman he could have possibly married."

"Aww, that's sweet. You're just saying that because we're friends."

"No. I'm saying it because it's the truth!" Macey's earlier fatigue seemed to disappear; she was getting fired up. "You will make the right man very, very happy. Now, maybe this new plumber is that man. But maybe not. Don't get hung up on dating 'Mr. Right.' Date 'Mr. Right Now.' Heck, if all this Trevor guy has going for him is his good looks and a little flirting, that's enough for now. It will get you back out there. Every new relationship is a chance to refine what you are looking for in a partner. Are your likes compatible? Do you somewhat agree on politics, on key issues? Do you get along? Does he treat you like the queen that you are? All those things. I say, get out there. Go out with this plumber. Trevor, right? Go out with him as soon as you can and report back to me pronto."

"Yes, ma'am." Paige laughed. She loved it when Macey got riled up.

"Well, I gotta go. I agreed to go strawberry picking with my mom in the morning before it gets too hot. She'll probably be pounding on my door at six. I got to get some sleep."

"Sure." Paige stretched and yawned. "Hey, thanks for listening. I appreciate you."

"And I you."

Paige hung up and glanced down at the book in her lap. Maybe Macey was right, maybe dating Trevor would be beneficial for her. More relationship experience, more data. What did she like? What didn't she like? With Caleb, it had just been easy. Comfortable. They got along; he was nice. He had been nice before he stomped on her heart.

SUNDAY MORNING, PAIGE grabbed a cup of coffee and asked if her dad was awake.

Sue laughed. "He's been up for hours. He's in the studio. Walk out there and see if he wants to come in for breakfast. Tell him

I'll make blueberry pancakes if he comes inside in the next fifteen minutes."

"I didn't hear him get up. And I was up early, reading. I'm surprised. I'll go out and tell him."

Paige walked through the back door and passed the barn that was used for storage and her mom's yoga studio. When she was a kid, it had been a frequently used play area for her and her brothers. Her dad's painting studio was past the barn. It was a small ten foot by ten foot room at the very back of their property, next to their neighbor's cornfield. He appreciated the distance from the house; it was quiet and he could lose himself in his art.

Paige knocked lightly on the door before entering. She waited until she heard him call for her to come in. "Hi Dad. What are you working on?" She stepped around the canvas to see what he was painting.

"It's the third and final in a series: *Contemplations on Aging*. I'm talking to a gallery owner in Chicago about a show this winter. I'm jazzed about the idea. Been a minute since I've been in a show." Frank yawned and looked at the wall clock behind him.

Paige looked at the canvas and nodded. "Fascinating." She discovered over the years that this was one of the best responses to her dad's art. It didn't provoke a lot of discussion. "Mom says if you come in soon, she'll make blueberry pancakes. How early did you get up? I didn't hear you."

"Long before sunrise early. Maybe four a.m. I woke to use the restroom, then came out. I don't like the lack of light that early, but I turned on all the lamps and made it work. Help me turn everything off. I'm starving for your mom's blueberry pancakes!"

Outside the studio, Paige glanced at the sky and noted the darker clouds in the southeast. "Think we'll get a storm today?" She thought about loading furniture in the rain and didn't like the idea.

"Doesn't look great. Let's hustle and load the van before we go in to eat. Just in case." Frank headed toward the garage. "Go get Logan to come out and help."

They loaded the van right before the rain fell. Paige gave herself a virtual pat on the back for paying attention to the weather. Her parents always sounded surprised when it stormed. They either had no confidence in weather reporters or couldn't be bothered to worry about how they might be affected by the weather.

The four of them drove to Bloomington to move her furniture into the apartment. Logan and Paige rode in her car, and her parents drove the van. Logan kept Paige laughing during the drive, telling her about his experience detasseling corn. He talked about kids losing shoes in the mud and their races down the long rows of tall corn. He said he came home every day ready to shower and fall into bed for a much-needed nap. Paige was glad she never agreed to do that job. The money was great, but the work was hard.

Izzy and Nica were home from Mass when they arrived, and Izzy prepared a chicken Caesar salad for lunch.

Paige walked her family to their van after lunch and gave them tight hugs before they left. Sue kissed her on the cheek and whispered in her ear, "I really like your roommates. Enjoy yourself, hon. Have fun this summer. You can throw yourself back into your studies in the fall. But live life now. Date this Trevor guy. I have a good feeling about this."

CHAPTER TWELVE

NICA ASKED PAIGE to take her shift at In Bloom on Tuesday so she could go home with Izzy for a visit. Paige was settled in after having all day Monday to unpack, so she jumped at the opportunity to work.

Anna Lee had several wedding consultations scheduled, so Paige was monitoring the retail store. She was grateful she was the only one in besides Anna Lee. No chance for the other girls to tease her about Trevor and being up front meant she wouldn't run into him a lot.

Anna Lee finished a consultation and walked the bride-to-be to the door. The young woman gave Anna Lee a hug before saying goodbye. Paige smiled seeing the exchange. Anna Lee was such a caring person; strangers became friends quickly.

"I've been so rushed this morning I haven't caught up with you, Paige. What's new?" Anna Lee put her work order binder under the counter and locked eyes with Paige, giving Paige her full attention.

"Well, I am renting the spare room at Nica's, and I unpacked yesterday. Thank you for that tip. I think it's going to work out well." Paige picked up the dust rag and began dusting the countertop.

"Glad to hear. Your summer must be looking up already." Anna Lee leaned over and rested her forearms on the counter.

Her yellow reading glasses slid off her head and landed on her nose with a soft plop. She laughed, removed them, and put them in a side pocket of her yellow dress.

"Yes, that's one book closed. I am looking for another job, so if you have any more insider knowledge to toss my way, I would appreciate it. Not getting the internship this summer made a mess of my budget. I've lost hundreds of dollars and need to make it up."

"Are you interested in waiting tables? I know the owner of Max's Coffee Shop on North Main Street, and they are hiring." Anna Lee checked her watch. "It's lunch time. Go on. I can watch the store."

"I can wait tables. Haven't done it since high school, but I have experience. I want to stay busy and make extra money. After I get off here today, I can stop by there and put an application in. Will they be open at four?" A surge of adrenaline rushed through her; another task to add to her to-do list.

"Yes. I'll call the owner while you're on break to vouch for you. Though I worry we'll be fighting over your shifts." Anna Lee smiled, and Paige was proud that Anna Lee saw her as a hard worker.

"Thanks, Anna Lee. Oh, I meant to ask," Paige looked over her shoulder to see if Trevor was around, "what happened with Trevor on Saturday? Tilly said that he got a phone call and rushed out."

"Oh, his nephew got hurt at a soccer game." Anna Lee replied. "I asked him yesterday, and he said the poor boy fell on the bleachers and got a nasty cut somewhere on his face. You know how badly head wounds bleed. Needed a few stitches, but all better now."

"Oh! Glad to hear that." The tension in Paige's shoulders eased. "I'll go on lunch break now if that's okay. I skipped breakfast this morning and my stomach is rumbling."

"Go on. I got this."

PAIGE GRABBED HER lunch bag with the leftover taco salad that Izzy had made the night before and went out to the picnic table with a book. If she kept her nose in her book, maybe she could avoid Trevor.

No such luck. In less than five minutes, Trevor joined her at the picnic table with his own lunch. Her pulse raced as he sat down. She kept her eyes turned down towards her taco salad and the book she had propped open on the table, but she could not miss his body movement as he sat directly across from her, his long legs raising and lowering onto the bench.

"Hello. What are you reading?" he asked as he sat down, taking a sucker stick out of his mouth and dropping it into his lunch box.

"Hi. *The Fifth Season* by N.K. Jemisin. She is one of my favorite authors, she's brilliant!" She held up the book for him to see the cover.

"Ah, cool."

"Have you read it?"

"No, but the cover is cool." He smiled and the lines around his eyes crinkled.

Paige couldn't help but smile back. He seemed genuinely happy. "Do you read?" she asked.

"What you really want to know is, can I read? Right?"

"I assume you can read. Can you?" her smile was a challenge.

"Yes, I can. I don't usually read the classics, but I enjoy a good novel. John Grisham, Jack Reacher, to name some favorites." He took a bite of a neatly prepared turkey and bacon sandwich. Paige wondered if he'd made it himself or bought it at a deli.

"You know Jack Reacher is a character, not the author, right?"

"Yes, I do. But there are a bunch of them. Jack Reacher works when I ask at the library for a new book."

"You use the library?" Paige's eyes widened with surprise.

"Seems like the most economical and environmental thing to do. I hate to waste anything. Last we talked, you didn't agree to go on a date with me. I would like to clear that up today. I have a plan. Hear me out." He paused.

Macey's suggestion that Paige just try it, date for dating's sake, echoed in her head. "Fine, I'm listening. I didn't agree, but I'm listening."

"That's a start. Okay now, first we go to the library. I have a book overdue, and I thought if I take a pretty girl like you in with me, they may forgive my fine."

"A pretty girl like me?"

"Did you miss the overdue book part? Whew! I thought that would be a strike against me in your book. Ha! Your book. Yes, a pretty girl. A beautiful girl, if I'm being honest. Anyway, after you get me off the hook with my library fine, I would like to take you to a delicious steak dinner." He paused as she wrinkled her nose. "No to steak?"

"Steak is fine, but it sounds like a fancy dinner. Are you sure? We could do a casual dinner. I'd be happy to pay my share." Paige didn't plan on this lasting more than one date and she didn't want him to waste his money on a fancy dinner. Plus, she worried about dating someone at work. What if it didn't work out? It would be awkward to be forced to see him. At least his time at In Bloom would be temporary.

"No way. I'm not going cheap on a first date with you. Quality requires quality. A steak dinner, that's firm. Then, if you'd like, we'll go to the cinema uptown and catch the weekly movie there."

"Cinema?"

"I feel like you are an echo," he smiled, and Paige blushed. "Yes, it's a movie theater. I thought you'd know that."

"I know what a cinema is, but I didn't know there was one uptown. I only know about the ten-screen theater off the highway."

He shuddered. "Yeah, I know that one, too. But this is a classy, classic cinema."

Paige giggled at his alliteration. "Classy? Classic movies too?"

"Yes, classics. This week they are showing *Casablanca*. Have you seen it?" He finished his sandwich and pulled out a giant chocolate muffin.

"Yes. My parents are classic movie buffs. That muffin looks divine." She tried not to lick her lips.

"Great, it's a date!"

She smiled. First alliterations, now rhymes. Why wasn't he an English major? "I didn't agree! It sounds like a lovely date, though." If she was being honest, she was going to say yes, Macey would be proud. But she wasn't letting Trevor off the hook easily.

"Lovely date? It's almost perfect. I noticed you haven't taken your eyes off my double chocolate muffin. Agree to the date and I'll let you have half."

"Deal!" she shouted, wanting to jump across the table to grab the muffin.

"Shoot," he said, "if I knew it was that easy, I would have started with the muffin. Friday at six?" He split the muffin in half and put half on a napkin, sliding it across the picnic table to her. She put the rest of her taco salad back in her bag.

"Friday at six," she agreed, taking a bite of the giant muffin. "And you must tell me where you get these muffins."

"Delicious, right? I'm not that easy. You don't get all my secrets before the first date. I'll save the chocolate muffin secret for the third date."

Paige rolled her eyes. "That's mean," she said, sighing with contentment.

CHAPTER THIRTEEN

THE NEXT FEW days passed quickly and finally Friday night arrived. Paige was pleased when Trevor arrived on time to pick her up.

After settling into his truck, she pulled a sucker from the open bag on the seat in between them.

"You really like suckers, don't you? Are you a kid at heart?" she asked, pulling the wrapper off and putting it in the small garbage bag hanging from the dash, filled with wrappers.

"Not particularly. But it's a much better habit than the one I'm trying to break." He grabbed a sucker as well and handed her the wrapper, which she placed in the trash.

"You smoke?" Paige turned in her seat to watch him drive. He was not in his usual blue t-shirt. Tonight, he had on a pair of black pants and a short-sleeve, button-down, checked shirt. He looked like a slightly older college student.

"Haven't for three weeks," he responded, pulling the sucker out of his mouth and resting his hand on his thigh. "But I've been a smoker."

"It's good that you're trying to quit."

"Yeah, it's important to me."

"Why?"

"I lost my dad to lung cancer earlier this year. It was torture watching him struggle to breathe. He ignored a chronic cough for two years, refused to go to the doctor about it. Guess he stuck his head in the sand. It infuriates me to this day." He sighed and flipped on the turn signal for the library parking lot.

"I'm so sorry. It has to be devastating to lose a parent." She thought about her own parents and made a quick mental note to hug them a little tighter the next time she saw them.

He grunted but didn't elaborate.

Paige had been looking forward to this library visit. She spent countless hours in the university library but had never been to the local library. Her eyes took in the nearly deserted parking lot. "Are you sure they're open?" She looked at the clock on the dash 5:50 p.m.

"They close at six. We have plenty of time."

Paige raised an eyebrow. "Ten minutes? You don't know me very well."

"No, but I'm excited about learning more! Let's go." He shut off the engine and opened his door, grabbing the overdue book as he jumped from the truck.

Inside, they approached the front desk together. Paige's eyes roved around the bright space. Their summer reading program was highlighted on a large bulletin board to the left of the desk, displaying colorful pictures of ice cream and beach balls. Trevor leaned over and put an elbow on the desk, looking the young clerk in the eye. She didn't seem to notice Paige's presence.

"Good evening, Miss. I believe this book may be past due. I know I'm a terrible person and I wish to make amends." Trevor spoke low, and Paige melted at his smooth cadence.

"Amends, huh?" the young lady behind the counter lifted a shoulder and gave an attractive smile to Trevor.

"Amends, Miss Colleen," he said, reading her name tag.

She clicked a few buttons and scanned the book. "You owe eighty cents. You are eight days late."

Trevor stood slowly and glanced at Paige. "Got eighty cents?" he asked.

Paige was confused. He asked her here to pay his fine? Worst date ever.

"I'm kidding, I'm kidding!" he said, pulling a folded stack of bills from the right pocket of his pants.

Paige turned away from him to look at a rack of new releases near the counter. She browsed the titles until Trevor moved next to her. He didn't touch her but stood close enough that she could smell either his laundry detergent or cologne. She wasn't sure which.

"Did you find a new book for me?" he asked.

"You said you like Grisham. Did you see this new release?" she asked, pointing with her sandal at a book on the lower shelf.

"No, I didn't. Thanks for pointing it out–cute polish on your toes, by the way–but I think I'm going to wait before checking out a new book. I'm going to be busy in the next few weeks. Are you ready to go?" He shifted his weight slightly and Paige could feel his upper arm touching her shoulder.

"Busy? Another big job coming up?" Paige started for the door.

"No, not work related. Something fun."

"Oh, I see." Paige wondered what he had planned but didn't know him well enough to ask.

Trevor took a few strides to get in front of her and open the door. He turned towards the librarian at the desk and gave a quick wave. Paige wanted to shoot daggers at the girl but didn't know why.

"Well, the library didn't appear to be a natural habitat for you. Where do you normally hang out?" Paige waited for Trevor to open the truck door for her as he reached for the handle.

"Here and there. I play pickup basketball with some friends. I hang out at a bar close to my house to watch live music a couple of times a week. When I'm home, I tinker around. I bought a fixer-upper and it's still in the fixer phase." Trevor shut her door and walked around to the driver's side, sliding in and grabbing another sucker from the bag.

"Is driving a smoking trigger for you?" Paige resisted the urge to grab one herself.

"Absolutely, the worst one. Sorry if it bothers you."

"Not at all. Better than smoking, I guess."

"Sure, sure."

AFTER PLACING THEIR orders with the server, Trevor pulled out a folded index card from his back pocket. It was covered front and back with meticulous print handwriting.

"Okay, now that we've ordered, I have a game for us." He said with a sly smile.

Paige's eyes locked on his. "A game?"

"Game. Twenty questions. A Q. and A. Call it what you will. Are you ready to begin?"

"That's a list of questions?"

"Yes, but I'm supposed to ask the questions."

"That doesn't sound fair."

"Fair is relative. If after you answer a question, you want to ask the same of me, you just say, your turn. Got it?"

"And if I refuse to answer?" Paige wondered what types of questions were on his list.

"You can say pass, but you lose a point for each pass."

"You're keeping score?"

"Why are you asking all of these questions? And yes, I keep score."

"So, there is a winner and a loser."

"Naw, we both win. We find out more about each other."

"Okay. I'm game."

"Number one. Who's in your immediate family?"

"My mom, Sue. Dad Frank. Brothers Jack, twenty-seven, married to Becca; Brian, twenty-four, single, but he's been dating his girlfriend Lily for several years; and my younger brother, Logan, is seventeen. Your turn." Paige took a sip of her iced tea and prepared for his answer.

"Dad, Pete, deceased. Mom, Ruth, lives in Florida. One sister, Tricia, lives in town. Her husband Erik is in the service. Unfortunately, things are not going well. They've separated and I don't think they can reconcile. The hardest part of it is that they have two young boys, Waylon and William. Four and two. They're my little buddies. You forgot to mention your age. I'm twenty-seven, though you didn't ask."

"Anna Lee said that one of your nephews got hurt the other day. What happened?" Paige hoped she wasn't being too forward.

"Yes, the youngest, Willie." His eyes softened, and he smiled. "He slipped climbing the bleachers. Nasty cut right below his nose. Took a few stitches. It freaked my sister out and then she needed help with Waylon at the hospital."

"So, you rushed to the rescue." Paige pictured Trevor hoisting a little boy on his shoulders and melted at the thought of it.

"Always. Anytime my sister needs me, or the boys need me, I'll be there."

"Aww, that's so sweet." Paige smiled. "I'm sure your sister appreciates the help. Do you volunteer to babysit? They are pretty young."

"Of course, I babysit." Trevor leaned closer to her. "I go to their games and cheer them on. I fix things at her house. I mow the lawn. I want to be very involved in their lives. I'm glad they are still in town. For a while it looked like Tricia's husband wanted them to move out of state. I'm grateful that didn't happen."

"Wow, you are an amazingly amazing brother. Your sister is very lucky to have you in her life. So are your nephews."

Trevor actually blushed. "Stop it. You're embarrassing me. It's family. You have to be there for your family no matter what."

Paige reached over and squeezed his hand. "I'm not sorry for embarrassing you. I think that most of the time men don't get enough recognition for helping out their family."

"Fine. Maybe you're right." He flipped his hand over and squeezed back.

"Hold on," Paige released his hand and held her hand up in a stop gesture. "You and your sister are Trevor and Tricia, and her kids are Waylon and William? What's with the matching first initials?"

"Family tradition. My mom and all her sisters are Rs. My sister followed the trend." He shrugged.

"Are you required to follow this trend?" Paige was curious.

"I didn't sign a contract or anything. Now, back to my questions. Age?"

Paige laughed. "I'm twenty-one. I noticed you didn't order a drink. Do you drink?"

"Well, yes, but again, a smoking trigger, so I've cut back. Not out, merely back. I think we're even so far. Question three. Who broke your heart?" Trevor set his card down as the server put salad plates in front of them.

"Wow. Softball questions one and two. Hardball question three. I see how you are. What makes you think I've had my heart broken?" Paige picked up her fork, not planning to tell him about Caleb.

"You said you broke up with your fiancée at Christmas. And it took a minor miracle to get you on a date. I assume your heart got broken in the breakup. You have a wariness about you that makes me believe your ex was a jerk. Who was he?" Trevor's voice sounded playful, but there was a seriousness in his gaze.

So much for holding back. She twisted the ring from her grandmother, it gave her the courage to answer. "Caleb. You know I thought I had dealt with the breakup and all that, but I recently found out that he's already engaged again!" Paige rubbed her forehead.

"Dang. That blows. How long were you engaged?"

Paige watched the forkful of salad pass through his lips. "Two and a half years. We got engaged soon after high school graduation. He was going to school at Northwestern, and I was going here, so…" she dropped her gaze down to her salad. Why was she giving this much detail?

"Ah. High school sweethearts. That's tough. Was he your first boyfriend?"

"No. I dated a couple of guys before him. But they weren't serious like Caleb. What about you? Have you been in love?" Paige held her breath.

"Yes. Next question."

"Whoa. Aren't you going to elaborate?"

"Darn. Thought I could get away with the short answer. I've been in love. Never engaged, though." His eyes looked as if they held a challenge.

"Well, I understand that." Paige's spine straightened. "I've decided that I won't marry before thirty. It was foolish to get engaged so young. Besides, I have my career to focus on now; there's no time for a serious relationship." There she said it. This was going to go nowhere. Might as well be clear about that up front. Protect her heart, though her mind wasn't convinced.

Though this was only their first date, she liked how Trevor took charge. Once he knew she was a reader, he suggested the library. He insisted on a fancy dinner. He brought conversation starters so there wouldn't be a lull in the conversation. Never mind that he was handsome like a modern-day Fitzwilliam Darcy from *Pride and Prejudice*. Though her words said one thing, he excited her, and she hoped this wouldn't end with a one and only date.

"No serious relationships. Noted. Question four," he repeated. "Favorite sport."

"Baseball. I love the history of it, the strategy."

"Cards or Cubs?"

"The White Sox," she grinned. "You?"

"Cardinals all the way. So that's good. Our teams don't go head-to-head too often."

Trevor finished his salad and eased back in his seat. Paige relaxed and enjoyed his company. Trevor's twenty questions game was lighthearted, a perfect way to get to know each other without awkward pauses in the conversation.

"So," she asked, "is this your standard first date index card? Are there cards for dates two and three? Do all the girls enjoy these questions?"

"I'm glad you're enjoying it. Actually, I've never done this before. I had a feeling I would have to be on my toes with you. You're not my normal dating demographic."

"Oh, yeah? I'm not going to ask what your normal dating demographic is. Why would you ask me out if I'm not your normal dating demographic?" Paige wasn't sure she wanted the answer.

"It was time to upgrade."

Paige liked the sound of that.

AFTER THE MOVIE, Trevor drove her home and parked on the curb. He pulled the keys from the ignition and opened his door. Paige wondered if he expected to come in. She hadn't talked to Izzy and Nica about visitors, so she wasn't sure what the rules were. But even if it was all right with them, she wasn't ready to have Trevor in the apartment. It was a great evening getting to know him, but it was too soon to invite him in.

She was considering how she could not invite him in without being rude or hurting his feelings when he opened her door. He held out his hand to help her down.

"Watch for the curb. It's pretty dark here, not a lot of streetlights," he said as she climbed down from the truck. He adjusted his hand after she was out of the car; now he was holding it. Paige liked the warmth of his hand around hers. Turning him away would not be easy.

They reached the top of the stairs, and Trevor turned to her. Paige sensed a knot in her stomach. "I should have said good night to you in the truck. You didn't need to walk me all the way up here."

"That wouldn't have worked," he responded.

"Worked?" she asked.

"I couldn't have kissed you properly in the truck."

"Properly?" she repeated. What was with all the questions? Was she incapable of making a statement?

"Properly." He let go of the hand he was holding and put his hand on the back of her neck, softly pulling her closer. His eyes sparkled as he leaned down.

Paige closed her eyes, and heat flooded her body when his lips touched hers. His kiss tasted like the cherry sucker he ate in the truck, the sweetness on his lips was intoxicating. She placed a hand on his stomach to steady herself, and he grunted like someone had punched him. She pulled back from him quickly. "Are you okay?"

"Fine, just fine. You shocked me, is all."

"A static shock?"

"No, a surprise shock. I didn't expect it. You surprise me." He smiled as he leaned over and rested his forehead on hers. "You are full of surprises, Paige. I'm enjoying getting to know you. Now, go in, have a great night, and I'll call you soon." He gave her a quick kiss on the cheek and started down the stairs.

"Good night, Trevor," she called.

"Night."

Paige replayed the date in her mind as she entered the quiet apartment. Trevor was full of surprises. She loved getting to know him and was excited about seeing him again. She noticed a television light coming from the living room. She found Nica asleep on the sofa with the TV on mute. She shook her roommate softly. "Nica, do you want to go to your bed? The couch doesn't look that comfortable."

"It's okay. I'm waiting for Izzy to get home. She'll wake me when she comes in. How was your date?" Nica rubbed her eyes and sat up.

"It was nice. But don't get up. I'll tell you about it in the morning." Paige was afraid the spell would break if she divulged too much too soon.

"Sounds good. Night." Nica appeared to fall asleep again before her head hit the couch pillow.

In the room, Paige got out her laptop and jotted a note to herself in her diary file.

First Date with Trevor
* twenty questions over dinner—fun
* Casablanca movie—he didn't talk during the movie—thumbs up
* walked me to the door—two thumbs up
* the kiss—too quick but dreamy nevertheless
* overall date score—A+

After typing the list, she closed her laptop and picked her cell phone up. It was late, but she sent a quick text to Lauren, who would be on a flight to Paris in the morning.

PAIGE: Have a safe flight & a great big adventure in Europe. I'll miss you!

She wondered if one of them would be setting the other up on a blind date at the end of summer. If things didn't work out with Trevor, she wondered if Lauren would have someone in mind for her. The date with Trevor tonight had worked out well. Maybe she *was* ready to put Caleb behind her.

CHAPTER FOURTEEN

PAIGE STARTED WAITING tables at Max's Coffee Shop on Monday after a quick orientation. The manager promised her three days a week and said he'd work around her schedule at In Bloom. He said he had a lot of respect for Anna Lee, and he would not tick her off by poaching a quality employee.

The shift started slowly but picked up with the lunch rush. It shocked her to see Anna Lee and Trevor standing at the hostess desk and it thrilled her when they were seated in her section.

Trevor had called on Saturday, said he had a full weekend, but that he enjoyed their date and asked if she did too. She agreed. Paige was disappointed that he had a lot going on over the weekend, but understood he had a life, and she didn't want to get too entangled too quickly.

"Hello!" she called as she approached their table. Trevor's eyes captured hers, and she wanted to melt into their toffee-colored goodness. Anna Lee cleared her throat and Paige turned to her. "Hi, Anna Lee. What can I get you two to drink? Are you ready to order?"

"We'll both have a BLT and an iced tea. We discussed on the way over."

Paige turned to Trevor and raised an eyebrow. He laughed and agreed with Anna Lee's order.

"Coming right up," Paige said.

Anna Lee turned to Trevor once Paige was out of earshot. "If I'm not mistaken, I think there is a spark between you two. What gives?"

Trevor rearranged the silverware on his napkin. "I like her, Miss Anna Lee. Not going to lie. But she said she's not interested in a serious relationship. Guess I'll have to take it slow. Do you have any advice for me? You know her a lot better than I do."

"Are *you* interested in a serious relationship?"

"I am. With the right person. I think Paige could be that person."

"Then don't give up!" Anna Lee smacked her hand on the table for emphasis. "She's a great person. Quiet. Caring. A hard worker. Be patient. Woo her. Young people simply want to swipe up, or down. Whatever. With their app for this and their app for that. What happened to dating? Respecting a woman? Wooing her?"

Trevor laughed. "Yes, ma'am. Message received."

After their quick lunch, Trevor stood and took money out of his pocket. He put a bill on the table and told Paige he'd call her that evening. Paige said goodbye and watched them leave. She turned to clear off the table and saw that he'd left a twenty-dollar bill as a tip. "Ugh," she mumbled. "This is way too much. I'll tell him when we talk later."

"I'M GOING FOR a run. Do you want to join me?" Nica asked. Nica and Paige sat at the dining table, drinking tea and working on their laptops. Nica was browsing kitchen makeovers on Pinterest and Paige was typing an email to her academic advisor about increasing her fall class load to ensure she would have the needed graduation credits, in case she got the spring internship.

"No, I'm not much of a runner. All right, I haven't run since high school." Paige hit send on her email and leaned back in her chair.

Nica closed her laptop and stood up.

"If you'd like to get back into it, let me know. I can help you ramp up."

"Thanks. I'll keep that in mind. I know I should build a better exercise habit. Especially when I work in a corporate environment and have to sit all day. Sitting is the new smoking someone said. Not healthy."

Nica smiled. "I can help you with that whenever you're ready. I'll be back soon."

Paige heard the email notification ping on her laptop and looked at her in-box. An email from Leslie Maron. Paige took a breath before opening the email.

Dear Ms. Bell,

I want to apologize again for the internship mix up. That had to be a disappointment to you. I hope you decide to apply for an internship next year, either in the spring or summer. Please let me know if you do.

On another note, I want to see if you would be interested in some freelance work this summer. We need proofreaders and copy editors. Attached is a chapter of a novel from one of our authors. If you are interested, take a run at proofing this piece and return it. If you're a fit, we will negotiate hourly rates with you and discuss availability.

Sincerely,
Leslie Maron, Director of H.R.
Garland Wilson Publishing

Freelance? Hourly rate? Interesting way to start in the publishing business, but what if they labeled her a freelancer? That would not be good. Paige needed full-time employment after college. A job with benefits. A job with a steady paycheck. All the years of financial uncertainty growing up had turned her off to the idea of freelance.

But for extra money this summer and a chance to show off her skills? That could work. And could it help her get the spring internship? Likely. Worth the risk. She printed off the attached chapter to read closely and she replied to Miss Maron that she would start on the assignment right away.

TREVOR CALLED AS Paige finished reading the chapter Leslie had sent. Paige was ready to read it a second time with a pencil in hand but was happy to take the call instead.

"What are you doing tonight?" he asked after she said hello.

"No plans, but I have an early shift at Max's."

"When will you be back at Anna Lee's? I miss seeing you there."

"I'm scheduled Thursday through Saturday. Won't you wrap up there soon?" Paige realized she was pacing around the living room and sat down so she wouldn't sound out of breath.

"Another week or two. I had to wait for parts to come in." He paused. "Now, about tonight. There is a new hot dog stand that recently opened near the airport, and I've heard great things about it. Would you like to take a ride with me and check it out?"

Paige had planned to cook a grilled cheese for dinner. "Sure, sounds yummy."

"Pick up you in twenty minutes?"

"Make it thirty? I didn't shower after my shift today and I think I smell bacon in my hair."

"Mmm, bacon. Sure, sure. Thirty minutes."

CHAPTER FIFTEEN

PAIGE ANSWERED THE knock on the door while towel-drying her hair. Trevor looked like he had showered as well; his dark hair was wet and combed back.

"Looks like you're not quite ready," he said as she held open the screen for him.

"I will be in two minutes. Come on in."

"Are your roommates home?" he asked, one foot over the threshold.

"No, they're both out," she said.

"I'll wait here on the porch then." He stepped back and closed the screen door.

"Why?" she asked.

"Don't want to cause a scandal. What will the neighbors say and all?" He stepped backwards and closed the screen door.

"Are you worried about my reputation or yours?" Paige called as she walked to the bathroom to put the towel away.

"Yours, of course. Mine is already shot."

Paige pondered his comment and frowned. She thought he'd been honest with her at dinner about his past relationships, but was he? She grabbed her purse out of her bedroom and tossed her cell phone inside. In the kitchen, she lifted her keys from the hook and put the door key in the deadbolt, pulling the door closed.

"Your reputation is that bad?" she asked, turning to Trevor after locking the door.

"I'm kidding. It's not that bad. Hungry?"

"Yes."

Trevor started down the stairs first, saying he wasn't crazy about the shape they were in, and he wanted to be in front in case she tripped and fell.

Paige was quiet on the drive. She thought about his reputation statement. He said he was joking, but was he? Anna Lee apparently trusted him, but was that because she knew his dad? The thing about dating men from home is she knew all about them, the good and the bad. With Trevor, she knew very little.

She tried not to let on that something was bothering her while they enjoyed their casual dinner but she knew she was more reserved than usual when Trevor called her out.

"You're bothered by my stupid joke, aren't you?" he asked when she didn't respond to his comment about the waffle fries.

"Um, no. Not at all. Why should I be?" She reminded herself that she would not get into a serious relationship with him, so his comment shouldn't bother her.

"Come on now." Trevor held up his hands. "I said something that concerned you. That's easy to see. I don't know why I said it. I was genuinely concerned about your reputation but worried it would make me sound old-fashioned, so I tried to deflect it by making fun of myself. When the words were out of my mouth, I realized how rotten it must have sounded to you. I don't have a sleazy reputation. I've dated, had a few serious relationships, but I'm not a dawg."

Paige laughed at how he emphasized the word dog by drawing it out. "Fine, you got me. Yes, I was concerned. It's hard to date a stranger, someone you didn't grow up with. Someone your family doesn't know."

"Yeah, but it doesn't sound like that worked out well for you either."

"Ouch. You're right about that." Paige sighed.

"Now I made you think about your ex." He shook his head. "Bad move, Trev."

"You call yourself Trev?"

"Only when I'm in trouble." He smiled. "Which is more often than I care to admit. What do you call yourself?"

"I."

"Aw, come on. You never call yourself a nickname? Pay? Pagett? Pagey? Gee, not easy to come up with a nickname for Paige."

Paige grinned. "My parents didn't like nicknames, hence Jack, Brian, Paige and Logan."

"Did your parents have a crystal ball?"

"No. Why?"

"Paige. And you're a bookworm. Funny how it fits."

"Maybe," she shrugged. "I have a lot of memories reading with both my parents when I was young. They probably read with me more than my rowdy brothers. What are some of your early memories with your parents?"

"My mom left when we were young." He took a deep breath. "My parents married right out of high school, and we came along right away. Mom was nineteen when she had me and she had my sister eighteen months later. I think she soon decided that she wanted to live a little, without all the responsibility. So, she left. Left my dad to raise us. He did all right. My early memories are with my dad, tinkering on stuff. There was always something that needed fixed. Plumbing, carpentry. He taught us all he knew."

"Your sister too?"

"Oh yes. She's not afraid to tackle home maintenance and repairs."

"Great life skills." Paige finished her fries and put the basket on the tray.

"True, true. That's why I was excited about buying my first home. It was going to be demolished, but I saved it. It's a late 1800s farmhouse, which had been in the country, but now the town has expanded around it. Two stories, three different additions over the years. In other words, a hot mess. The tinkering keeps me out of trouble."

"It's great that you own a house. Financially, it's usually a smart move."

"I'm not so sure about that." He shifted on the bench seat. "It's a bit of a money pit right now. But when I'm done, it'll be worth it."

"I hope to get to see it someday."

"You will. You will." He smiled

"Hey," Paige's voice rose in excitement, "if you're fixing up your house, Nica wants to flip houses after college. I don't know a lot about her skills, but I bet she would love to help you so she can learn some new things. We had a creaky spot in our living room floor and she figured out a way to shift and glue a board to stop the creak. If she's not watching a Jennifer Lopez movie, she's watching HGTV or she's on Pinterest, reading before and after posts about home improvement."

"Really?" Trevor replied. "I'll talk to her next time I see her. Sounds like it could be a win-win situation. Thanks for that heads up."

Paige's phone beeped. She pulled the phone out of her purse to check it. It was a text message from her oldest brother, Jack. Odd. She rarely heard from him directly.

JACK: big news sis

PAIGE: ??

> **JACK:** Becca's pregnant–ready to be an aunt?

Paige squealed; her eyes were wide. She looked at Trevor with a huge grin. "Oh, my gosh!"

"What is it? Good news, obviously." He smiled back.

"I'm going to be an aunt!" She squealed again.

"That's terrific! Being an uncle is the coolest. My nephews are great, they're curious and full of life. Congrats auntie."

Paige turned back to the phone.

> **PAIGE:** YES!! Congrats!!! Do mom and
> dad know?

> **JACK:** Yes, we're home. Told them in person.
> Wish you were here.

"Wow. They drove from Chicago to tell our parents in person. On a weeknight! They must be super excited. I wish I was there tonight."

"I bet you do. Could you run home tonight? You said it was only an hour away, right?" Trevor put his napkin on the tray, signaling he was done.

"It is, but no, I can't go. I work early tomorrow, remember? I'll find out how long they're staying. Maybe I can go later in the week. I'm off Wednesday. Well, after a rough start to the summer, losing the internship, things are really looking up."

"I would say they are." Trevor locked eyes with her and Paige blushed. This was nice, but she had to remember this was temporary. She couldn't fall for Trevor now. She intended to get that internship in the spring and she knew how well her last long-distance relationship had gone. Nope. She wasn't going to fall and get the rug pulled out from under her again.

CHAPTER SIXTEEN

TREVOR WAS STILL tingling from kissing Paige good night. He'd held her longer than he probably should have this early in their relationship but holding her was like crossing the finish line first in a tough race. He wanted to punch his fist in the air and celebrate.

After a rough start to the evening, she turned around once she got the news that she would be an aunt. The light that flipped on inside of her was awesome to watch, and he basked in the warmth of it. He wanted to make sure she was always like that with him. No more sticking his stupid foot in his mouth. But if he had said what was actually on his mind, it would have scared her. He knew this had the chance to be more than a brief fling, even if she didn't see it. But why did he have to say what he had? He saw it put Paige on edge right away.

Why did this girl churn up his insides like this? He enjoyed being single. He was in no hurry to get married. Right? He had his hands full taking over his father's business, rehabbing his house, helping his sister, who was raising her boys on her own. He didn't think she would reconcile with her husband. He wouldn't be able to find his way back if his spouse cheated.

At home, he walked into the dining room and surveyed the in-flight projects–scrapping hideous yellow metallic wallpaper off the walls and stripping four layers of paint from the crown molding. Yes, he wanted Paige to see this place, but not in its current state. Once he finished the dining room and living room, he'd have her over. Not until then.

Paige had lit up when she heard her brother and his wife were going to have a baby. Trevor already suspected that Paige would make a great mom someday. She was smart and kind and cautious. But seeing the joy in her eyes, hearing the news about becoming an aunt, solidified it for him. Sure, she had another year of school and she talked about this internship, but once she saw he was serious about her and their relationship, surely she'd stick around. Plans changed all the time. He knew he must step up his game and show her how he was feeling, show her how much she meant to him, and show her he'd do whatever it took to make her happy. How to show her? That was the question. He needed to get to know her better, to figure out what made her tick and what would make her happy.

His phone rang, and he hoped it was Paige. It was his sister Tricia, instead.

"Hey Sis," he said, putting the phone on speaker.

"Trev," she said.

"Oh no, am I in trouble?" He smiled.

"What?" He could picture the look of confusion on her face.

"Never mind. You called. What's up?"

Tricia sighed. "Hey, I need a favor. Can you keep the boys Saturday night? I have a date."

"I'm not ready to keep them here. This house is too torn up. Too dangerous. But I can stay at your place with them. Would that work?" His eyes swung around the room at the various tools lying around.

"Well, I guess that would work. I was hoping the date might end up here."

"Trish, you're not divorced yet. Are you sure that's a good idea?"

"Don't get high and mighty with me, bruh. But fine, you can plan to stay here."

"You don't want to give Erik any ammunition to ruin things in a divorce. If it comes to that."

"Isn't that a given? Besides, he's the one that cheated and left. I don't know how he can gain any ammunition at this point. But, sure, I get your point."

"Who's the lucky guy?"

"Someone I met at the grocery store. I'm not getting my hopes up. Just looking to have some fun. How are things going with your flower girl?"

"She's not a…never mind. Things are good." He wouldn't make a big deal about this with Tricia, yet. But truthfully, he thought things were much better than "good".

Trevor looked at his watch. It read 8:30 p.m. He could finish removing the wallpaper from one wall tonight. By the weekend, he might be able to paint the walls and refinish the woodwork. Then he could start in the living room. "Hey Sis, I want to get some stuff done before I call it a night. I'll stay over Saturday night and we can catch up when you get home, or Sunday morning if I'm zonked out when you get in. Sound good?"

"Sure thing. I want to hear more about this girl you're seeing. Can't wait to catch up."

AFTER SHE GOT off work on Tuesday, Paige stopped at The Book Nook, her favorite independent bookstore in Bloomington, and bought several books for her future niece or nephew, including *Goodnight Moon, Where the Wild Things Are,* and three Little Golden books. She picked out a blank card with an illustrated baby crib on the cover and wrote "Congratulations 'Mommy'

and 'Daddy'! I'm super excited for you and can't wait to meet my niece or nephew! Remember 'Don't Panic,' I've heard babies are 'mostly harmless'! Love you, Paige" on the inside.

She knew Jack would get *The Hitchhiker's Guide to the Galaxy* references, but he would probably need to explain them to Becca.

She stopped at the post office on her way home to mail the books and card. Back at the apartment, Izzy asked if she wanted to go to the mall with her, but Paige declined. She had a phone call to make. She couldn't wait to fill her best friend Macey in on Jack and Becca's news.

Macey answered on the third ring. "Hey Paige, what's up?"

"I have exciting news," she answered, kicking off her sneakers and lying across her bed.

"Yes?"

"Becca's pregnant. I'm going to be an aunt! I'm so freaking excited!"

"Aww, that's awesome! Congrats to the family. You'll love being an aunt. I know I do."

"Speaking of, how are Adam and Lisa's twins?"

"They are adorable," Macey replied. "They turned six months last week and they're babbling and rolling around. When you're home next, maybe we can go and see them. They always appreciate extra hands to hold the girls. Speaking of, when are you coming home next?"

"I'm not sure. Trying to get all the extra shifts that I can this summer. I need the cash. And then there's the Trevor situation."

"And how's that going?"

"Pretty good so far. I like him but I don't want to get serious. It's just a diversion, helping me shake off the Caleb drama."

CHAPTER SEVENTEEN

TREVOR WAS ALREADY working at In Bloom when Paige arrived on Thursday. She was grateful that Anna Lee was there when she got in. She wouldn't have liked it if Trevor and Tilly had been in the store alone. Trevor seemed to be into Paige, but Tilly was so darn cute, always wearing trendy clothes and accessories, and though she had a boyfriend, she loved to flirt.

Shortly after Paige arrived, Anna Lee went home. She expected a slow day and wanted to rest up for a full weekend.

"What's new, Tilly?" Paige asked once Anna Lee left.

"Not much," Tilly sighed. "They haven't opened the pool in my apartment complex yet and I'm miffed. I'm going to have absolutely no tan this summer."

Paige hated sitting by the pool, getting sunburned in the summer; she never tanned. She'd rather be at the library, browsing the shelves. "Bummer," she replied.

"I know, right? If they don't open soon, I'm going to ask my parents if they'll send me to Florida for a week. I need a tan."

"Couldn't you lay out without a pool?"

"Well, I could, but I love jumping in the water when I get hot. Know what I mean, Trevor?" She smiled, flashing her perfect teeth, and her eyes focused past Paige's shoulder.

Paige hadn't heard Trevor approach. She spun her head quickly, hoping to see his reaction. He was probably imagining Tilly in a swimsuit.

"I'm not much of a pool guy, Tils. Too much sitting around. I get the shakes if I'm not doing something."

"Ah, I like to stay occupied, too. Even in the pool," Tilly purred.

Paige wanted to roll her eyes and stick her finger down her throat. Could Tilly be a bigger flirt?

"Hey Paige, can you help me back here?" Trevor smiled at her, holding two wrenches. Paige knew nothing about plumbing, but if it meant spending alone time with Trevor, she was game.

"Sure. Yell if you get slammed, Tilly," she said, following Trevor to the workroom.

Once she knew she was out of earshot of Tilly, she asked, "Tils?"

Trevor grinned, "When I think Tilly, I think silly. It's how my brain works. Tilly plus Silly equals Tils. I think it's better than calling her Silly Tilly."

"Well, it didn't stop her from flirting with you, so she must not mind it."

"You think she was flirting?"

"Well, *yeah*," she drew out the word, making the "duh" meaning apparent. "She thinks you're scrumptious, so she's flirting."

"She does?" Trevor knelt beside the hole in the floor and latched one wrench on to a pipe. He gestured for Paige to grab it as he maneuvered the other wrench onto the same pipe a foot away. Paige grabbed a towel off the counter, dropped it on the floor, and then knelt on it.

"Yes," Paige replied. "It was the first thing I heard about you."

"And what about you?"

"What do you mean?"

"Do you think I'm scrumptious?" He trilled the word, over-exaggerating it.

Paige groaned, "I walked myself right into that, didn't I?"

"You did bring it up."

"Chocolate cake is scrumptious. Good-looking men are handsome. I would never say a man was scrumptious." Paige shook her head to emphasize her point.

"So?"

"Wow, you're genuinely fishing for a compliment, aren't you?"

"I'm trying to get a sense of where I stand with you. I'm not sure if you've gone out with me just to shut me up or if you might actually like me."

"We've only been on two dates; can't I wait to form an opinion?"

"Only looking for initial impressions, not asking for a letter of recommendation." Trevor gave a pull on the wrench in his hand to tighten it. Paige admired the muscles in his arms. She wondered if he worked out or if was a bonus side effect of the job.

"I think you're friendly, outgoing, handsome, warm, funny." Paige trailed off. He was these things and a great kisser. If she wasn't leaving for New York as soon as she could get there, she could see herself investing in this man.

"Sounds like you think pretty highly of me."

"You are looking for a letter of recommendation, aren't you?"

He laughed, a low throaty sound. "No ma'am. Gauging if I think you'll go out with me again. Like, maybe tomorrow night?"

"What do you have in mind? For the third date."

"Have you ever been to a CornBelters game?"

"No. What are the CornBelters?"

"They're a collegiate baseball team in Normal. The games are a lot of fun and it's a beautiful baseball field. The game is early, six p.m. If we don't fill up on ballpark food, we can grab dinner afterwards.

"That sounds fun."

"You'll go?"

"Yes."

"Great, I'll pick you up at 5:30?" Trevor loosened his wrench from the pipe.

"I'll be ready." Paige gestured towards the wrench in her hand. "Did I honestly help you with something here?"

"Naw, was just a trick to get you back here. Alone." He smiled and Paige felt an adrenaline rush. He held out his hand for the wrench and when Paige held it out, he held on to her wrist instead, pulling her closer. She leaned forward and lost her balance. Her eyes widened, and she glanced down at the wrench in her fist. She stopped herself from falling over by putting both fists on Trevor's thighs. Luckily, the wrench tilted up and didn't hit a leg. It could have left a bruise.

"That was close," she said as she looked up into Trevor's face.

He smirked and shook his head. "Why is it every time I go to kiss you, I worry about physical harm?"

"You're going to kiss me?" she asked.

He smiled and leaned forward until their lips touched. He tilted his head to deepen the kiss. Paige worried about Tilly walking in but decided she wouldn't mind it if she did. Maybe it would prevent Tilly from flirting with Trevor. As Trevor elongated the kiss, Paige forgot all about Tilly and focused on Trevor's scrumptious, her word now, lips.

PAIGE FLOATED THROUGH the rest of her workday. Trevor kept finding reasons he needed help in the back – hold this, hold that. Tilly asked at one point if Trevor was going to pay Paige for all the work he was making her do.

After work, back at the apartment, she gathered her dirty clothes together so she could go to the laundromat. She was walking out the door with two laundry bags, a tote with snacks and two novels, and her purse when her cell phone rang. "Dang it," she muttered, dropping all the bags and pulling her purse around to fish out her phone. It was her brother, Brian.

"Hey, Sis. I have news!" he said as soon as she answered.

"This is the week for news, I guess. What's up?" she asked.

"I asked Lily to marry me!"

"And?" Paige said, being a bit snarky. Brian getting engaged was wonderful and Paige was happy that he was marrying his high school sweetheart, but his engagement evoked the memory of Caleb breaking up with her. Paige felt like someone had punched her in the gut.

"She said yes!"

"Well, congratulations. It's about time. I love Lily and am excited to get another awesome sister-in-law. Any ideas on a date?" Paige hoped he wouldn't say spring. She hoped to be in New York then.

"Lily wants a fall wedding. Pumpkins, yellow leaves, a bonfire. We may even have it at her mom and dad's place. We'll see. Well, I have a few more phone calls to make, so I'll let you go."

"All right. Congrats again, big brother. Let me know how I can help."

Wow, first the news that Jack and Becca were going to have a baby and now Brian and Lily were engaged. This was the summer of good news. Maybe she'd get to add a spring internship to the list. Things were starting to look up.

Paige hung up the phone and looked at the clock. In Bloom was still open. She called the store and ordered an engagement gift basket to be sent to Brian and Lily. She asked Tilly to write on the card, "Congrats! Can't wait to celebrate your special day. Welcome to the batty Bell family, Lily!"

That task complete, she gathered her bags. Trevor flashed into her mind. If they continued to see each other in the fall, she could invite him to the wedding. She didn't want to go alone because Caleb and Moria might be there. Even if she and Trevor weren't together, no way was she going alone.

IT WAS LATE when Paige got home from the laundromat. Nica and Izzy were watching the Jennifer Lopez movie *Second Act* in the living room. Paige put her clean clothes away and then joined them. She pulled out her laptop, checked her emails, and was excited to see an email from Ms. Maron. She had been waiting for a response on her first editing assignment.

Dear Ms. Bell,

I received a message from the editorial director with feedback on your freelance assignment. He said your work was superb, exactly what he was looking for! Congratulations on successfully completing your first proofreading assignment!

If you will continue freelancing, we have plenty of work. I've given your contact information to Ed Billings, the editorial director. He will reach out to you with an assignment or two each week.

Sincerely,
Leslie Maron, Director of H.R.
Garland Wilson Publishing

"Woo hoo!" Paige exclaimed after reading the note.

"What's up?" Izzy asked.

"They liked the freelance assignment that I did." Paige stood up and did a little dance. She was no J. Lo but she could shimmy around. "They've offered me more work. Hopefully, this will help me get an offer for the spring internship and I'll make more money this summer. If I get the internship, I'll be required to take a heavy class load this fall to graduate on time, so I won't be able to work a lot during the fall semester."

Paige flopped back on the couch, thinking about the financial gap that losing the internship caused. With more freelance work, she could close that gap and not be as stressed out. Maybe free-lancing wasn't so bad after all.

Nica gave her a high-five and hit pause on the remote. "Congrats! That's great news. What does Trevor think about the internship?"

"Well, we haven't talked about it much. But it's okay, I'm not going to get serious about him. I am too young, and I have my career to think about. I don't think it is going to matter." Paige looked out the window to avoid Nica's gaze.

"Girl, I think you need to check in with your emotions," Nica said. "And I think you need to re-look at Trevor. I see the way he looks at you. I think he's falling. Hard. You may not want to get serious, but it may be too late for him."

"No way. We've gone on a few dates. He can't be serious about me."

"Oh, yes he can! He can't keep his eyes off of you. When you're not at In Bloom, he asks all sorts of questions about you. What do you like to do, what kind of jokes do you laugh at, etc., etc."

"Really?"

"Yes!" Nica nodded her head emphatically. "When are you going out with him next?"

"Tomorrow night. We're going to a CornBelters game."

"Okay, but pay attention to the signs. He is into you. I think you need to have a deeper conversation about your plans. Tell him how much your career means to you and what happens *when* you get that spring internship."

Paige didn't see it. But could Nica be right? Could he be more serious than she was? Should she slow things down? There were so many decisions to make. It took some of the joy out of the email from Ms. Maron.

CHAPTER EIGHTEEN

TREVOR PICKED HER up on time Friday night. He came to the door as usual, dressed in cargo shorts and a light-blue, short-sleeve, button-down shirt with tennis shoes. Paige looked him up and down. "Am I under-dressed?" she asked. She had on a pair of white shorts, white tennis shoes with no-show socks, and a yellow blouse.

"No, you look great." His eyes lingered on her legs a little longer than necessary before he started walking down the stairs. Paige followed, trying to suppress a smile. His lingering look at her legs spoke volumes.

"I didn't look it up, but I thought yellow would be the color of the CornBelters."

"That's right. You'll fit right in. I thought after the game, we could go to a drive-in movie. There is an 80s movie double header tonight, two John Hughes films. I forget which ones. But the fun is the drive-in part." He reached the bottom of the stairs and turned to her, raising his eyebrows quickly.

Paige laughed and swatted at his arm. "You're terrible. I've never been to a drive-in. Sounds fun. But I don't know how much damage it could do to my reputation. I've heard things, you know."

"Your reputation is safe with me, Paige."

Paige considered the remark. If her reputation was safe, then didn't that mean he wasn't that interested?

"Got it. The drive-in sounds fun. Can we get popcorn?"

"Yes," he answered, "if you don't stuff yourself with hot dogs at the ballpark."

"That may be a problem. I'm hungry and I love a great ballpark hot dog!"

At the truck, he opened the door for her, and she climbed in, dropping her drawstring backpack on the floor.

Trevor got in the driver's seat and Paige had a sucker ready for him.

"You are very thoughtful," he said, taking the sucker from her. He pulled the wrapper off and placed it in one of the cup holders. He glanced at her. "Ready?" he asked.

"Yes, I am. I've been looking forward to this date." She decided there was no reason to bring up the seriousness of the relationship like Nica suggested.

They cheered for the ball team from behind home plate. Paige enjoyed the game and the company even more. Trevor was easy to talk to and affectionate, resting his arm across her shoulders every chance he got. It was fun to enjoy herself and not worry about next week, next semester, or the possible spring internship. They were supposed to decide on June first, a few days away. To ease her guilt about not sharing the potential internship with Trevor, she told him about the freelance work instead and he had lots of questions.

"That's great," he said. "Of course, they were happy with your work. I bet you never give less than 110%."

"I try not to."

"Why the overdrive?"

"Good question." Paige shifted in her seat. "All my brothers and I are overachievers. It probably comes from not having a financially stable up bringing. We all started working early to earn money to get the things we wanted. Mom and Dad couldn't provide the extras."

"What do they do?"

"My dad is an artist, a painter. He's getting ready for a gallery show in Chicago in a few months. It's sort of feast or famine. He could get several sales in a show and we'd be fine for months, but then things would dry up. He has a few clients that he works on commission for; it's more stable now than it was when we were kids."

"I see. And your mom?"

"She's a yoga teacher. She has a steady clientele now, but again, as kids, it wasn't like that. I think my brothers and I decided we wanted more stable careers and we've always thrown ourselves into schoolwork so we could get scholarships and better paying jobs. I'm not complaining. I hope it doesn't sound like that. My parents taught us important life lessons and I appreciate them for it. We had a ton of fun growing up. They helped us excel at the non-academic stuff too–art, athletics, theater. They cultivated my love of reading and stories. I'm happiest when I'm reading a great book. And I'm lucky there are many careers in the area I'm passionate about. Competitive careers, yes, but careers. If I work hard, I should be able to do exactly what I want to do and get paid a decent living at it."

"But," he strung out the word, "isn't publishing primarily on the East Coast?"

Darn, he said it. "Yes, the big houses are in New York. I'm hoping to go there once I graduate. I am vying for an internship at Garland Wilson Publishing and hope I get it."

"Could you find similar work here?"

"Adjacent careers, sure." Paige looked down at her ring and twirled it so the Celtic tree of life symbol was back on top. When her grandmother gave it to her, she had said, "Do great things with your life, but never forget your family and your roots." Paige continued, "But not the big publishing houses."

"How can you be sure that's what you want if you haven't done it before?"

"There's a chance that it's not what I expect. That's true. But that is partly what the internship will help me discover."

The batter for the CornBelters stepped up to the plate and missed the next pitch. It ricocheted off the catcher's mitt and hit the net at eye level. They jumped in response.

"Whoa," Trevor laughed. "Even knowing the net is there, it's still a jolt to your reflexes."

"Right," Paige agreed. She appreciated the interruption to their conversation. Trevor's questions made her wonder if he would be disappointed when she left. Time to change the subject. "Speaking of extracurricular..."

"We were?"

"Well, sort of. I was curious what sort of things you like to do in your free time. What gets you excited?"

"Besides pretty strawberry blondes?"

"Hey, I guess I sort of set myself up for that, didn't I? What do you enjoy doing besides work?"

"Hanging out with friends."

"What do you do?"

"Lots of things–bowl, hunt, pickup basketball games, parties. The usual."

"And what are your friends like?" she asked. "Who do you hang out with?"

"What kind of crowd do I run with?" he clarified.

"Yes. Respectable types?"

"Sure, sure. For the most part. Most are guys I went to high school with. We stuck close to home. Not everyone is itching to leave the state."

"I know." Paige could understand the appeal of staying, of falling in love with someone and committing to where she was.

But it was too soon after the split with Caleb. Five months had not been enough to heal her heart.

Trevor took a hold of her hand. "Hey, ready for another hot dog?"

Paige put her other hand on her stomach. "No. Two was plenty."

"Well, I need one more. Let's go."

AFTER THE BALLGAME, they stopped to get ice cream to kill time before heading to the drive-in. Paige wondered if she'd have room for popcorn after two hot dogs, a shared pretzel and ice cream.

At the drive-in, Trevor navigated into a parking spot. Paige was confused why he parked backwards from the screen. He jumped out of the truck and grabbed a duffel bag from behind the seat. Outside of the truck, he took a box from the tool chest in the truck bed.

"What are you doing?" she asked, approaching the tailgate.

"I brought an air mattress. Thought we could lie in the truck bed to watch the movies. Here, hold this while I hook up the pump." Trevor walked around to the cab and plugged the pump into the cigarette lighter holder. Paige did as he instructed and held the air pump on the mattress as it filled.

She pushed on the mattress and declared it full. Trevor turned off the pump and came back to check out the mattress. "Perfect."

"I thought you were worried about my reputation. What will people think?" she teased.

"We're out in the open, surrounded by people. I don't think people will assume anything."

"I'm not sure about that. I certainly won't tell my mom what we're doing. She wouldn't believe it was so innocent."

"Because you're not innocent?" he teased.

"I didn't say that!" Oh boy, this was going down a path she didn't want to go down.

"Here I have pillows and a blanket in the duffel bag. Why don't you get them out while I go and buy a large tub of popcorn?"

"Sure. Extra butter, please."

"Wouldn't be popcorn without extra butter."

He walked off and Paige climbed onto the truck bed to lay the blanket on top of the air mattress and prop the pillows against the toolbox. Satisfied with the arrangement, she climbed across the mattress and sat with her back against the pillows and relaxed. The sun was setting, and the stars were coming out to make the night magical. Paige promised herself that she would focus on the movie and not mess around with Trevor. No sense in taking things too far when she planned to leave in the spring. She was not getting her heart broken again so soon after Caleb.

Trevor kept his word and didn't try anything during the movie. They left before the second movie because Paige started yawning.

At the apartment, he walked her to the door and kissed her goodnight. This time, Paige was ready for the kiss. She stepped into his arms like it was the most natural thing in the world and raised her lips to his. She let herself fall into the kiss and put all thoughts of New York out of her mind. The fresh scent of his shirt filled her nose as she concentrated on every aspect of him. The feel of his back under her hands, the pressure his lips applied to hers, and the sweet taste of cherry on his tongue from the last sucker he ate on the ride home.

The smell of lilacs wafted up to her from the overgrown hedge behind the apartment building, and when she heard giggling from inside the apartment, she decided it was time to go in.

CHAPTER NINETEEN

ANNA LEE HAD created unique designs for each of the two weddings on their Saturday schedule. The first wedding would be in the Miller Park pavilion, a small wedding with forty-eight guests. The In Bloom team was making centerpieces in low compote vases filled with layers of greenery and champagne-colored roses. Paige admired the simple and elegant design. She was arranging the bouquets and boutonnieres and was looking forward to delivering the flowers. She had been in the shop when the bride ordered the arrangements and had helped Anna Lee with design suggestions. The bride made quick decisions and the process was easy and efficient, the same way Paige imagined her wedding would be. Wait, why was she thinking about getting married? That was several years away, according to her life plan.

The second wedding was a two-hundred-guest affair at the legendary Woodberry Inn on the edge of town. The table arrangements featured silver candelabras with a wreath of red roses at the base. Twenty-five of them meant it was an all-hands-on-deck morning. Nica, Tilly, and Paige sat around the worktable, talking as much as they were working, but it helped keep the rhythm needed to get everything done on time. Anna Lee oversaw the work, kept them supplied with flowers, greens, ribbons and wires as they needed them. All while monitoring the store.

She stopped at Paige's workspace. "Are you all right with running these to Miller Park and setting up on your own?"

"Yes, I will be happy to. You have the address for where they are getting ready, right? I didn't put that in my phone yet." Paige finished her fourth arrangement, two to go.

"The paper is on the side table. I meant to ask if you've heard about the spring internship yet."

"Not yet. They will make the announcement around the first. Hopefully I'll know next week."

"And it's still what you want to do?" Anna Lee asked.

Paige hesitated. "Yes. Why do you ask?"

"I've seen how you are with Trevor. I was thinking you've been on a date, even."

"We have. Three dates, to be exact. You don't have a problem with that, do you? Mom always said dating in the workplace was a big no-no."

"I understand where your mom is coming from. As a general rule, I agree. But this is different–you don't really work together, you both happen to be working in here, in different capacities, at the same time. It won't last very long and you're not causing scenes or doing anything disruptive here. Besides that, I've known him a long time and I knew his dad well. He's a decent person. And as long as he makes you happy and treats you right, I don't have a problem with it. Do you think it could get serious?"

"We're keeping it light."

"Both of ya?" Anna Lee lowered her brows, looking doubtful

"Well, we haven't talked about it, but I think it's light."

"Remember, Paige. We reap what we sow. If you water and fertilize a relationship, you get a relationship. Three dates in a couple of weeks? Sounds like a relationship to me."

"I know you're right. I need to set things straight with him. He knows about my career goals; we've talked about it."

"And what does he say? Does he support it?"

"He's hard to read on that. He asked if there are other options for a career that doesn't involve the East Coast, so I guess he's not jazzed about it. But I'm speculating. I have to have the discussion."

"I think it sounds like the right thing to do. Keep me posted about the internship, too. I'm rooting for you, kid."

"Thanks. I will."

Well, there was no getting out of it now. She'd committed to Anna Lee to talk to him, so now she had to. She would, just as soon as he called her again.

PAIGE WORKED IN the restaurant on Sunday morning, then proofread a novel manuscript all afternoon and evening. She was grateful they gave her additional work, and with her upcoming schedule, she wanted to get it done as soon as possible.

She finished at eight p.m. and went to her room to call her mom to check in–they hadn't talked since Paige got the news that Brian was engaged.

"Do you think they'll get married this fall?" Paige asked once the conversation moved to her brother.

"Yes," Sue answered. "They stopped by here yesterday with Lily's mom and we knocked out a lot of the planning. Lily needs to check on dates in October with catering companies. The ceremony and reception will be at their farm. They'll rent a large outdoor tent, tables, and chairs. It will be beautiful."

"Well, I'm glad. If they had it in the spring and I got the internship, it would be hard for me to get home for all the festivities–showers, rehearsal, and what not. Do you think they will invite Caleb?"

"We reviewed the guest list, and he's on there. He's close to Lily's family. Maybe he won't go. Are you nervous about seeing him?"

"Yes, I am. It can only be awkward." Paige thought it would be horrible, embarrassing, humiliating, and awful. Was there a word for the combination of all of those things?

"Not if you're over him. You are over him, right?"

"I think so." Paige shifted on the bed and grabbed a pillow to hold in her lap. "I've been seeing someone. The plumber I told you about. Trevor."

"How's that going?"

"It's going well."

"But?" Sue challenged.

"Well, he may be more serious than I am. I don't know what will happen if I get the internship and then a job in New York. I don't think he'd consider coming with me. Seems like he's set on staying here. He has his business, and he helps with his sister and her kids. I hope we can stay together until Brian's wedding; he'd make a great date."

"Paige, don't stay with a guy because he would be a great date for your brother's wedding." Sue paused and Paige waited. "Date a guy who gets you, who makes you happy, who you are thrilled to see, who makes you smile. Life is hard enough. Don't stay with someone because it's convenient."

"It's not like that," Paige insisted. "He makes me happy. But he's older. He's twenty-seven, and he may want to settle down soon. That's not on my agenda right now."

"Honey," Sue dragged out the word like she wasn't buying Paige's speech, "weren't you engaged and planning a wedding last fall?"

"Well, yes, but not now. I've decided to double down on my career and put off marrying until later. There's no reason to be tied down this early." Paige wondered when this topic would stop being a part of every conversation with her mom. She couldn't wait for the time when her engagement to Caleb was a distant memory and no longer talked about. It was time to wrap up this call. "Well, I should go. I want to do a final review of my notes on this book before I send it off."

"What book review?"

"Oh, I forgot to tell you, the publishing company is sending me some freelance proofreading work. Sort of a consolation prize, I guess, for not getting the internship. It's cool. I did a sample for them last week and they sent me a full manuscript, which I've worked on all afternoon."

"How exciting! That's a great way to learn more about the industry and keep you involved even without going for the internship. Do you think you could do it full time, from here?"

"Maybe, but no way would I do that. I want a full-time job with benefits, to work for a company. I do NOT want to freelance."

"I think you should keep it in mind as an option."

To appease her mom and cut the call short, Paige mumbled something like agreement, but she knew that was not in the cards for her.

CHAPTER TWENTY

AYLON AND WILLIAM splashed around the bathtub, squirting each other with rubber clownfish, as Trevor watched from his seat on the bathroom vanity. His job scrubbing the sticky mess left by his famous *grilled* peanut butter and jelly sandwiches was done, and now he let the boys play while he took a breather.

"Uncle T, I'm going to be a firefighter when I grow up." Waylon said, out of the blue.

"Really, Way? That's cool. It's an important job. What about you, Willie? Do you want to be a firefighter too?"

Willie looked at Trevor and smiled. He squeaked out a yeah, but Trevor couldn't be certain that the two-year-old was responding to his question.

"Okay, bedtime, boys. Let's get you dried off and into your PJs." He grabbed the two towels that were hanging on the back of the door. He knew Tricia's system–Waylon used the blue towel and Willie used the green one.

"But. But. We're having fun!" Waylon pouted.

"Yes, I know. But you're going to be prunes if you don't get out soon. Besides, I brought new books to read to you once you get into bed. *Hurry. It. Up*," he said.

The boys stood up once Trevor pulled the plug. Willie was afraid of the water rushing down the drain so he jumped, and Trevor caught him before he could fall.

"Whoa, kiddo! Make sure I'm looking at you when you jump like that!" Trevor laughed as his very wet nephew clung to his neck with his short legs wrapped around his waist.

Getting the boys dressed and into their matching toddler beds was completed without incident. Before Trevor finished reading the three books he'd brought for them, they were both asleep.

He rose from sitting on the floor, between the beds, and turned off the overhead light. The boys' faces were illuminated softly by a night-light on the nightstand. Trevor stood in the doorway and watched them sleep for several moments, enjoying the soft sighs that Willie made in his sleep and the frequent shimmies that Waylon made, as if he was still running around the house instead of fast asleep in his bed.

TRICIA WALKED THROUGH the front door as Trevor sat down on the couch with a glass of ice water in hand.

"You're home earlier than I expected," he said as he leaned forward to put the glass on the coffee table.

"Well, the date was a bust. We didn't click." She dropped her purse on the coffee table and sat on the opposite end of the couch to pull off her high heels. "Any trouble with the boys tonight?"

"Nope. Easy peasy."

"You're becoming a pro!" she exclaimed. "Glad I have your support. Never thought I'd be a single mom. Not this early any-way. Were we doomed by our parents' crash and burn marriage?" Tricia stretched across the couch and put her head on Trevor's leg.

He rubbed her head playfully. "No, sis. Not doomed. Your husband was a first-class idiot. Wasn't your fault, and it wasn't because of a family curse or anything."

"Maybe. Not sure I buy that. There's hope that one of us will have a good marriage. Speaking of, tell me about this flower-shop girl."

Trevor smiled, thinking about the day he first saw Paige behind the counter. She'd captured his attention immediately. There was an air of inquisitiveness about her, like she wanted to know everything about everything. Her eyes had swept over him quickly, like they were cataloging his features for future recall. He thought about how quickly she blushed when he called her out about her roving eyes.

"Stop calling her that," he said. "Her name is Paige, and she's a literature major. She's more of a book girl than a flower girl. She just happens to work at the florist. Thank the lord for that. Otherwise, I don't think I would have met her."

Tricia yawned. "There's a great job perk. A literature major, huh? What else?" Tricia closed her eyes and Trevor wondered how long this conversation would actually last.

"She's quiet, reserved. Beautiful with long, strawberry-blond hair and green eyes. About five and a half feet tall. She doesn't wear a lot of makeup; goes for the natural look you could say. She's both book smart and street smart. She doesn't take any guff. I think she gets that from her three brothers. She surprises me, too. She doesn't have to be taken care of and she's not looking for anyone to take care of her, but when I'm with her, I want to take care of her. I want to know everything about her."

"She's surrounded by boys? I can relate. Sounds like you're into her. When do I get to meet her? I have to approve of your relationships now that dad is gone." Tricia's eyes opened, and she rolled onto her back to look up at him.

"Oh, ya think so? I don't need your approval, sis, but you will meet her. Soon. I was thinking about having a cookout at my place. You could bring the boys. I'll invite a few more friends. Small, casual. But I'd like you to meet her. I think this could certainly be something, Trish."

"Have you told her how you feel?"

"Not exactly. But I think she gets me."

Trevor thought it was too soon. Only three dates. He couldn't tell her he was falling for her this soon. He'd never said those words first. It was better to wait. Once he knew a girl was into him, then he could let his guard down. And though their dates were perfect, he sensed Paige was holding back. Maybe she didn't trust him yet. He knew she was weary of relationships after her called-off engagement. He wanted to know more about how that ended so he could prove to her that he was different, that this relationship was different.

"You can't assume that. Tell her how you feel and see how she feels. Don't assume." Tricia yawned. "Are you staying the night or going home?"

"I'm going home. I have a lot of work planned for the house tomorrow. If I'm going to have that cookout, I have to get my house presentable."

"All right. Then go already. I must get some sleep. The boys will be up at the butt crack of dawn."

CHAPTER TWENTY-ONE

PAIGE DIDN'T SEE Trevor again until Tuesday. He said he was almost done with replacing the pipes at In Bloom. He would take on a new job the following week and she wouldn't be able to see him at work.

"Well, at least when we see each other after this, it will be without the distractions of work," he said.

Paige was working the register while Anna Lee conducted several consultations with clients in the consultation room. Trevor came to the front on breaks when no customers were in the store.

"That's true," she replied, arranging the pens in the green flowerpot by the register. Some of the girls and customers put pens in upside down, which was annoying.

"Speaking of seeing each other. Do you have plans tonight?"

"I need to work on proofreading a novel tonight. It's not due until Friday, but I want to take the first pass reading it tonight. Then I'll have the next two nights to reread and make notes."

"That sounds interesting. Who are you doing that for?"

"Oh, I didn't tell you? Not sure how it slipped my mind. I'm doing it as freelance work for the publishing firm that I was going to intern at this summer. They sort of threw me this as a bone to make up for the mix-up. But I'm liking it."

"That's cool. So, you can do what you want to do, remotely."

"Well, it's a start. There's a lot more I need to learn that I'll pick up when I can be there in person. In the internship."

"Sure, sure. So, you're reading tonight."

"Yes."

"Want company?"

"Seriously?" Paige raised an eyebrow.

"Sure. I can come over, bring dinner. We can sit on the couch and read."

"But you didn't get a book from the library when we went. What will you read?"

"I actually own five books of my very own." He held up his right hand, spreading his five fingers out. Paige wondered if he was serious. Who owned just five books? "They are in my house. I could stop and get takeout on my way. Chinese food?"

"I don't know how I can concentrate while entertaining you."

"You won't have to entertain me. I will have a book. I will read. You will read. We will read together. Quite brilliant, if you ask me."

"A reading date. That would be nice. Let me check with my roommates–make sure they don't have plans and don't mind the company. I'll let you know."

"Sure. Sure."

Trevor went back to work and Paige texted her roommates. Izzy had a date and Nica had a softball game. Paige promised to watch Nica's next game. She was feeling guilty because she hadn't been to a single game yet.

Anna Lee finished her latest consult and walked the client to the front door. They stood chatting about the fairy garden on display in the front window. When the conversation ended, she held the door open and watched the bride-to-be walk to her car.

Paige was cleaning a glass display case to the left of the counter when Anna Lee turned around.

"Any news on that internship, Paige?"

"No, not yet. Waiting patiently. They are supposed to make their decision today, but I don't know how long it will take to notify the selected intern."

Salty came out from behind the counter and circled around Anna Lee's legs. "Someone's hungry. Hold on a minute, Salty. Let me know when you know. Are you getting enough hours this summer between here and at Max's?" Anna Lee bent over to give the cat a scratch on his head.

"Yes, plenty. I'm also getting some freelance proofreading gigs, so I'm all set. Thanks for checking. I appreciate you giving me hours here this summer and for the recommendation at Max's. You've been a blessing." Paige thought about the fact that she got to meet Trevor because of Anna Lee, too, but she didn't want to make a big deal about that to her.

"I'm happy to help. Now, why don't you take your break? Salty and I can manage the store. My next client isn't due for another hour." Anna Lee walked behind the counter and scooped some dry food out of the container for Salty.

"Will do. I'll be outside if you need me."

Paige grabbed her lunch and a book out of her backpack. She passed Trevor on the way out to the picnic table and told him she was taking her lunch break.

Trevor followed her outside and walked towards his truck, saying nothing. Paige watched the way he moved and practiced breathing normally. She worried he might jump in the truck and take off, but he grabbed his lunch off the front seat and joined her at the picnic table. He sat on the same side as her, looking out toward a clump of trees behind the property.

"Nica and Izzy have plans tonight, so it won't be a problem if you want to come over and read." She stressed the word read. "And I would love it if you brought Chinese. I haven't had any for weeks. Sounds yummy."

"Well, then it's a date. Number four, by my count." He smiled at her and she admired the way the little lines gathered around his eyes.

"You keep count?"

"Sure. Why not? Helps me judge how well a relationship is going."

"And?" Paige wasn't sure she was ready for this assessment of their relationship.

"I think this one is going very well. You're beautiful, smart, kind. You make me laugh."

"I do?"

"Yes. After I leave you, I smile for thirty minutes, thinking of the things you said and how you made me feel. Like I said, funny and kind. Top priorities on the list of qualities I look for in a girlfriend."

"I see. Well, I'm glad to hear that."

"Do I meet any of your criteria for someone to date, or are you merely stringing me along?" Trevor took a bite of his sandwich and a crumb lingered on the corner of his lip. Paige reached over and wiped it away before responding.

"My list. Well, kind is top of the list, and you meet that. A check there. Handsome. Double check. Thoughtful. Check. Humorous. Check. Responsible. Double check."

"Responsible?"

"You know. You show up on time. Keep your commitments. You've been stellar working for Anna Lee, as far as I can tell. Those things are important to me."

Paige thought about the one area where he did not check off the box on her scorecard–"steady job with benefits." While plumbing was highly skilled and highly in demand, being self-employed, he must have lull periods where the work was unreliable. And did he even have health insurance? Dental? A pension plan? She forced herself to not shudder, thinking about it.

"Where did you go just now?" he asked, nudging her shoulder.

"What?"

"You got a faraway look in your eyes. And you didn't respond to my remark about the 'handsome–double check' remark."

"Oh, did I double check that one?" she asked playfully.

"Yes, you did. You know I'm more than just my good looks. I can read a book and I'll prove that to you tonight, Miss Bookworm. I may not even ask you for any word definitions. Then you'll certainly be impressed with my looks and skills."

Paige laughed. He was honest in a way most men her age weren't. He made fun of himself and actually listened to her. How was she going to leave him if she got the internship she wanted? "Don't borrow tomorrow's troubles"–one of her mother's favorite expressions–came to her mind.

"I'll be home by five tonight," Paige said. "What time do you think you'll be able to come over?"

"No later than 6:30. I want to take dinner to my sister on the way."

"That's nice of you. I'm sure she'll appreciate it. I hope I get to meet her someday. I'm not sure what your rules are on meeting family. Does that occur after the tenth date?" she teased.

"Oh, you will definitely meet her. Soon. I think you two will get along great. She's sassy though. I'm giving you a fair warning. She's had a rough couple of years, and she's put up a barrier. Shoot, I shouldn't be talking about her like this. You should form your own opinions."

"Rough years?"

"Yes, her husband cheated on her. Broke their marriage up. She's an awesome mom and a wonderful person, but she's still aching. She's starting to act like her old self, though. I hope she's finally healing."

Paige finished her salad and put the container back in her lunch bag. Thinking about Trevor's sister, she wondered if he had overshared information. She wouldn't want him telling her life story to others and tried to decide if it was a red flag. She appreciated his honesty with her but wasn't sure his sister would agree.

"I hope she doesn't mind you sharing this with a stranger."

"You're not a stranger," he protested.

"To her I am."

"That's true. Maybe I shouldn't have shared but I'm comfortable talking to you. I feel like I know you so well and I trust you. I'll tell my sister what I said, so she'll know what you know. Keep things on the up and up."

"That I can accept."

"You have pretty high standards of loyalty. I like that."

"Sounds like it's important to you, too."

"Definitely. Because of the way my mom split when we were kids and the way Tricia's husband cheated on her. Trust and loyalty are important to me."

"Noted." Paige couldn't imagine being disloyal to Trever or to anyone. Once that line of trust was broken, it was nearly impossible to get it back.

WHEN TREVOR KNOCKED on the screen door, Paige rushed in from the living room, where she was setting the coffee table for their dinner. She bought a handful of pink and purple tulips from Anna Lee before leaving In Bloom and arranged them in a white pitcher. She laid a bright pink tablecloth on the coffee table and set out Izzy's blue and white checked plates. She loved the energy the colorful tableau gave off.

Trevor walked in with a bag of takeout food and a six-pack of assorted soft drinks. "I wasn't sure what kind of soda you like, so I brought a variety pack." he said, putting the food and soft drinks on the kitchen counter.

"What a great idea!" Paige looked through the soft drinks. "Black cherry sounds like a winner. Are you okay if we eat at the coffee table? We have comfortable floor cushions and I thought it would be easy and casual."

"Sure. Sure." Trevor pulled his work boots off and left them by the door. "I didn't have time to go home and shower. Took longer at my sister's than planned. My nephews were spun up, so I took them outside to toss a ball around while my sister showered. It is surprising how much trouble two little boys can get into when you don't have your eyes on them constantly."

"I'm sure she appreciated the help. I put plates in the living room; we'll take the food cartons with us. Hey, I don't see a book–I thought you were coming to read with me."

Trevor reached behind his back and pulled a slightly tattered paperback out from where he'd tucked it into the back of his jeans. "Tada! Book!"

Paige smiled when she saw the book, *Fahrenheit 451,* by Ray Bradbury. "Wow, that's one of my favorites. 'It was a pleasure to burn'," she quoted.

"Oh? I had no idea."

"Have your read it before? In school?"

"No. I found it in the attic of my house. Looks interesting."

"I can't wait to hear what you think about it." Paige led the way into the living room. She was thankful that her roommates had other plans tonight, and she had the place to herself. She had a lot of reading to do but hoped they could have a few romantic moments between dinner and reading. It had been four days since their last date, and she could remember the feel of his lips kissing hers. The memory was fading, and she longed to recreate the experience.

They sat on the floor on square floor cushions with their backs against the couch. Paige had music playing softly on the stereo.

"I didn't peg you for a classic rock person," Trevor said, finishing an egg roll.

"My parents love to have music playing all the time and this is what they listen to."

"I thought kids and teens were supposed to reject their parents' music."

"Sure, we all went through those phases. For my brother Jack, it was hip hop, for Brian, it was country, modern country at that." She shivered. "And for younger brother Logan, it's punk."

"And you?"

"My rebellion was top forty pop. Bubble gum pop, you could say. I'm over it now. And my parents' music is in my blood. What about you? What kind of music do you listen to?"

"Classic rock all the way."

They finished dinner, and Paige stood to clear the makeshift table. Trevor grabbed her hand and pulled her back down. "That can wait a few minutes, right? I've been wanting to kiss you since I walked in, but my stomach had priority over my heart."

He leaned in and pressed his lips against hers, putting a hand on the back of her neck to pull her in close. Paige sighed and closed her eyes. Her hand rested on his thigh to steady herself. She had been hoping for this moment since he walked in. It seemed as though her insides were glowing the perfect shade of pink and her heart did a double beat when his lips parted to intensify the kiss.

"Mm, yummy," she said when she sat back to breathe.

"Yes, yummy. Wait, do you mean dinner? I'll try not to be offended."

Paige giggled. "Obviously, I meant dinner. Though the kiss was pretty decent, too. Now, I need to read, sir! You're becoming a distraction."

"Kissing you is a distraction. And I'd love to be distracted all night. But I made a promise that I would let you work and not be a distraction. Let me clean up so you can get started." He stood and picked up the food containers.

"I have time to help. Besides, you may put things away in the wrong place."

"You're right. I don't want to make you or your roommates mad. I might not get invited back. So please supervise me."

"You're on."

In the kitchen, they fell into a comfortable routine. Laughing and joking about the neat kitchen with frilly curtains and dish towels. "Izzy is frilly. And fun. And a superb cook." Paige said as she dried the dishes that Trevor put into the sink drainer.

"You lucked out with the roommates, didn't you?"

"I did. I worried I was going to be moving home for the summer. Glad this worked out."

"What would you have done if you'd gone home for the summer? Hook up with an ex-boyfriend?" Trevor had a teasing tone, but it made Paige a tad uncomfortable.

"No. I'm sure *that* wouldn't have happened." The image of Caleb that flashed through Paige's mind was unwanted. "I don't know what I would have done if I went home. Worked in retail or fast food for the summer. Hung out with my best friend."

"Who's your best friend?" Trevor asked, rinsing out the sink.

"Macey Nelson. We have known each other since kindergarten."

"What does Macey do?"

"She's studying to be a teacher. She's planning to join Teach For America when she graduates."

"What's that?"

"It's a program that sends new teachers into underserved communities for two years. She's passionate about teaching. It's inspiring."

"Wow. That's great. I think that's it on the cleanup. Did I

miss anything?" Trevor wiped his hands on a towel and looked around the small kitchen.

"That's it," Paige replied. "Thanks for helping with the cleanup. You're pretty adept in the kitchen."

"I'm a bachelor, remember? I get to do *all* the cooking and cleaning at home."

"Tell me more about the house you're rehabbing."

"She's a beauty but needs a lot more work. I have some projects that I want to finish before showing it to you. I've had it for a year and while I've made progress, it's far from done. With my dad getting sick, helping my sister out, and work, the house repair and refinishing tasks fall to the lowest priority. But the house is functional, comfortable for a bachelor who doesn't bring guests around very often."

"Not often?" Paige wondered how many women had seen his house.

"Well, I can't have my sister and her kids over. There are too many active projects and tools lying around. It's not safe for little guys. I've had friends over to watch sports. And contractors for a few tricky things that I wasn't ready to tackle. Like electrical. I'm trying to learn it all, but I also don't want to burn the house down."

"I see," Paige said. He didn't mention women, but he could be keeping that to himself.

Almost like he read her mind, he said, "You'll be the first lady guest." He leaned over and nudged her with his shoulder. "I bet you were curious."

"Sure, a bit." Paige was glad he could read her so well. "Ready to read?" she asked, happy to change the subject.

"Yes! Let's do this."

Back in the living room, they each took an end of the couch and turned towards each other, their feet touching in the middle of the couch. Paige decided she would peek at him after every page she read, an incentive to keep reading. Every time she looked up; he was looking at her.

Finally, the fifth time she looked up, she asked, "Are you honestly reading? I haven't heard a page turn."

"I'm making progress. Not as much as I would if I was alone, but I'm reading. This book is interesting. How's your reading going?"

"Good! I'm going to have a lot of notes, but the story is engaging. I wish I could talk about it with the author, but I simply hand in my notes and the editorial director will have the follow-up conversations. I would like to know how the author came up with the idea. And I'd love to hear them talk. Reading their written words is one thing, but I would love to hear how they speak, too. I hear their voice in my head as I read, but I don't know how close it is to their actual voice. I'm curious."

"Like a cat."

"Yes," she laughed. "Curious like a cat."

Paige imagined what married life with Trevor could look like. Curled up on the couch together, reading, talking about their day. Talking about their dreams and plans. She felt that Trevor would encourage her and challenge her in all the best ways. If she had a dream that felt too big, he wouldn't let her get overwhelmed; he would encourage her to pursue it and he would do what he could to help her.

The picture in her mind of being married to Trevor was idyllic, like all the good parts from her favorite books rolled into one.

CHAPTER TWENTY-TWO

PAIGE STOOD AT the kitchen sink, filling the coffeepot with water. She had to be at Max's Coffee Shop in forty-five minutes for the breakfast shift. She yawned and stretched, waiting for the coffee to finish. As soon as the coffee stopped dripping, she grabbed her mug and filled it with milk and a teaspoon of raw sugar for the extra kick. She took the mug to the bathroom and turned on the shower.

She reminisced about the evening reading with Trevor. It was charming that he wanted to hang out with her. And she believed he did read a couple chapters of the book he brought, in between the times he sat gazing at her.

After showering and getting dressed, she looked at her watch. She had five minutes before needing to get in her car to make it to work. Enough time to check email. The publishing company said they would decide on June first, yesterday, about the spring internship. They didn't say how long it would take to notify applicants, but Paige hoped it would be quick. She was not disappointed when she saw an email from Ms. Maron in her in-box.

Dear Ms. Bell,

I am thrilled to inform you that we have chosen you as our spring intern! I hope this is some consolation with the mix-up over the summer internship.

The internship will begin on January 5th. Please let me know by June 15th if you accept this position or not.

Congratulations!

Sincerely,
Leslie Maron, Director of H.R.
Garland Wilson Publishing

Fantastic! She got it! It was real this time! Losing out on the summer internship still stung, but at least she got to meet Trevor because of that mix-up, so it wasn't all bad. She thought about whom to notify first. Macey and Anna Lee wanted to know, and she had to tell her mom right away. It was early, so she sent a quick text.

PAIGE: Hi mom! I got the spring internship at Garland Wilson! Super excited! I'll call tonight to talk–off to work at the coffee shop. Luv U!

It was way too early to call or text Anna Lee and Macey–she would call each of them once she got off work at the Max's. She responded to Ms. Maron, accepting the offer and felt a rush of relief and a hint of sadness when she hit send. She pushed the sadness aside. This is what she wanted. Right?

She grabbed her purse and keys and hustled out of the apartment.

AFTER WORK, SHE drove to her favorite taco stand and purchased two soft chicken tacos with a side of chips and salsa. It was a gorgeous day, so she drove to the park and sat at a picnic table in the shade. Devouring her food so it wouldn't get cold, Paige watched kids running back and forth, on and off playground equipment.

A young boy in blue shorts and a yellow t-shirt with a T-Rex on the front slid down the slide and ran back to the ladder as soon as he was down, over and over. Paige looked around to see who he was with. She liked to guess parents or caregivers and the kids they were watching. She finally pegged a young teenager as his sitter. She was paying more attention to her phone than any of the kids. Since the teen wasn't keeping a close watch on her charge, Paige did. He was still wobbly on his legs, and she worried he'd slip on the stairs.

Finally, the sitter called to him, and he ran to her for a drink from his sippy cup. Paige decided her role in the situation was over, so she gathered her lunch wrappers and walked them to the garbage can.

She wasn't in a hurry to go anywhere, so she started walking on the path around the park. She put an earbud in and called Anna Lee.

"Anna Lee, I got the spring internship!" she squealed when Anna Lee answered.

"Well, of course you did. I knew you'd come out smelling like a rose. This calls for a celebration. And I'm in the mood for baking another chocolate cake! When are you working in the store next?"

"Tomorrow," Paige replied.

"Well, I better get going on that cake." Paige could hear the smile in Anna Lee's voice. "We'll celebrate tomorrow! Everyone loves a celebration."

"Oh Anna Lee, you don't need to do that. You baked a cake for me already. It's unnecessary. I certainly appreciate your support and encouragement."

"Nonsense. This calls for cake!" Anna Lee hung up without goodbye. Paige shook her head and smiled.

Thinking about the last chocolate cake Anna Lee made for Lauren's going away party made her think of Lauren. She sent her a text.

PAIGE: Hey Lauren, I got the spring internship in NYC! How's Europe?

She didn't wait long for a reply.

LAUREN: I knew u would! Congrats! Last day in London, leave for Dublin tomorrow. Miss u!

PAIGE: Any romantic developments? Miss u!

LAUREN: Not yet. How's Trevor?

PAIGE: Good so far.

LAUREN: ♥

Paige wanted to share her concerns with Lauren about Trevor's potential reaction to the internship. It would be too complicated to discuss over a text message. Besides, she didn't want to disrupt Lauren's adventure in Europe.

She called Macey next and relayed the news.

"Oh, my gosh, Paige. I'm very excited for you! Your plans are falling into place. What does Trevor say?"

Why did Macey go there right away? Paige was feeling excited but thinking about telling Trevor put a twitch in her stomach.

"I haven't told him yet. To be honest, I haven't talked to him about the internship very much. I don't have a lot of faith in long-distance relationships. It didn't work out so well with Caleb."

"Just because it didn't work with Caleb doesn't mean all long-distance relationships are doomed. Besides, Caleb's a poor choice to compare anything to. From everything you've told me about Trevor, there is no comparison," Macey said. Paige knew she was right.

"True. But that doesn't mean Trevor is going to even want to try it. He may break up with me when he finds out."

"Don't go there. You don't know that. Give him a chance to surprise you. From what you've told me, it sounds like he's into you. I can't wait to meet him."

"Well, hopefully you'll meet him at Brian's wedding, if not before. I hope he'll be my date. I don't want to go alone in case Caleb and Moria are there. Again, if Trevor hasn't dumped me by then."

"Hey now. That is not the optimistic, driven Paige I know. I gotta run. And I think you need to call Trevor and have a talk."

"I can't. He said he was going to be with his sister and her boys today. He wouldn't be available. I'll need to tell him tomorrow."

"All right. Good luck when you talk to him. And let me know how it goes."

Paige hung up and walked to an empty swing. She sat and pushed herself backward. She thought about Macey's advice and wished she could talk to Trevor right away. The uncertainty sat in her stomach like a ball of too many caramels eaten just before a roller coaster ride.

CHAPTER TWENTY-THREE

TREVOR SHIFTED IN his green folding chair, deciding it was time to invest in a newer one. The seat was one sneeze away from ripping in half and he would be on the ground, looking like he was in a *Saturday Night Live* skit. No thanks. He hoped Willie wouldn't want to sit on his lap tonight; he couldn't imagine explaining the precarious state of his seat to the two-year-old.

Tricia stood and cheered as Waylon ran, kicking the soccer ball back and forth with a teammate, a small girl with brown braids. Trevor thought the girl was named Carrie, but it was hard to keep them straight.

"Did you see that? Waylon was passing the ball, not hogging it to himself." Tricia smiled with pride at Trevor.

"You remind him every day, Sis. But give the kid a break. We're a pretty competitive family. Always have been." Trevor thought back to his high school sports days. He wasn't against team sports, but he preferred his times in cross-country, track and field, and wrestling over the one year he played basketball.

"I love rugged individualism, but I am required to teach my kids to share and play nice and get along. God, some days it's just tragic." She looked at Trevor and winked.

Trevor laughed. "You are raising them right, I guess. Might

keep the boys out of scuffles and fist fights. Dad preferred teaching self-defense over diplomacy."

Tricia smiled and turned serious. "Do you think he would have been a little softer if Mom had stayed?"

"I don't know." He shrugged. "But I think we would have had a better balance if she had. We could have learned the softer skills from her. But it is what it is."

Trevor thought about all the childhood fantasies where he played out the "what if" scenarios with his mom. What if she'd stayed with their dad? What if she had left dad, but stayed in the same town where they could see her weekly? What if she had made more of an effort to stay in touch from Florida? How expensive would a weekly phone call be? Heck, a monthly phone call? They considered themselves lucky if they got a card on their birthday and a gift at Christmas.

To her credit, she came back for their graduations. And ever since her husband died five years ago, she tried to call at least once a month. Trevor couldn't build the relationship that he wanted with his mom. She'd left, and after all the time that had passed, it was impossible. But he appreciated what he had now. He was thankful that she was trying to stay in touch with Tricia's boys. She may not have been the best mom, but she was turning into a pretty good grandma.

Tricia stood and cheered again, as best she could with Willie on her hip. Trevor came out of his seat and cheered as the game ended and both teams came off the field.

Twenty minutes later, they sat in a booth at their favorite pizza place. The boys colored on the white paper that covered the table.

Trevor took a drink from his glass of water as he drew a truck for Willie. Willie responded with a loud "vroom, vroom!"

Tricia tapped on her phone and eyed Waylon's drawing. "Hey Trev, you mentioned a cookout at your place so I can meet the young lady. Do you have a date in mind?"

"I was thinking about Father's Day. Gives me a couple weeks to get the living room finished. Any concerns?"

"Not with me. It's a reserves weekend for Erik, so I'll have the boys all weekend. But you said Paige's dad was still alive. Won't she go home to see him?"

"Maybe. I'll check. I'll also invite some other friends, so I'll have a cookout whether she can make it or not. But I hope she can. I'll plan for the evening. That will give everyone a chance to hang with their families during the day and will hopefully get a few people out to my place that night."

"That sounds nice. I dread this Father's Day. The first one without Dad," she sighed. "Sucks."

"Yep, yep." He looked towards the door, not wanting his sister to see the emotion on his face.

She reached across and squeezed his forearm lightly. She didn't address the sadness of the moment out loud, which he appreciated. "What do you want me to bring?"

"Make your deviled eggs and bring a dessert. I'll grill burgers, hot dogs, and be well-stocked with beverages and chips."

"Wow, you're going all out. I hope this girl is worth it." She teased.

"She is, you'll see."

"Why? What about her is so special?"

"It's hard to say. I feel happy and content when I'm with her. Like last night. I went to her apartment. She had to do some reading for a work assignment."

Tricia interrupted, "Botany for beginners?"

"Not for the flower shop. For a freelance gig with a publisher in New York. She's proofreading a book. She said she couldn't go out last night because of it, so I offered to bring takeout and a book to read so I wouldn't disturb her."

Tricia nodded and handed a brown crayon to Waylon.

"It was great," Trevor continued. "Low-key. It felt homey. Comfortable. At peace. Is that weird?"

"Yes, you've never talked like this about a girlfriend. As much as I thought you were into Gwen, you never talked about being comfortable. Quite the opposite. You couldn't figure her out half the time."

"Gwen was high maintenance. I thought I wanted that, but I don't. I want someone who is down to earth, warm, caring. I want Paige."

Tricia's eyes whipped back to his. "What? You are serious!"

"I am." He didn't know if it was wrong to tell his sister before telling Paige, but it was done. Hopefully, Paige wouldn't break his heart when he told her.

CHAPTER TWENTY-FOUR

KNOTS FORMED IN Paige's stomach, thinking about telling Trevor that she got the spring internship. Would he think it was worthwhile to have a long-distance relationship? Or would he suggest they end it? She felt like a coward for not calling to tell him before now. The fact that his truck was not in the parking lot when she arrived didn't ease her angst. It meant prolonging the conversation.

Anna Lee was true to her word and baked her delicious chocolate cake *again*. Paige inhaled deeply as she walked through the back door of In Bloom. She smiled when she saw the familiar "CONGRATULATIONS PAIGE!" banner hanging in the workspace. There were blue tablecloths and two glass vases with yellow roses on the worktable. Knowing Anna Lee, the vases would go into the retail store after the party.

"Congrats, Paige!" yelled Tilly. "Knew it would happen for you. You are going to kick butt in New York. And we're glad that we get you for six more months before you go. Please remember your friends when you hit it big."

Tilly gave her a high five, and then Nica hugged her tight. "I'm glad you didn't get the internship for this summer. I wouldn't have gotten you as a roommate and a friend. You would probably have preferred being there now, but I think it was fate. Plus, you got to date Trevor. Now that's a bonus!"

Anna Lee approached. "Let's cut this cake," she said. "I'm not getting any younger, ladies."

Paige leaned closer to Anna Lee and whispered, "Is Trevor coming in today?"

"He said he had to work an emergency call this morning and he'd be in this afternoon." Anna Lee pulled her reading glasses off her head and put them in a pocket of her smock. "He's pretty much done here. The water is running fine. He needs to run a few tests and pick up his tools. You seem on edge. He knows about the internship, doesn't he?"

Paige shook her head slightly. "I didn't call and tell him, thinking it would be better to tell him in person. I was hoping he'd be here when I got in."

"He'll be here soon." Anna Lee gave her shoulder a squeeze.

They stood around the worktable talking and laughing while they ate cake. Paige got wrapped up in the conversation and was just as excited as she had been when she got the email from Ms. Maron. Her hard work was paying off, and the excitement from the others heightened her own joy. She momentarily forgot about the pending conversation with Trevor.

Everyone finished their slices of cake, so Paige went around to pick up their paper plates. She walked to the garbage can next to the back door, stepped on the button that opened the lid and dumped everything in. She was turning back to the group to answer a question Tilly had asked about her lodging in New York when the door opened, and Trevor stepped in.

He looked at the room, the banner, flowers, and the glitzy tiara on Paige's head. The look of hurt that flashed over his face pierced Paige's heart. The laugh that was itching to burst forth died on her lips.

"Trevor," she started, but he didn't give her a chance to say anything else. He turned on his heal and left without speaking. The door banged shut.

Paige pushed open the door and called for him again as he made his way to his truck. He ignored her and opened the door. She ran to catch up to him, putting her hand on his shoulder before he climbed in. He stood motionlessly but did not turn around.

"I'm sorry," she started. "I wanted to tell you in person, not on the phone."

"Don't," he replied as he climbed into the truck without a glance at her. He shut the door and turned on the ignition.

Paige waited and prayed he wouldn't drive away. Leaving would be the answer to her question. It would tell her that he wouldn't tolerate a long-distance relationship. Without saying a word, he made it clear–it was the internship or him, not both. Paige took a deep breath. He turned to look at her as he put the truck into gear. The anguish on his face matched her own.

He drove off and Paige turned back towards the building. She was thankful that no one was outside, watching her humiliation. She opened the door, and they were all standing close, seeming to hold their breath. No one spoke.

"He didn't even give me a chance to explain. He just left." Paige fought back the tears that threatened.

"Oh Paige, he's in shock. Give him a bit to process it. He'll come around." Anna Lee put her arms around Paige's waist, Paige hugged her back, the other girls gathered around for a group hug.

"It'll be okay, *Chica*," Nica said, patting her on the back.

"Yes, you'll see, Paige!" Tilly said. "He knows you're amazing. He looks at you like he's holding his breath, waiting for whatever you're going to say next. He is immensely into you. I think this calls for another piece of cake for all of us! Let's keep the sugar rush flowing."

Paige finally laughed. "Who can say no to more cake? I'm in."

She said it so they wouldn't worry or pity her. She could put on a cheerful face, even if her future with Trevor was in question.

After work, she sat in her car and considered her next steps. She could call, but would he be cooled off enough to answer? She could text, but that was cowardly. Showing up at his house was not an option; she didn't know where he lived. She sighed. *I'll give it another day,* she thought, *give him some time. Maybe in the meantime, I can figure out what to do to make him understand how much I care for him and that I'm more than willing to try the long-distance thing.*

TREVOR REACHED FOR a sucker as soon as the truck was in gear. The urge to smoke was palpable. He yanked the sucker's wrapper off and tossed it on the floor, shoving the sucker in his mouth. Without thinking, he chomped down on it and swore. He hoped he didn't break a tooth.

He told himself to calm down and pay attention to the road. He navigated quickly to the interstate and headed north on Interstate 55. It was early afternoon; he could easily drive to Chicago and be back before bed. There wasn't any place in particular he wanted to go to in Chicago, but driving for hours would calm the rage warring inside him.

He thought about how today was supposed to go. He was going to ask Paige out to dinner and have a heart-to-heart talk with her. Tell her how he felt. Put it on the line. Let her in. He wasn't sure how she would react, but he wasn't going to wait for her to show her cards first. She was still recovering from her broken engagement. He assumed that was what drove the reservation he saw in her eyes.

He had hoped that she would be content with the freelance work and would change her mind about going to New York to intern. He was certain of it, but maybe he saw what he wanted to see and not what was right in front of him. He didn't ask her about the internship, and when she didn't bring it up again, it was easier to forget about it. He put his guard down and got comfortable.

Now, though? Now, what? Was this why she appeared to hold back from him? Sure, she said that she wanted financial stability because she didn't have that as a kid, but did she really need to go to New York to find that? Wasn't New York an expensive place to live?

He wondered if this is how his dad felt when his mom left them. Surprised. Angry. Hurt. How did he let this happen? When he'd walked in on her party, he felt like he'd been sucker punched. The blowback sent a shock wave through his whole body and rather than fight back, there in front of Anna Lee and the other girls, he was the one that ran.

Thirty minutes later, Trevor was mulling over these questions when he saw an exit sign for Pontiac, Paige's hometown. Taking the exit and driving east through town, he passed a Burger King, and his stomach growled. He meandered through the streets of Pontiac and drove until he found the high school. *This is where she went to school,* he thought. He wanted to drive by her parents' home, but other than knowing she lived in the country, he didn't have a clue about where to start. He wouldn't go into a store and ask around. He wasn't a stalker.

After an hour of driving up and down the streets, he decided to drive back to Bloomington instead of Chicago. The detour through Paige's hometown took some of his anger away. He wasn't sure why, but he was thankful. Better a drive to Pontiac than Chicago in his gas guzzling truck.

Once he was back on I-55, heading south, he called his sister.

"What do you want? I've got my hands full," she said when she answered.

"Sorry to bug you at work, but I wanted to see if you had plans tonight. I could use a listener."

"I can't tonight. I'm meeting with Erik to talk. See if there is a chance we can salvage our marriage." She sighed.

Trevor grabbed another sucker. "Wow. I'm shocked."

"I know. But don't get your hopes up. I'm not. Tomorrow's our usual Friday night pizza night. Can we talk then?"

"Sure. Sure. What can I bring?" he asked.

"A bottle of red."

"You got it."

He hung up with his sister and called Anna Lee next, asking if he could come in after the store closed to finish up and get his tools without running into Paige. He wasn't ready for that conversation. First, he wanted to talk things over with Tricia.

CHAPTER TWENTY-FIVE

$\mathcal{P}$AIGE WAS HOME in her apartment, puzzling over a gesture to show Trevor how much he meant to her already. She had only known him for three weeks, but she knew there was something special between them. With him, she felt safe and excited. He was kind, funny, and strong. Not only physically strong, but emotionally strong. He knew what he wanted and how to get it. He supported his family, and she could see the way he loved his sister and her kids by the way he talked about them. She could not wait to meet them. Now, she worried she wouldn't have the opportunity.

She attacked the apartment with a dust rag, cleaners, and a mop. The challenge she found living with roommates, as wonderful as they were, was that they weren't all on the same page with housekeeping. Maybe they needed a chore chart. Lists made everything better.

She finished dusting and was sweeping when her phone beeped with a text message.

NICA: Izzy and I are taking you out tonight to celebrate and to get your mind off Trevor. 8pm. We'll both be home by 7 to get ready. ♥

Paige's finger hovered over the keyboard for a moment. She didn't want to go out. But she didn't want to stay in and feel sorry for herself, either.

PAIGE: Sounds great–I'll be ready

She placed furniture mover disks under the couch legs and moved it towards the middle of the room so she could sweep where the couch had been. She swept the dust bunnies and lint into a pile, feeling better that the junk was being removed. Clean house, clean mind.

NICA AND IZZY took her to High Jinks Bar, a popular college hangout. The bar was jam-packed, typical for a Thursday night. They grabbed the only available high-top table near the back. Izzy went to the bar to get drinks as Nica surveyed the crowd.

"Do you think my next boyfriend is in here tonight?" Nica asked.

"What exactly are you looking for in a boyfriend?" Paige responded.

"Someone who is kind, warm, funny. Someone who is shy would be great."

"You are such an outgoing person; don't you worry someone who's shy would be a shadow to you?"

"Two outgoing personalities can be too much. Believe me, I've seen a lot of them. An outgoing and a shy person balance each other out. But we're talking boyfriend material, not marriage material, so for a boyfriend, I don't care." She smiled and shrugged a shoulder; her small gold hoop earring caught the light as she did.

"It's funny that you differentiate boyfriend from husband material. I never thought about that, and I've been engaged. Maybe I should have. Maybe I would have recognized the issues in our relationship sooner."

"Well," Nica replied, "that's the past. You've learned from that relationship. Makes you better equipped for each new relationship."

"I guess," Paige shrugged.

Izzy brought three bottles of Modelo to the table and perched on the open barstool. "Ladies, the bartender *es muy caliente*. I will get all the drinks this evening."

"Which one?" Nica asked.

"The one in the red shirt, dark hair. *Díos Mio*! I will flirt with that man tonight!" Izzy scooted her bar stool closer to Paige to see the bartender better.

"We were talking about boyfriend material, Izzy. What is on your list of criteria?" Paige asked.

"Tall, dark, and handsome. Look at exhibit number one," Izzy responded, nodding toward the bartender again.

"And besides looks?"

"For now, it's all about the looks. I'm not ready to settle down. Then I'll worry more about other qualities. For now, I'm just looking for arm candy!" Izzy gave a broad smile, and her eyes lit up. Paige thought that Izzy was arm candy. She was stunningly beautiful. She probably had guys fawning all over her.

Nica raised her beer bottle to clink Izzy's. "Snap your fingers, Izzy, and that bartender will ask for your number. You have a way of making them fall all over you. Now, I would like to toast our roommate and the next New York publishing executive, Paige. Congratulations on your internship and I know you're going to do great things!" She held up her bottle again, and the others joined her.

"Yes! To Paige! Congrats!" called Izzy.

Paige clinked their bottles. "Thank you both. I know we've only lived together for a few weeks, but it has been great. You are both sweet and fun. Thank you for letting me move in."

"Do you think you'd like to stay with us for the fall semester?" Nica asked. "You know you're a pretty cool roommate yourself. I noticed you scrubbed the apartment this afternoon. It smelled like vinegar and lemons when we came in."

"I love to clean when I'm stressed. Helps me burn off the adrenaline or whatever spikes under stress. And yes, I would love to stay with you for the fall semester. That would be fantastic!"

"What are you stressed about?" Izzy asked. "You got the internship you wanted!"

Nica jumped in to answer. "Trevor didn't seem too thrilled when he showed up in the middle of our party today."

"Oh no. What did he say?" Izzy asked.

Paige took a moment to gather her thoughts. "He didn't even talk to me. When he walked into the store and saw the celebration, he got a pained look on his face, and he turned around and walked out. I followed him to his truck and tried to talk to him, but he left without saying anything. Yes, I should have talked to him more about the possibility of the internship. I mean, I mentioned it, but I didn't talk to him about how much it meant to me. I have loved spending time with him, getting to know him, and I didn't want to bring up anything that might have put a damper on how well things appeared to be going." She took a long drink of the cold beer.

"The honeymoon phase of a relationship." Nica said. "Everything is blissful. But you have to have some meaningful conversations to ensure compatibility at some point. I don't want to invest too much time or energy in a relationship if it can't go anywhere long-term. I'm not saying it's a first or second date conversation. But usually within a month or two."

"I haven't even known Trevor for a month!" Paige responded. "I don't see why he would seem so hurt or disappointed."

"Gosh, Paige," Izzy raised her hands in an 'I don't know' gesture, "I'm no relationship genius, but I think that means he really likes you. What are you going to do now?"

Paige thought Izzy probably was a relationship genius. She had much more experience than herself. Trevor was only her third boyfriend; Izzy probably had three boyfriends every few months.

"I don't know," she responded. "It seemed like he needed some time, so I chickened out of calling him today, and a text felt too impersonal. I thought I would let him cool off before I call."

"Why don't you go to his place to see him without an audience?" Nica asked.

"That's a great idea, but I don't know where he lives." Paige admitted. "He hasn't taken me there or given me the address. Anyway, can we change the subject?"

"Okay, yes," replied Izzy, standing up. "Time for round two. Wish me luck." She grabbed their empty bottles and sashayed towards the bar.

Nica and Paige talked about weekend plans while Izzy got their drinks. As Izzy came back to the table, Paige looked up and saw Trevor sitting at the far end of the bar. He appeared to be alone. Her pulse raced. Should she go to him now? Wait for him to see her first? Pretend he's not there?

Izzy sat the bottles on the table. "Success! The bartender asked me for my phone number and already texted me to make sure it was a legit number."

"Does he have a name?" Nica teased.

"Yes, it's Mark. Let's see if he remembers and contacts me tomorrow."

Paige tried not to stare at Trevor. She debated telling the girls that he was there. But they would probably make her go talk to him. If the ideal place to talk to him was alone, without an audience, this wasn't it.

"Of course, he'll contact you, Izzy," Nica replied. "He'd be crazy not to."

Paige shifted her gaze to the bartender, not wanting them to catch her watching Trevor. She nodded in agreement with Nica.

Izzy started talking about her job at a beauty supply shop. All the employees in her store location received a beauty gift bag from one of the major retailers and Izzy detailed out all the products included. Paige tried to follow the conversation but kept finding her mind and eyes drifting towards Trevor. She watched him sip a bottle of beer, but he tossed back a couple shots of an amber colored liquid. That didn't bode well for his state of mind and kept Paige from approaching him. She hoped tomorrow would bring a chance for them to talk so they could clear the air and find a path forward.

CHAPTER TWENTY-SIX

PAIGE SLEPT LATE on Friday and had to rush to get ready. She took a quick shower and mentally ran down a list of possible opening statements to make to Trevor.

* Trevor, I'm sorry for not talking to you about the internship in more detail
* I'm sorry the party caught you off guard
* Trevor, I'm surprised at how upset you were
* I should have contacted you about the internship before you showed up
* What the heck dude, we've only dated for a few weeks!

No matter what she came up with, they all sounded wrong. They didn't convey the depth of her emotions or how her feelings for Trevor were growing. She was as sad about leaving him as he seemed to be about her leaving. But her career goals were older than their relationship. Surely, he'd understand that. He was career focused, happy, and proud of what he did for a living. Shouldn't he want that for her, too?

There were no events on Friday that required flowers from In Bloom. But Fridays were steady retail days, so both she and Tilly were on the work schedule. When Paige arrived, Anna Lee was sitting in the workshop bay with several buckets of fresh flowers, creating arrangements to sell in the store. She greeted Paige and asked if there was an update on the Trevor front.

"No, not yet. We haven't talked since he left here yesterday. Is he coming in today?" Paige asked.

"No, he came last night to pick up his equipment and deliver the final bill." Anna Lee said, turning an arrangement of yellow tulips and greenery. It appeared as though she was checking for balance.

"He came back? I was here until close."

"He called me and asked if he could come in after we closed."

"Oh. He didn't want to risk seeing me," Paige murmured.

Anna Lee grabbed another vase from the wire shelving unit behind her. "He didn't say that exactly." She paused. "But that would be my guess."

Tilly walked in the back door, carrying a small box of donuts from Mama C's Bakery, their favorite. "Good morning! I brought donuts! Anyone want one?"

"I think we could all use a cup of coffee and a doughnut. Thank you, Tilly," Anna Lee said, rising from the workbench. "Paige, let's carry the ready arrangements up front to tag and put out."

Paige grabbed two arrangements and followed Anna Lee to the retail side. "Do you think I should call him?"

"I think you need a face-to-face discussion." Anna Lee said as she sat her arrangements on the counter. "Why don't you go see him? I have his payment ready. Perhaps you could drop it off on your way home tonight?"

"I don't know where he lives! He's never taken me there or given me his address." Paige thought that statement sounded ridiculous. How serious could he be about her if she didn't even know where he lives?

"I have the address and see no harm in giving it to you. I know hurt when I see it, and that boy is hurting. You are too." Anna

Lee created price tags for each arrangement and handed them to Paige to add to the vases before placing them on the shelves.

"I am," Paige agreed. "I've made a complete mess of this situation. Should have been more up front about my plans."

"You can fix this. You gotta tell him how you feel. Let's see what sort of donuts Tilly picked up." Anna Lee would give brilliant advice, but she wouldn't belabor a point or get caught up in endless debate. She'd speak her mind and move on. Paige admired that about her.

She grabbed a blueberry doughnut and an extra-large cup of coffee. She wished she could take the sugar surge and go to Trevor now, instead of waiting the seven hours until her shift was over.

PAIGE WAS OUT the door at five o'clock. Tilly waved her off, saying she'd handle all the closing activities on her own. Anna Lee had given Paige a white envelope with Trevor's name and address on the cover. She laid it on the passenger car seat and tapped the address into the GPS on her phone. Ten minutes away. Convenient. Paige hoped he would be home by now. He didn't give Anna Lee any information on the location of his current assignment or if he even had something lined up after his work at In Bloom.

Paige zipped down Hershey Road with a gnawing pain in her stomach. She stopped thinking through what she might say, deciding she would wing it when she saw him.

She arrived at the address on the envelope and parked at the curb. She stared at the house for a minute, puzzled. This was a brick ranch house, with a neat, well-tended yard. Not the type of fixer-upper farmhouse that Trevor described. Did Anna Lee have the wrong address or had Trevor lied to her about his project house? Why would he lie about his house? That didn't make sense. Anna Lee must have the wrong address. There was only one way to know for sure–knock on the door.

She walked to the driveway, which was on the far side of the house. She could not see the full length of it from her car. When she got to the drive and started walking towards the house, she saw Trevor's truck parked at the back, in front of a detached garage. This must be the right place.

She rang the doorbell and admired the front door–a craftsman-style brown wood door which paired well with the light brown brick. She thought she heard voices from inside before the door opened. A beautiful woman with brunette hair, long slender legs in cutoff shorts, and a white tank top opened the door. *My word,* Paige thought, *could this woman be any prettier?*

"Um," Paige spat out over her dry tongue, "is Trevor here?"

"Yes, he is," the lady holding the door open replied. "He's in the shower. Can you wait a few minutes?"

Paige blushed. Obviously, this was someone who was intimately familiar with Trevor. A past girlfriend that he rebounded to after he found out Paige was leaving? Someone he met at the bar the night prior? Paige had never been so embarrassed in her life. Trevor would probably break down in laughter once he knew she stopped by and saw his beautiful friend.

"No, I can't. Sorry, I'm an employee at In Bloom and Anna Lee asked me to drop off his payment." She stuck out her hand with the envelope and prayed the lady would take it fast so she could run.

"Oh, okay. That's nice of you to stop by. Hope it wasn't any trouble." She took the envelope and Paige turned to go. As she did, she heard the water shut off. She hadn't recognized the sound of the shower until it stopped.

"No trouble. Thanks for giving it to him," Paige called as she walked away.

Back in the safety of her car, she fumbled getting the key into the ignition. Her hands were shaking. On the positive side, she didn't need to figure out what to say to Trevor to apologize. There would be no need to speak to him now.

As she pulled away from the curb, she glanced in her rear-view mirror. It startled her to see Trevor step out on to the porch, wearing only a pair of basketball shorts. He looked towards her car and Paige almost stepped on the brake. Instead, she applied more pressure to the gas pedal.

CHAPTER TWENTY-SEVEN

"DANG IT!" TREVOR yelled as he stepped back inside the house. Tricia raised her eyebrows at him. "What? I didn't cuss!"

"But you yelled, and William is still napping," Tricia replied. "If you wake him up, you can deal with his crankiness. Who was that?"

"That was the woman I've been telling you about. Paige."

"Oh, I should have guessed, the pretty strawberry blonde you have been talking non-stop about for weeks." She smirked and walked to the kitchen.

Trevor followed, pulling on his t-shirt. "What did she say?"

"Not much. She asked if you were here. I said you were in the shower, and she said 'give him this', and she handed me the envelope. Oh, she said she works at In Bloom and this was your payment."

Trevor looked at the envelope again. In Bloom was the return address. His name and the current address, his dad's house where his sister and two kids were now living, were in the mailing address. He made a mental note that he needed to change the address on his invoices to his new house. And change the name of the plumbing company from "Peter Morrison and Son Plumbing" to "Morrison Plumbing," or something else.

"Ah." He nodded. "Anna Lee asked her to drop it off. Did she ask who you were?"

"No. She didn't seem like she wanted to chitchat. Maybe she was in a hurry. Didn't you say you guys had a spat?"

"Not a spat. But I turned and ran when I walked into a celebration at In Bloom wishing her well on her internship. It caught me off guard."

"When's the internship?"

"Not sure–she was up for one for this summer and something happened so she couldn't go. I knew she was reapplying, but don't know when she'll go."

"Well, if it's next summer, why are you so concerned? You're not the long-term boyfriend type."

"This is different. I think I could be long-term boyfriend material. I think I could be husband material with Paige."

"Wow. That is serious. But if she wants to do this internship, shouldn't you be supporting her and not shutting her out?"

"What if she meets someone else while she's there?" His hand tightened into a fist.

"Then you, my silly brother, are not the right person for her and isn't it better to know that *now*, before you're married with a handful of kids?"

Trevor knew she was right. He knew it because he watched the pain and distress she had gone through when her husband decided he was in the wrong relationship and left. And he wasn't being fair to Paige, acting like a jealous boyfriend, only concerned with what it meant to *him* if she went to New York. He hadn't been thinking about her and what *she* wanted. She told him that her career was important to her, to be able to be self-supported and self-sufficient if she had to be.

Trevor had been focused more on his feelings than hers. He saw that now. He wanted to be with her, protect her and take care of her. But he couldn't put his desires above hers, he needed to support her dreams too. He wouldn't be the kind of guy that made her choose between a career and him. He hoped to convince her they could have both.

"Point taken," he answered. "Clearly. You're right. If it's meant to be and all that."

Waylon ran into the kitchen with an airplane in hand. "I'm a pilot. I'm a pilot. I'm a pilot."

"Whoa, Mr. Pilot," Tricia said, picking him up when he reached her. "Slow down in the house, okay? Or I'll send you home with Uncle T."

"Can I go with you now, Uncle T?" Waylon asked, wide brown eyes pleading.

"Not tonight, kiddo. I have work to do in the morning." He looked to Tricia, "And I think I have a dating mess to clean up. I shouldn't have left without talking to her."

"Explain that to me in more detail. What happened exactly?" she put Waylon back on the floor and he ran off to his bedroom again with his airplane.

"I walked in. They were celebrating. I walked out."

"Did you say hello when you walked in?"

"No. I left." Trevor looked out the back window.

"When was this?" Tricia opened the dishwasher and started putting clean dishes away in the cabinets.

"Yesterday afternoon."

"And she hasn't called or texted since?"

"Well," he didn't want to admit this part, "she followed me to the parking lot. To my truck. She said she was sorry she hadn't told me yet but wanted to tell me in person."

"And?"

"I left."

"Without a single word?"

"I said 'don't' and then I left."

"You walked out without talking to her. You're a loser. That is the most shameful thing I've heard you do in a long time. She came after you and you didn't talk to her? That's awful. You walked out on her like Mom did to us." She shook her head. "This isn't going well."

Trevor felt that. Felt it to his core. Was he like his mom? He never thought he was. Tried all his life to do better. Be better than that. He ran his hand through his damp hair. "Yes, I know that."

"Stop being your stubborn self and go fix this." She picked up a towel and started spraying cleaner on the counter.

"I hate it when you're right."

"I know you do." Tricia threw her towel at him. "You need to fix it, dummy."

CHAPTER TWENTY-EIGHT

PAIGE SLAMMED ON her brakes at the last moment to avoid running a stop sign. She wiped the tears from her cheeks and turned off the radio because it was playing sappy love songs.

"I will get over him. I am almost over him already. What a jerk. Only a day later and he's already got some beautiful girl over. She's probably nursing his hurt feelings. Well, he can just suck on those hurt feelings or whatever he's feeling. He hasn't even given me the courtesy of telling me what he's feeling!"

Paige felt better ranting at the top of her lungs in her car until the man in the car passing her gave her a sideways look.

Paige glanced at her watch. 5:20 p.m. Izzy and Nica had plans tonight, so the apartment would be empty. But would staying home be wise? She could call her mom or Macey and ask for advice. But they had more important things to do.

She thought about the latest novel that she had to proofread. She could work on that tonight. Throwing herself into a book was always a balm when her spirit ached. But working in the apartment was too restricting. She'd go to Denny's, get an endless cup of coffee, a stack of warm, sweet pancakes and a dessert to ease her heartache. Then she'd camp out for hours if needed to get through the first read-through.

She stopped at the apartment to get her laptop and left a note for her roommates. At Denny's, her mind kept wondering to Trevor. After two hours, she gave up and left. She drove to her apartment and was happy to find Nica at home.

Nica was in yoga gear and stretching in the living room. "Hey, I saw your note. You're home sooner than I expected."

"Yes, I thought the novel I'm proofreading would take my mind off Trevor, but it didn't." Paige dropped her backpack on the floor and plopped on the couch. "I gave up. I work at Max's coffee shop in the morning, so I shouldn't be up late reading and drinking coffee, anyway. As it is, I may not get to sleep for a few hours." Paige yawned.

"*Pobrecita.*" Nica sighed. "No word yet from Trevor?"

"No. And get this: Anna Lee asked me to drop his check off for him. She had his address. I didn't. Sounded like a good idea. But I go to the address. His truck is in the drive, but a gorgeous woman answered the door. She was barefoot, and it seemed like she was right at home."

"Gorgeous?" Nica moved into a downward facing dog pose.

"Yes, tall, a few inches taller than me. A brunette with chunky blonde highlights. Tan. Perfect hair. Skinny with boobs. Ugh. Gorgeous. I wonder if he picked her up at the bar last night. Or if he knew her already."

"Was he there at the house?"

"Yes, in the shower! They probably just did it."

"Paige! You don't know that. You're jumping to conclusions. Did you talk to him at least? And wait, what do you mean about the bar last night?"

"He was at High Jinks," Paige admitted. "I saw him sitting at the bar. I'm surprised Izzy didn't notice him when she went for drinks. Well, she only had eyes for the bartender. Anyway, no, I didn't talk to him. I handed the goddess at the door the check and I took off. I was pulling away, and I saw him come outside, only wearing shorts, holding a t-shirt in his hand."

Nica released her yoga posed and sat cross-legged on the floor. "Why didn't you tell us you saw him last night? And why didn't you go talk to him? Was he with a girl?"

"No, by himself as far as I could see, drinking." Paige noticed she was using a lot of hand gestures; she sat down and tucked her hands under her legs. "No way would I start *that* conversation in a crowded bar. And while we were both drinking. Nothing good could come out of that conversation. But now, I don't even want to talk to him. I mean, who was that girl? He's obviously moved on. I will too."

"Haven't you heard looks can be deceiving? Maybe she was a friend. Or maybe she was a cleaning lady, or…"

"Or maybe I was born yesterday. He was in the shower, and she was barely dressed." Paige found that her hands had taken flight again.

"What do you mean, barely dressed?" Nica came out of her latest pose and sat on her butt, staring at Paige.

"Cutoff shorts, a tank top, no shoes. Barely dressed."

"It was ninety-eight degrees today, Paige. She was dressed for the weather. You have an overactive imagination. Maybe you read too many books." Nica smiled. Paige felt the warmth from across the room. She knew Nica was giving solid advice, but Paige wasn't ready to let go of her suspicions yet.

"Thank you for listening. I'm trying to be open-minded but, I don't know. It's unsettling. Besides, you can never read too many books. That's it. I'm going to bed. And I'm going to bury my nose in a good book."

Nica smiled. "Night, Paige."

AFTER HER EARLY shift at Max's, Paige stopped at In Bloom to talk to Anna Lee. The parking lot was full of employee and customer cars, typical for a Saturday. Paige went in the back door and found the work room bustling. The girls were working on wedding centerpieces.

"Anna Lee, can I help?" Paige asked when she saw the full room and all the flowers in the middle of the worktable.

"See if you can help Nica up front. The front doorbell has been jingling non-stop. We've got things under control in here."

In the retail space, Nica was ringing up a customer and there were two more customers waiting in line. Paige waved to Nica and walked around the store, asking customers if they needed assistance. She helped a man who was shopping for flowers for his 30th wedding anniversary and then she helped a young girl pick out a small bouquet to take to her grandmother, who was in the hospital with a broken wrist.

After all the customers were taken care of, there was a lull in traffic. Nica ran to the restroom for a much-needed break and Paige kept an eye on the store. Anna Lee came out front to check on things.

"How's it going?" she asked as she scooped Salty up off the floor for a head rub.

"It's fine now. Nica was slammed when you sent me up here. Can I ask you a question?"

"Well, you just did. The answer is yes. Got another one?" she replied, setting Salty back on the floor.

Paige smiled. Leave it to Anna Lee. "Well, first, I dropped the check off for Trevor."

"Good. Thank you. Did you talk to him about how you feel?"

"No, the thing is, there was another girl there. It was awkward. Anyway, I think it's over between us and I could use a few days at home. Lick my wounds, I guess. I'm scheduled here Tuesday. If I can find someone to switch Tuesday with me, would you mind?"

"Of course not. Though I am not sure running away ever solves a problem." Anna Lee checked the clock on the wall, the clock with the swinging cat tail and shifting eyes.

"Maybe not," Paige agreed. "But I need some home time. Time to get together with my best friend and see my family too. Hope it will help heal my hurts."

Nica joined them at the register as Anna Lee responded, "Home usually helps in matters such as these. Of course, I'm fine if you can switch your Tuesday shift. Thanks for asking first. Since everyone is here today, you can ask around."

Paige gave Anna Lee a hug. "I will. I know Nica is already on the Tuesday schedule, so I'll ask in the back. Do you want me to stay and help with the wedding arrangements? There's a lot going on back there!"

"There is, but it is under control. Go on now, you're not scheduled today, get out of here." Anna Lee shrugged her off.

Paige turned to her roommate. "Nica, if I can get someone to cover or switch for my Tuesday shift, I'm going home. If someone picks up the shift, I'll go to the apartment and pack my bag. I want to get on the road soon."

"Okay," Nica responded. "Good luck."

Paige asked the girls in the workroom and Tilly volunteered to switch her Tuesday shift for Friday. Tilly tried asking Paige about Trevor, but she dodged the question and fled.

CHAPTER TWENTY-NINE

ONCE TREVOR WAS done with his Saturday morning job, he went home and started on the woodwork in his dining room. Using a heat gun, he labored to remove the layers of paint. Halfway through the project, he realized how thankful he was that there was no crown molding in the living room.

He kept turning over the last few days in his mind. His sister was right. He had been a coward when he left Paige without even talking to her. But he worried that if he had talked to her, he would have freaked her out. His passion for her had come on so fast, so quick, he couldn't understand it. How could he make her see that his feelings were genuine?

When the heat gun no longer removed additional paint, he went to the kitchen for a glass of water. He stood at the sink and stretched his back, bending backward, side to side, and forward, holding each stretch for a few seconds. He looked at the clock on the stove–four p.m., time to think about dinner.

A craving for Chinese food reminded him of the night at Paige's apartment, reading with her. He loved the image of her on the couch, her laptop propped up on her knees. The way she lightly chewed on her lower lip and the way her forehead pinched together. He wondered if that meant the reading wasn't going well, but he didn't want to ask and interrupt her when he promised he wouldn't be a nuisance.

Why couldn't she make a career of proofreading like she did that night? If they could send her books to read through email and she could read and proof from anywhere, why did she have to go to New York? She didn't act like it was only for the internship; she acted like she would move there after college, and she would probably never look back.

He thought back to his sister's words the night before–"fix it". She was right, but how could he fix it? How could he explain his feelings to Paige without making her run, run fast, run far away? He was crazy for falling for her in a matter of weeks.

Trevor ruminated on the last three relationships he'd been in. First was Amanda. They dated when they were both twenty-one. They fell hard for each other, but it fizzled out faster than a damp sparkler on the fourth of July.

Then there was Marley. They met right after he broke up with Amanda. He told Marley right off the bat that he was not looking for a long-term relationship and she agreed. They dated for two years and finally went their own ways, amicably.

Finally, there was Gwen. He was twenty-five and his sister had recently had Waylon. For the first time, he thought about marriage. The emotions he had holding his nephew for the first time surprised him. Sure, he had friends with babies by then and he'd held babies before. But holding his nephew and talking to his sister and dad about what family traits Waylon had, it was different. He started imagining what his babies would look like. Would they have his dark hair or Gwen's blonde hair? His brown eyes or her green eyes?

He even looked at engagement rings and dropped hints that an engagement may be imminent. And then Gwen cheated on him. Maybe he should be thankful that it happened before they got engaged. If they had been engaged, would he have worked harder to forgive her? Would he have forgiven her and gone through with a wedding? It was hard to say.

Trevor shook himself out of his reverie. "Time to get back to work," he said to the empty kitchen. "You said you wouldn't have Paige over until the dining and living rooms were done, so let's get them done. Then, when you figure out how to get yourself out of this mess and back in her good graces, you can invite her over."

CHAPTER THIRTY

PAIGE HELPED HER mom around the house and yard on Saturday and woke up Sunday morning with the sore muscles to prove it. She was thankful for the pain, as the busyness had helped keep her mind off of Trevor. Her mom tried to get her to join in on a yoga class, but Paige declined, saying her muscles were already like Jell-O, and elected to take her dad to breakfast.

After breakfast, they stopped at the grocery store to pick up a few staples. Standing in the checkout line, Paige heard someone call her name. She turned to look at the line of customers behind her. Standing behind three other people, was her first boyfriend, Rick Townes. She smiled and waved.

"Wait for me, okay?" he called, holding up a jar of maple syrup.

Frank finished paying for their groceries and told Paige he would walk to the hardware store to grab a few supplies and he'd meet her at the car when she was ready.

After Rick paid for his purchase, he approached Paige and gave her a big hug. Paige closed her eyes and breathed in his familiar scent. It had been years, but the hug felt like a homecoming. It was comforting and warm. "How are you doing, Shorty? I haven't seen you in ages!"

Paige scrunched her nose at the nickname. At six feet four inches, Rick could call most people Shorty.

"It has been a while, hasn't it? I'm all right. How are you?" Paige stepped back to look him in the eye. He had the same mischievous squint around his big blue eyes.

"I'm great! Working hard, playing hard, staying hard." He double tapped his stomach muscles. "I work out four days a week," he boasted.

Paige wanted to roll her eyes. Rick was outgoing and boisterous. It was hard to take life too seriously when he was around. He didn't. He was the life of the party and everybody's best friend. It had amazed Paige when Rick asked her out sophomore year. She was one of the "smart" kids, not a partier. But they had a lot of mutual attraction and she fell hard for him. They broke up their junior year and Paige started dating Caleb soon after.

"You're a nut," she said.

"Almond Joy, baby! How long are you in town for? What are you doing in town? Did someone die?" His eyebrows came together, and he almost lost the gleam in his eye.

"No one died," she answered. "Just home for a brief visit. I'll go back to Bloomington on Wednesday."

"Oh, you're here for a few days. Are you totally booked, or could I take you out to dinner one night? I'd love to get caught up."

"Well..."

"Oh, do you have a boyfriend? I'm not trying to be too forward. Sorry if it seems that way. I thought two old friends could catch up. What do you say? Dinner tomorrow night?"

Paige laughed. It was like Rick to rattle off several questions before she could answer the first. She wasn't sure how to answer the first question honestly, so she ignored it. She thought about Trevor and while they never talked about relationship status, she would have thought they were *something*. But now, after his silent treatment, she wasn't sure what to think.

"Dinner tomorrow night would be great," she answered. "I'd love to catch up."

"Perfection. I'll pick you up at six."

PAIGE STRESSED OVER what to wear to dinner with Rick. She had called her best friend to find out what she could about Rick. According to Macey, there were no rumors of him dating anyone seriously. He always had a date for weddings, but rarely the same date for two different events. Not that he had a loose reputation. The general word was that he was a gentleman. Rick was doing very well for himself selling cars, and he bought his first home at twenty. He had an investor's spirit and flipped his first house at twenty-one, upgrading to a larger house.

Paige thanked Macey for the low-down and promised to call her after the dinner with a play-by-play.

Rick knocked on the back door and called out before opening the door. Paige was helping her mom wash the fruits and vegetables they had bought at a farmer's market that morning.

"Hi Rick. It's lovely to see you again." Sue said as Rick gave her a hug.

"Great to see you, Mrs. Bell. It's been a while. How are you and Mr. Bell doing?"

"Mr. Bell is great," Frank said, entering the kitchen. Rick turned to shake his hand.

Sue laughed. "I'm well too, Rick. We keep seeing your name in the paper. Your work with the youth center has been fantastic. It's wonderful to see younger adults step up and help out."

"I love it. Absolutely love it," Rick smiled. "You know, I've been wanting to ask you about a possible yoga class for the high schoolers. Can I call you later this week to discuss?"

"Of course," Sue responded. "That sounds fun."

"Well," Rick said, turning towards Paige, "are you ready to go?"

Paige nodded. She took in his attire–long cargo shorts and a polo. Must have a casual evening planned. She was thankful she went with the maxi dress–it could go either casual or fancy.

As they made their way out to his car, a sporty red Chevy Camaro, she asked, "How can you afford the insurance for this? A young single guy, red sports car...."

He laughed. "I work extra hard."

He opened the car door for her and waited for her to settle in before closing it carefully. The banter on the way to the restaurant was light. They caught up on where their mutual friends were–who continued to live in Pontiac, who had moved off to other cities or states, who had not been heard about in a while.

It pleasantly surprised Paige when he pulled into The Big Steer. It was the nicest restaurant in town, a popular place for prom nights, date nights, and other special occasions.

Rick told the hostess that they were reliving sweet memories and asked if they could have a booth in the 'back forty' room. She said it wasn't usually open on a Monday night, but she would make an exception.

The room was chilly, and Paige wished she had a sweater. When Rick saw her rub her arms after they sat down, he asked if she wanted him to sit beside her for body heat.

"That would be great," she said. He slid in next to her and casually dropped his arm around her, rubbing her shoulder. "Thanks. I'll warm up in a minute, adjusting to the a/c."

"No sweat. Ha. Pun not intended. Now, tell me all about the hearts you've been breaking."

The waitress came to take their order, and Paige was grateful for the interruption. Unfortunately, Rick did not forget. "So?" he prompted once the waitress left.

"Well, I'm sure you heard about my engagement to Caleb and

the disastrous ending." Paige thought about the disadvantages of living in a smaller community.

"It would be hard not to. I'd have to be a hermit to have not heard about it. I'm sorry." He gave her shoulders another squeeze.

"Thanks. I guess in hindsight, it wasn't a good match. I sometimes wonder what I was thinking when I started dating him. But it was easy. It was comfortable. But I learned a lot." Paige straightened up, she would not degrade herself in front of Rick for the failed relationship.

"Yeah? What d'ya learn?" he reached for the beer in front of him and took a long drink.

"I learned that I'm way too young to be engaged. I need to focus on my career first and just because something is familiar, doesn't mean it's right." She sighed and picked up her diet soda.

"Ouch. That hit a little close to home. But are you really?"

"Really what?" she asked.

"Too young to be engaged. A lot of women marry before they're twenty-one. Shoot, half of our graduating class is already married. I think you and I would be if we'd stayed together."

"You think so, huh?" Paige grew uncomfortable and wondered if it would be rude to ask him to go to the other side of the booth.

"We were perfect together, Paige. Your beauty, your brains, and my personality. My ambition and your ambition. We'd be running the county in no time."

"I don't want to run a county."

"It's only a hypothetical. Sorry, I think I'm making you uncomfortable. Didn't mean to do that. Tell me about college, how is it going? What's your life like these days?"

"Do you know you ask a lot of questions?" She smiled at him, hoping he had some self-awareness.

The waitress brought their salads and Rick moved to the other side to give them room, after asking Paige if she had warmed up.

"Do I?" he asked, responding to her question. "You're right! I do." He laughed at himself, and Paige couldn't help but laugh too.

"Yes, you do. But you're cute and charming, it's not bothersome."

"Ah ha! You think I'm cute and charming. Cool. Now please tell me about your life." He took a bite of his salad and waited.

Paige rolled her eyes. "It's been an interesting few weeks. I thought I had a summer internship locked up for this summer and lost it at the last minute."

"What kind of internship?"

"A publishing house, in New York," she answered.

"Wow! New York! I never pictured you in New York."

"Well, I never thought about how books were made until I had a conversation with my adviser back in January. We talked about it, and I was all in. It sounds exciting. I can't wait to get my chance to go. I found out last week that I have an offer for a spring internship. Same publishing house. They messed something up, that's why I lost the internship for this summer."

"And, you came up with this pursuit in January…"

"Right," she said.

"Right after your broken engagement with Caleb at Christmas…."

She bristled. "What are you getting at?"

"Oh, I don't think I'm getting at anything. It's just interesting timing."

"They're not related. I didn't know about this career path before."

"Are you more attracted to the job or to the fact that it's in New York?"

Paige turned over his words in her mind. No, that was not it at all. New York had always fascinated her. She'd been there several times for her dad's art shows. She loved the hustle and bustle, though the noise was hard to get used to, but she knew she'd learn.

"I love New York! It's full of culture and interesting people."

"There's not enough culture and interesting people here?" The teasing in his eyes made her smile. He wasn't trying to offend her, just trying to keep her honest with herself. He was always the one to cut through any baloney.

"There's plenty of interesting people here." She raised an eyebrow and tried not to smirk.

"Ha! You've got me there. But seriously, P. I think you're running *from* something, not to something. Caleb was a jerk, and he didn't deserve you. I wish I had made a better decision about our relationship when I had the chance. Stayed with you instead of letting you go." He looked away wistfully.

"Rick," she whispered, reaching for his hand. "I..." she didn't know what to say. Several emotions were fighting for her attention. There was an ache in her heart, thinking about what might have been; and there was a warning in her mind, thinking about what could be. And finally, a stirring in her gut, thinking about Trevor and wondering what he was doing tonight. Still regretting that she hadn't tried to contact him yet.

He turned to her and put his hand on top of hers. "Paige, I think about you often. I see your brother Logan around town a lot, and I always ask how you're doing. You are the one that got away."

Paige admitted that she felt comfortable and safe with Rick. She always had, but was that enough? Maybe it didn't need to be enough, but maybe it was good enough for now. Seeing Rick would help distract her from thoughts of Trevor.

"This is a little awkward to bring up now, but I've been seeing someone."

"Yeah? But..."

"Well, I think he's mad at me because I didn't tell him about the spring internship. It's complicated to explain, but he came into the flower shop where I work right in the middle of a party the owner was throwing for me to celebrate. He looked around, realized what was going on, and he left. He wouldn't say anything to me, he simply left."

"When was this?"

"Thursday."

"No peep from him since?"

"No."

"Ouch."

"I know. I think that tells me everything I need to know."

Their dinners came and Paige welcomed the distraction. Rick told her about his job at the dealership, some of the new ideas he had implemented successfully, and his volunteer work. His drive impressed her, and she told him so.

After dinner, they walked three blocks to the Dairy Barn, where they indulged in ice cream. One of the local soccer teams came pouring out of a few vehicles as they were leaving, and Rick turned back around and offered to pay for their ice cream.

"That's generous of you," Paige said as they walked about to his car, eating their ice cream.

"Good PR. Some of those minivans need to be upgraded," he said and gave her a wink.

THEY DROVE AROUND town after finishing their ice cream. Rick didn't like to eat in the car. "It's a loaner," he explained.

They drove to their old high school and saw a baseball game in progress, so they stopped to watch. Rick walked through groups of people smiling, chatting, and shaking hands. Paige watched him schmooze and thought he could be a politician.

They found seats in the bleachers and cheered for the home team. After the sixth inning, Rick went to the concession stand to get bottles of water for them. Though the sun was setting, it was ninety degrees.

While waiting for Rick to return, she wanted to send her mom a quick text, letting her know they were hanging out, and she'd be home late. She pulled her phone out of her purse where she'd left it all evening and saw that she missed a text from Trevor an hour before. She debated responding and saying she couldn't talk, but she didn't want to have to explain where she was and what she was doing, so she ignored the text. She could always respond later.

She sent the text to her mom and checked for her reply as Rick came back with water and sat down beside her.

"Everything okay?" he asked, nodding towards the phone.

"Yes," she said, "I'm updating Mom. Didn't want her to worry."

"You check with her when you're on all your dates?"

Paige hadn't thought of this as a date, it was an evening with a friend. Did Rick see it as a date?

"No, but she rarely knows when I go out. Being at home as an adult has some awkward boundaries. I think parents still worry and we default back to our high school habits. Text when you get there, text if you're going to be late, text if…."

"One of the reasons I moved out as soon as I could," Rick replied. "Easier on them, easier on me."

"Do you date a lot?"

"I go on dates, but I wouldn't say I date a lot."

"Just the ladies that might need a new car?" Paige teased.

He laughed softly. "No, Paige, I don't mix business and actual pleasure."

"That's good. I won't be expecting a sales pitch when you look at my car with a hundred and twenty-five thousand miles on it."

"Hmm, maybe it's time to break this date off right now and make a sales pitch."

Oh boy, Paige thought, *that's the second time he's said 'date' in about as many minutes. I need to watch this situation. I don't know what's going on with Trevor, but this could get messy.*

The game ended, and Rick drove her home. He walked her to the back door and kissed her cheek before asking her to hang out the next night.

"I'm not sure." Paige hesitated. "Macey and I have loose plans for tomorrow."

"I understand. Well, let me know. I'll keep my evening open, just in case." He gave her a broad smile, and she relaxed. He was a friend, just catching up with a friend. She could explain that to Trevor if asked. She didn't feel guilty about it, hardly at all.

CHAPTER THIRTY-ONE

FTER A PRODUCTIVE weekend fueled by his anger, he had the wallpaper removed and the woodwork stripped in the living and dining rooms. He even had the walls patched and ready to paint. When he left for work Monday morning, he thought about paint colors while he drove. On his way home, he stopped at his favorite mom and pop hardware store and bought three gallons of paint, hoping it would be enough to give both rooms two coats of "Neutral Linen." Several nights after work painting the walls, then a few nights staining the baseboards and window molding, he'd be done. Maybe he could invite Paige over on Saturday. If he could make amends and she'd talk to him by then.

It had been four days since the party at In Bloom. And no word from Paige. He wished for the hundredth time that he had been available when she showed up at his sister's house. Just his luck, he took a five-minute shower and Paige arrived during that time. What would she have said? What would he have said to her?

Fix it. Tricia's words rang through his mind again. But how? Did he need a grand gesture or a simple apology? This was killing him. He unloaded the paint, paintbrushes, paint trays and drop cloths from his truck. After carrying everything inside, he decided he needed to do something where Paige was concerned.

He pulled out a wooden chair at his kitchen table and sat down. He took his phone out of his pocket and studied it for a minute before gathering the nerve to text Paige.

TREVOR: Hey. Can U talk?

Not the most eloquent text message, but it was a serve into her court. He stared at the phone, waiting for, and expecting, a quick reply. It did not come. After several minutes, he stood and tossed the phone on the kitchen counter and he went into the living room, ready to paint.

TREVOR OPENED HIS eyes Tuesday morning and grabbed his phone. His shoulder ached, reminding him of the four hours he'd spent painting the night before.

No text message response or call from Paige. He swore under his breath and rolled out of bed. She usually worked at In Bloom on Tuesday, so he would stop there on his lunch break. He was working on a new house build not far from In Bloom–it could be a quick trip.

He thought about stopping at another florist so he could show up with a dozen roses, but Anna Lee would probably whack him over the head for not buying flowers from her store. *Hmm, maybe I could make Paige jealous and buy a dozen roses from her, not letting on they are FOR her,* he thought, chuckling to himself. *No, you idiot. That's not the way to fix this. Be upfront, be honest, be a man for god's sake.*

The hours on his jobsite seemed to drag on. He knew the foreman was eager to get all the plumbing done that day so he could start the drywall crew on Wednesday, so Trevor decided he might need to work until midnight, but he had to take the time at noon to go talk to Paige.

At In Bloom, he scanned the parking lot, but didn't see her blue car. *Maybe she rode with Nica, I don't know what she drives.*

Inside the store, he saw Tilly behind the register. He waited for her to ring up a customer and then he approached. "Hi Tils. Is Paige in today?"

"No," Tilly answered, "she asked for someone to switch days and I volunteered."

"Do you know why she asked for the day off?"

"No, but Anna Lee might. She's in the workroom if you want to check with her."

"Thanks. I will."

"You bet."

He entered the workroom and found Anna Lee staring out the garage windows to the street. "Everything all right, Miss Anna Lee?"

"Oh, yes. I'm woolgathering. What can I help you with, Trevor?" Anna Lee stood up and stretched, shaking out her legs.

"First, everything all right with the water pressure?" He didn't want to jump to Paige right away.

"Yes, perfection. You did good work. Your daddy would be proud."

"Well, thanks for that. It's a high compliment."

"What did you honestly come for?" Anna Lee's eyes pierced his.

"I was looking for Paige. I'm surprised she isn't here today."

"Ah, Paige. No, she asked for someone to trade her days."

"Why? Did she say?"

"I'm not sure how much she wants me to share. Have you tried calling her?"

"No, but I sent a text last night. She didn't reply."

"Oh, my stars and garters. What is it with you young people and all this texting? Pick up the darn phone and call someone," Anna Lee huffed.

Trevor wondered if she was mad at someone else for not calling and taking it out on him. "You're right. I should and I will. Did she say anything about me? I know I shouldn't have turned and left the other day. That wasn't the right thing to do."

She raised an eyebrow at him.

"I know, I know," he continued. "I've been kicking myself ever since. And I'm pissed I missed her when she dropped off the check. Thanks for that, by the way. You could have mailed it."

"Hmm, I thought it might help the two of you if you talked. Paige mentioned another girl there…" she let the rest of her thought remain unsaid.

"She brought that up?" he asked. "That was my sister."

"Did she know it was your sister?" Anna Lee tilted her head.

"I don't think they introduced themselves."

"Well, that might be part of your problem. She shows up at your house and there's another girl there?"

"Technically, it's not my house." Trevor explained. "That was my dad's place. My sister lives there now. I haven't changed the mailing info on the invoices yet. It's easy to pick up work mail from my sister's. I love to stop in and see her and her boys all the time, anyway. I thought it was fine, until Friday."

"Yeah," Anna Lee began. "I'm sure it doesn't sound like a great idea now. Maybe, just maybe, Paige jumped to a wrong conclusion when she dropped off the check. And maybe, just maybe, that's why she didn't respond to you last night. I don't know for a fact, only speculating." Anna Lee started walking towards the flower cooler in the corner. "All I know is that Paige's next scheduled shift is on the calendar in my office."

Trevor smiled at Anna Lee's back. She was an incredible person.

"Thanks. Maybe I'll see you whenever Paige's next shift is. And I'll probably come in the day before to buy a dozen roses."

"Maybe you will. And while I would usually say that roses sound like the bee's knees, Paige's favorite flowers are peonies. If you were shopping for her, that is."

"Ah, thanks for that tidbit. I'll be shopping for peonies." He smiled and turned for the door.

"Pink peonies, Trevor!" Anna Lee called after him.

He raised his arm with a thumbs up sign.

CHAPTER THIRTY-TWO

PAIGE PICKED MACEY up for lunch and shopping. Just like in school, Macey was waiting on the front steps when Paige arrived. She was the only person Paige knew that was always ready ten minutes early.

Closing the car door, Macey held up her phone. "I have a list of ideas for lunch. I was thinking we could go to the buffet, Subway, or Phil's. What are you in the mood for?"

"I say Phil's," Paige put the car into drive and pulled back onto the street. "It's downtown and then we can shop. I want to pick up gifts for my new roommates. We can go into the bath boutique and the gift shop."

"Sounds good." Macey began to mess with the radio tuner. Paige had stopped her audiobook when she pulled up in front of Macey's and now the car was quiet. "I would love to meet your roommates. Maybe I can get down to see you before school starts. This summer will be over before we know it."

"Always. Glad I picked up the extra job waiting tables; it's helping to fill the time."

"What about Trevor?" Macey asked. "He's helping to fill the time too, right?"

Paige sighed. "About that." She then told Macey about his running out of In Bloom and seeing the pretty brunette at his house.

The words poured out of her, and she finished the humiliating tale in the five minutes it took to drive downtown and park.

"Oh no. I can't believe it." Macey responded after Paige brought her up to date. "I'm surprised he had such a strong reaction about the internship. On the positive side, he obviously doesn't want you to leave, so he must really like you. On the negative side, no call, no nothing. That's not cool."

"He sent me a text last night. I didn't reply." Paige felt sheepish now, telling Macey. "Not sure what to say. I hoped we'd have a real conversation. You know, face to face. Sometimes it's harder on the phone. Texting or talking."

They arrived downtown and Paige found a parking space next to the fire department, not far from Phil's. They were greeted in the restaurant by a former classmate who sat them in a booth by the front window.

Macey glanced at the menu quickly. "I always get the chicken salad sandwich here. Anyway, back to the Trevor conversation, I agree, that should be an in-person conversation. Maybe you should text back and suggest that."

Paige browsed the menu. Now that her mind was on Trevor, nothing sounded appetizing. "Maybe, can we change the subject for now?"

"Sure. So, tell me what's going on with Rick."

"Not much. We went to dinner last night and caught up. Afterwards, drove around and stopped to watch a baseball game. Just old friends catching up."

"Come on," Macey groaned. "Rick's an old boyfriend, not just an old friend."

"I don't really think about him as an ex-boyfriend. We dated for a such brief time."

The server came and took their orders. Paige decided to have whatever Macey was having.

"Your lies are your own," Macey said with a twisted smile. "You dated a year. Which in high school is a lifetime."

"Can we talk about your love life?"

"Not when yours is so interesting! Besides I don't have one. After college, I will be sent off to who knows where to teach for two years so I don't want to get tied down here."

"Ouch. That's my issue with Trevor." *Dang it, that slipped out! I didn't want to talk about him or Rick.* "Same issue with the internship."

"But your internship is only a few months. The Teach For America commitment is two years. You'll be back in no time. And if each of you can make a trip or two to see the other, it'll fly by."

Paige shook her head. "What if they offer me a job? I'll have the credits to graduate in the spring. If they offered me a job, I could stay there. Come home for the graduation ceremony, then turn around and go back."

"But is that what you really, really want?" Macey leaned forward. "We've known each other since we were five. Moving to New York never came up–not once–until a few months ago. You know, after you and—"

"Please do not say his name," Paige put her head in her hand. "I'm listening. I really am. You're right. I've been flighty this year, changing plans. But it's fine to change plans when you have new information, you know?"

"Certainly. As long as you're true to yourself and not changing based on someone else's agenda." Macey laid a hand on Paige's. "That's all I'm saying. And I'm not saying this to hurt you. I just want you to do what YOU want to do because deep in your heart you know it's the right thing to do."

A woman in a yellow sundress passed by the window, the bold and happy color caught Paige's attention. Paige took a deep breath and exhaled. Macey was right, she needed to be honest with herself. Needed to decide what she wanted for herself, not for what Caleb might have wanted. Not for what Rick may want now. Not even for what Trevor wanted. She needed to know what she wanted first and stay true to that. Then the right relationship would complement her life, not be her life.

AFTER LUNCH AND shopping with Macey, she was home by four p.m. Her parents were taking Logan to an action movie after dinner, which left her free for the evening.

Paige checked her phone to see if there were any more messages from Trevor. None. Oh well, she didn't have the energy for the conversation she had to have with him. She would see if Rick was available instead.

PAIGE: Hi–R U still open tonight?

She watched her phone and saw the three dots showing he was typing. She waited a few seconds before seeing his response.

RICK: Heck ya! I'll pick you up 45 minutes. Dress sporty.

Sporty? What did that even mean? She looked through her closet and found a Pontiac Township High School Softball t-shirt. She was proud to have made the team her freshman year. It was her first and only high school sport. She pulled it on with a pair of shorts and tennis shoes. If she was woefully under dressed for whatever Rick planned to do, she'd make him wait while she changed.

He didn't even bother knocking tonight. He walked through the back door and yelled hello. He was wearing a polo, shorts, and tennis shoes. Expensive tennis shoes.

Paige and Sue sat at the kitchen table, drinking iced tea. Sue offered him a glass, but he refused. "Are you ready to go, Paige? We sort of have a timeline to keep."

"A timeline? That's interesting. Is this outfit all right?" she asked. "I can change."

"It's perfect. Let's go. Night, Mrs. Bell. I won't keep her out too late."

Paige rolled her eyes at her mom and followed Rick out the door.

"I wasn't sure what we were doing," she said.

"Well, it's a surprise. I hope you like surprises."

"Normally I do. But I'm a bit nervous tonight. Is this going to require some sort of athletic prowess?" she asked.

"Here you are, wearing your freshman softball t-shirt, and you're worried about athletic prowess?"

"Well, duh," she responded playfully. "I have little athletic ability, as you know."

Rick was a high school star athlete. He lettered in all the sports.

"That's not what I remember," he teased.

"Rick," she shrieked, "you can't talk like that. My parents could have heard."

They got into the car, laughing. Rick backed out the driveway. "Do you regret not doing it when we were going out?"

Paige thought she would audibly gulp. Wow, what a question. "No, I wasn't ready then."

"That's fair."

"So," she changed the subject, "what are we doing tonight?"

"Bowling!"

"Are you serious? That's what you call sporty?"

"Hey it's a sport. And I don't think it will stress your athletic prowess."

"Leave it to you to be so considerate." Paige relaxed. This was going to be a fun night.

CHAPTER THIRTY-THREE

PAIGE WOKE ON Wednesday morning with her brother Logan sitting and bouncing on her bed.

"Mom told me to wake you. Don't be hating on me," he said when Paige tossed her pillow at him. "It's 9:30."

"Shoot. Really? I'm surprised I slept this late."

"Were you up late smooching with Rick?" Logan started making kissing sounds on her pillow.

"You're a child," she said. "Get out."

He left, and she rolled out of bed and stretched. She picked her phone up off the nightstand. Three text messages, all from Rick.

> **RICK:** Good morning, Sunshine!

> **RICK:** I know you go back to Bloomington today–do you have time for lunch?

> **RICK:** Make time. I promise it will be worth it.

No messages from Trevor. Paige was disappointed. He made the one attempt Monday night and there was nothing since. She should have texted him back on Monday, or at least by Tuesday morning. Now he was probably assuming she was no longer interested.

Well, she thought, *it was fun while it lasted. But it's better this way. We weren't compatible.* She thought of how easy it had been to talk to Rick and hang out with him the past few days. Maybe there was something to that first love being a true love thing. The weird thing was Paige could almost picture herself dating Rick again. Maybe their timing had been off the first time. Maybe this time would be different.

He was ambitious, a go-getter. She wondered if he would consider moving to New York at some point. If she stayed there. She thought about coming back home to Pontiac and settling down. No, Caleb was still here. That would not work.

She got in the shower and considered Rick's lunch offer. She had plenty of time. It was only a forty-five-minute drive back to Bloomington. Yes, she had to be up and at the coffee shop at five a.m. Thursday morning. But as long as she was back in Bloomington by nine p.m., she'd be fine.

After the shower, she sent a text to Rick.

> **PAIGE:** Lunch would be great. Let me know what time.

Downstairs, she found her mom in the kitchen. She grabbed a "Got Milk" coffee mug and filled it with black coffee.

"Morning, hon. What are your plans for today?" Sue asked.

"Rick asked me to lunch. So, I'm going to lunch. Then I'll pack to go back. Anything you need me to do before I go?"

"No. Do you think you can stay for dinner before you go? You haven't spent a lot of time with your dad or brother. We can call Brian and Lily up, put them on a video call, and maybe we can nail them down on a date for their wedding."

"That would be helpful, and yes, I can stay for dinner. But I'll head out shortly after. I work at Max's at five in the morning." She sat at the table and put her phone down, checking for a response from Rick.

"Well," Sue started, "you've spent a lot of time with Rick the last few days. What's going on there?"

"I don't know, Mom. It's been a needed diversion. I haven't had to think about Trevor a lot. Rick has been super fun and sweet. Familiar is the right word, I guess."

Sue made a humming noise. "Sounds," she paused, "safe."

"That sounds so blah. I wouldn't say safe. Safe compared to what?" Paige's irritation rose, she wanted to pick a fight.

"Safe from having to confront Trevor."

"I don't see a reason to confront him. He is obviously pretty childish with relationship matters. Yes, I should have told him about the internship before the party, but he shouldn't have run out without talking. And then the girl at his house the next day. Obviously, I thought our relationship was further along than he did. I mean, I absolutely started having feelings for him. But that's me. And that's silly. I don't have time for feelings or a relationship. I need to go to New York in the spring."

"Need to? Or get to?"

"What do you mean?" Paige was confused. "Working on the relationship?"

"No. Going to New York. You said you *need* to go. Do you really? You just made it sound like something you weren't looking forward to." Sue stood and refilled her coffee cup.

"Oh, obviously I get to, and I want to go to New York. It's what I've been dreaming about for so long!" When was her mom going to understand?

"Didn't this internship idea just come up in January? I'm not trying to be confrontational; I'm only wanting to make sure you are looking at everything from all angles. Even the hurtful angles. That's what mature people do in relationships all the time."

Paige blew out a breath of air and knew it was the most imma-
ture thing she could have done. Her phone indicator beeped, and
she grabbed the phone, thankful for the distraction.

> **RICK:** I need to take a late lunch, does 1:30 work?

> **PAIGE:** Sure, want to meet in town to save time?

> **RICK:** Ah, you want to spend more time with me…. sweet. No, I'll get you.

Paige put her phone down and looked at her mom. "I hear what
you're saying, but it's been days! And nothing."

"Nothing?"

"Well, he sent one text Monday night, but I couldn't respond-"

Her mom cut her off. "Because you were out with Rick."

"Well, yes. And, sure, I could have texted when I got home
even though it was late, but I chickened out. The conversation we
need to have is too hard to do over the phone. Texting or talking."
Paige looked at the clock on the wall. It would be hours before
lunch. She hoped it wouldn't be hours talking to her mom about
this. "Don't you teach a class today?"

"Not during the summer. Stop changing the subject."

"Does Dad need some help in the studio?"

Sue set her coffee cup down on the table and walked behind
Paige. She put her hands on Paige's shoulders and started kneading
gently. "Oh honey, you are tight. Your shoulders are full of stress."

"Yes, because we're having this conversation, Mom! Look, I
don't know what's going on with Rick, but I like it. It's fun. I don't
have a reason to see Trevor again. He's done at Anna Lee's shop,
so that's over and I'm just trying to be happy. The breakup with

Caleb hit me hard. And it was a good reminder that I shouldn't get too serious about anyone right now. I'm too young." She finished her coffee and considered another cup.

"I don't know what you mean about too young. Love happens when love happens. Your dad and I were eighteen when we eloped. Our parents thought we were too young, and it was the only way we could see to stay together with your dad's art school scholarship in Chicago. It wasn't easy. It wasn't perfect. But we made it work. With blood, sweat, and tears at times, but we made it work. That's what you do for love."

Paige suppressed a groaned. "I think you and Dad are exceptions to most rules. Thank you for the advice. I hear you. Maybe things will look different when I get back to Bloomington, but right now, I'm in a good place. I'm going to go out to the studio and visit Dad. Should I take him anything?"

"Yes, take muffins. He'll have coffee in the studio."

PAIGE FOUND HER dad sitting in a chair, staring at a huge blank canvas. "What are you seeing, Dad?"

"It's still forming, Pumpkin. I can't articulate it yet."

"Can I sit with you for a while? It was getting stuffy in the house."

"Fighting with your mom again?"

"Not fighting. Disagreeing."

"I see. Boy trouble?"

"Isn't it always?"

"Anything I can help with? I know a thing or two about young men. Having been one. Having raised three, well, two so far. Logan is still growing into a young man."

"That's the truth. Sometimes I think he's seventeen going on twelve."

He laughed. "Exactly. Now what young man trouble are you having? The Rick kind? I have to admit it surprised me to see you spend so much time with him this week."

Paige smiled. "We're going to lunch today, too."

"Ah, I see. Rekindling an old flame. Not easy."

"I don't think we're rekindling an old flame. Simply hanging out."

"Has he tried to kiss you?"

"Dad!" she laughed. "Does a peck on the cheek count?"

"Counts. You may not think you're rekindling something, but I am guessing he is."

"Hmm." Could her dad be right? Could Rick be interested in more than just friendship?

"Care to elaborate?"

"No. Not yet. At lunch today, I'll look closer for signs."

"Paige," he said, raising an eyebrow, "that makes three days in a row. Rekindle much?"

"You're as bad as Mom. I'm going to go pick on Logan."

PAIGE WAS ON the front porch reading a book when Rick pulled into the drive at 1:15. She raised a finger to him, signaling him to stay put, then she tossed the book inside and grabbed her purse. She didn't want Rick talking to either of her parents who were in the kitchen.

"Sorry for being a few minutes early. Hope you don't mind. My appointment finished earlier than I expected," he said when she jumped in his car.

"Not a problem. I was reading. Where are we going for lunch?

And I'm buying today by the way. Wherever we go. Shoot, maybe I should have said that after you said where we're going. Now you can take advantage of my offer."

"I'll always do that," he laughed. "I won't allow you to buy lunch, and I'm taking you to Jonie's Diner. They have the best chili and I'm craving a chili dog."

"Chili? It's too hot for chili. And I'm buying lunch. No arguing with me."

"Never too hot for chili. You speak blasphemy."

Paige giggled. "Do you even know what that means?"

"Didn't I use it correctly, Ms. Dictionary?"

"Well, if you consider chili sacred, you used it appropriately. Is chili sacred to you?"

"As a Midwestern male, heck yes!"

"You are very funny. I miss that about you."

"You miss me, and you want to spend as much time with me as possible." Rick smiled, then sighed. "I wish you came home more often."

Paige looked at the dash, confirming the air conditioner was on. It felt like the temperature was rising steadily in the car. She had been reading Rick wrong. He was more serious than she thought.

Her thoughts turned to Trevor and the way he ran out the door at her party at Anna Lee's. She thought things with him were getting serious, but he chose to run rather than talk to her.

"Home more often? Um," Paige stammered. She loved home, and she loved Bloomington. She hoped she would love New York as well, but she hadn't lived there yet. Did she want New York because she loved it or because it was far away? "I've got a lot going on with working two jobs."

"Sounds like a poor excuse to me. I can make more of an effort to come see you, too." He parked the car in front of the diner and turned to her. "Paige, I think we should get back together."

Her jaw dropped. "What? Rick, that's…"

"Crazy I know. It's only been a few days together after several years apart."

"I wouldn't say *together*." Paige's stomach flip-flopped.

"Fine. We've been seeing each other for three days, not *together*. But that's not my point." He raked his hand over his short hair. "Spending time with you made me remember how much I care about you. I always have. Ever since the first day of high school when I met you. I was the new kid in town, and you were sweet to me. It was great dating you. But then I got comfortable and cocky and decided it was time to see other girls. But none of them were you and by the time I figured that out, you were with Caleb. When I heard that you two broke up, I was ecstatic. I've been waiting for you to come home to see you again. I know it's only been a few days, but I think we are perfect for each other."

"Rick," she tried to interject.

"No, hear me out first. You have a year of school left, you get your English degree and then you can come home to teach. We'll get married next summer, and you can take the summer off to settle into our new house before school starts. It'll be perfect."

Paige's head spun. Marriage? Rick? A new house? Teaching?

"Rick, teaching is not on my radar. I told you I plan to work in publishing. When I graduate, I won't even have the certification to teach. I switched away from being an education major. Look, this is way too sudden. I thought we were just having fun, old friends catching up. I am sorry if I gave you another impression. Besides, I told you I've been seeing someone."

"Right, and you told me you haven't heard from him in days. Didn't seem like that was going all so well." He let out a long breath. "Look, I'm sorry. I'm coming on hard, I know. But you're going back to Bloomington today, and I want to be honest with you. I'm serious and I'm not one to make rash decisions. I want you to know how I feel. Take some time, think about what I've said, we could make a great life together. Here."

Paige thought about "here." Pontiac. Home. Close to her parents. A couple hours from her brothers in Chicago and their growing families. Her future nieces and nephews. Home had a lot of appeal. This is what she had always thought she'd have. She and Caleb had planned to live in Illinois, possibly Peoria or Champaign or Bloomington-Normal. Close to their families where they could get good jobs. That was back when Paige thought she would teach and write. But Caleb shattered those dreams when he called off the engagement.

Her head swam with thoughts of kismet and destiny. It was maddening to rely on someone else when planning your future. Better to take control and only rely on yourself.

Rick continued talking. "I've shocked you. I can tell. Don't answer me now. Take some time and think about what I've said. I'm not looking for an answer today. This isn't an official proposal or anything. I don't have a ring. But I would like to try again. See where this takes us."

He pulled into the parking lot of the diner. Paige's head spun, and she wasn't sure she could eat anything. She managed to eat a bag of French fries, dipping them into her chocolate shake, enjoying the mix of hot and cold, sweet and salty.

She steered the conversation to Rick's dealership and sales quotas, all the while images of Trevor fluttered through her mind. She should have texted back Monday night or she could have called. Hopefully, he would be receptive to that when she got back. He did text after all.

PAIGE HOISTED HER duffel bag onto her shoulder and grabbed her tote bag with the other hand. She took everything out to her car and tossed them in the front passenger seat. She returned to the porch where her parents sat with after-dinner drinks in hand.

"Well, I'm off," she said as she leaned over to hug her dad. "Thanks for letting me come and hang for a few days. I needed the time to relax."

"Anytime you want to come home, you come home," her mom said as she stood to embrace her only daughter.

They stood in each other's arms for several seconds. Paige closed her eyes and inhaled, loving her mom's familiar scent of hay, brown sugar, and lavender. A country kitchen and open spaces.

"I will. Love you," Paige replied. "I'll text you when I get to the apartment."

The large ice ball clinked in her dad's whiskey glass. "Do."

Her mom followed her to the car. Paige opened the driver's door and turned to her.

"Paige," her mom took a deep breath, "reach out to Trevor. Talk to him. I think you're letting fear hold you back. You deserve to know, and not speculate, what happened at his house. I know that coming home and seeing Rick was comforting, but a well-lived life requires risk. It requires following your dreams and not settling."

"Mom," Paige whined.

"Think. That's all I ask. You have a quiet car ride ahead of you. Think about what you genuinely want. Even if that means taking risks. You deserve to have a full life. Full of passion, adventure, and big dreams. Don't settle for easy and familiar."

"I'll think about it." Paige didn't tell her mom that Trevor was all she thought about when she was alone. Or how frustrated she was with herself over the roller coaster she put herself on after Caleb's abrupt breakup. It was only a month later when she jumped at the idea of a New York internship for the summer. Once she declared that her plan, she hated to back away from it.

That wasn't like her. A declaration, her word, was final. There was no going back.

That's why she reapplied when the summer opportunity fell through. But now that she'd met Trevor, she was hesitant to go. But without telling him, without being open and honest with him, she messed things up.

"You'll think about thinking?" Her mom's eyes danced.

"Yes, I'll think. And I'll text when I get home." She didn't think there was anything new she could think about, but she had nearly an hour in the car.

"That's my girl."

Paige did a three-point turn in the drive and drove down the long lane. She watched the trees swaying in the breeze. At the end of the drive, she turned west, heading toward the interstate that would take her south to Bloomington and, perhaps, back to Trevor.

CHAPTER THIRTY-FOUR

PAIGE CLOCKED IN at Max's and tied her apron strings around her waist. She yawned and reached for a coffee cup, filling it with ice cubes and then pouring coffee on top, watching the ice cubes dissolve as soon as the steaming coffee hit them. She blew on the cup cautiously and took a sip. The caffeine jolt was exactly what she needed.

The hostess started filling her section as fast as her legs would carry her. By five minutes after six, Paige had three tables, and she was rushing. The movement helped wake up her tired body and raised her mental alertness.

Her tables had turned over by 7:00 a.m. and Paige wondered if things would slow down after this round of customers. She picked up two orders in the kitchen and walked through the swinging door with the tray over her shoulder. She saw movement out of the corner of her eye. The table in the corner had been seated while she was in the kitchen. She looked over to acknowledge the table and her breath caught when she saw Trevor.

His eyes held hers with a hesitancy she didn't recognize in him. Was he worried that she wouldn't talk to him?

She nodded at him slightly and delivered the hot food to waiting customers. One customer asked for hot sauce; she grabbed the bottle and a pot of coffee. She made the rounds to all her tables to ensure none of her customers were waiting for anything, and then she reluctantly went to Trevor.

"Hi," she said, filling his waiting coffee cup.

"Hello, Paige. I hope you're not upset that I ambushed you at work. You've been hard to track down this past week." He smiled hesitantly. Her heart beat a little faster. He was here. That meant something. Something positive, she hoped.

"I went home for a few days."

"Home, huh? Seemed sudden."

"I had a few days off in a row, so it was time for a visit." Paige would not bring up what happened at his house on Friday. "Are you ready to order?" She glanced over her shoulder at her section, wanting him to see that she didn't have time to chitchat.

"Only coffee this morning. Can we get together later and talk? I think we've had a misunderstanding that I want to clear up."

Paige raised an eyebrow. Misunderstanding? The beautiful woman at his house while he was showering didn't seem like a misunderstanding to her. "I don't think that's a good idea. If you're not going to eat, I can leave this check with you." She filled in the price of coffee with tax and ripped the diner check from her pad. She laid it on the table, and he covered her hand with his.

"Paige. I can tell you're upset. And I think you think my sister is someone she's not."

"Sister?"

"Yes. My sister Tricia was at the house Friday when you stopped by. That's who answered the door."

"Oh."

She knew he had a sister. But that didn't explain everything. He said he lived in an old farmhouse, not a brick ranch. This wasn't adding up.

"Look," she said, "I need to make the rounds. I'll be back."

She refilled coffee cups, picked up dirty dishes and delivered customer checks. She smiled and chatted with Doug, a regular customer that she had grown fond of already. He was a retired, widowed English teacher and they loved to talk about literature.

After taking a new order to the kitchen, she came back to the dining room and picked up a coffeepot. Customers needed their coffee this early of a morning. She stopped at Trevor's table first. "Refill?"

"Yes. Can I please take you to dinner tonight? I owe you an apology for leaving without talking to you last week. That made me look like an idiot. I overreacted. But you've given me the cold shoulder since and I want to know why. Why the radio silence?"

Her spine tightened up. She was giving *him* the cold shoulder? Trevor was the one that ran out of her party without a word. Sure, she didn't text him back after his brief text Monday night, but did that count as "radio silence"? She bit back the retort on her lips.

This wasn't the time or the place for this conversation. She was at work, and she would not act unprofessional. "Fine. Dinner tonight."

"Great," he smiled, and Paige could see relief on his face. "I'll text you later with the details."

NICA DANCED INTO Paige's bedroom. "You got flowers!"

Paige put the straightening iron down on the dresser. "I did?" She wondered if Rick had sent them. She really needed to have a conversation with him. While meeting up with him when she was at home was a nice distraction, he was not the one for her. She had to let him know before things went any further.

Nica bounced on her feet. "Yes, you did. Come on. Let's read the card."

Paige followed her to the kitchen. On the table stood a ceramic vase with a mix of pink peonies, white roses, and strands of ivy providing pops of green. "Did these come from Anna Lee's?"

"Yes, Tilly delivered them."

"Good." Paige didn't think Rick knew the name of the flower shop she worked at, but maybe he asked her mom. That would also explain why it contained her favorite flowers, pink peonies.

"Are you going to read the card?" Nica pointed at the tiny white envelope sticking up from the center of the arrangement.

Paige took a deep breath and grabbed the card. The flowers were beautiful, but she had to have a talk with Rick.

She opened the card and read the inscription. "I look forward to seeing you tonight and seeing if we can get on the same page, Paige. Trevor."

Paige smiled at Nica. "Trevor sent them."

"Fabulous! Does this mean things are back to normal between you two?"

"Not yet. We're going to dinner tonight. He came to the coffee shop this morning and asked me to go to dinner to talk. But the flowers are beautiful, aren't they?" She leaned over to take a deep breath of their sweet, intoxicating scent.

"They're gorgeous. If I were to guess, I would say Anna Lee made it herself. She's such an artist. Are you going to take them to your bedroom?" Nica asked.

"No. I think they're beautiful here on the table. I need to finish getting ready, though." She looked at her watch. "He should be here soon."

Paige was sitting at the table ten minutes later, admiring the flowers again. She was ready to go with her purse on the chair next to her.

Trevor knocked on the door and she called for him to come in, pulling her purse strap on her shoulder and grabbing her keys off the table.

"Hi," he said, with a half-smile on his face. His eyes were cautious. "I see you got the flowers."

"Yes, thank you very much. They are gorgeous. Did you know peonies are my favorite?"

"A little bird in a purple dress told me they were. Are you ready?"

Nica came in from the living room. "Hey Trevor, how's it going?"

"Great. How are you, Nica?"

"*Bien*. Excited to have the apartment all to myself tonight. Izzy is on a date." She turned to Paige. "With the cute bartender from High Jinks, the one she met Thursday night."

Paige's eyes enlarged. Shoot. Would Trevor catch the reference and realize they were in the same place on Thursday?

He turned to her and raised an eyebrow. He'd made the connection.

Paige busied herself by putting her cell phone in her purse. As much as she wanted to hear Trevor's explanation for running out of In Bloom, she knew she had a few things to explain to him as well. High Jinks, Rick, the internship. This could be a long night. "That's terrific. I can't wait to hear how that goes. See you later."

She walked towards the door and stepped in front of Trevor. He put his hand on her lower back, following her out. "Sounds like we have a lot to talk about at dinner."

CHAPTER THIRTY-FIVE

TREVOR TOLD HER what time he'd pick her up for dinner, but he didn't tell her he was taking her to his house. He didn't want server interruptions, restaurant noise levels, and other customers to disrupt their conversations. They had a lot of ground to cover. He was determined to end the night with no further misconceptions or misunderstandings. He knew he needed to address his behavior at the flower shop when he walked in on her party and promptly walked out. It wasn't going to be pretty, but he needed to talk about his abandonment issues.

After opening and shutting the truck door for Paige, Trevor settled himself in, started the truck and grabbed a sucker from the bag on the seat.

"Where are we going to dinner?" Paige asked in a soft voice.

"A quiet bistro on the east side of town," he replied.

"Oh," was all she said. He waited for her to speak, but when she didn't, he let the conversation drop.

Ten minutes later, he pulled into the long driveway and sneaked a peek at Paige. She was looking at everything at once, the drive, the trees, the old white house with a covered front porch that needed updating. He wished he had put a bench or a flower pot or something on it to spruce it up.

"What's the name of this bistro?" she asked.

"Trevor's Treehouse," he said, letting the name roll off his tongue. He was proud of coming up with the name on the spot.

Her head whipped around to him. "This is your house?"

"Yes. I told you I bought an old farmhouse and was fixing it up. Hence, the old farmhouse that needs fixing up." He grinned at her but saw the confused look on her face.

"But the address Anna Lee gave me—the brick ranch?"

"That was my dad's house. The business mail continues to go there. I gotta update it. Anyway, my sister moved in there with her two boys after our dad passed. I usually hang out with them on Friday nights, we order pizza, and I take the boys to the park to let them run off steam and give my sister a break." Trevor stopped the truck and turned off the ignition. "Ready?"

"Yes," Paige answered quietly. "I have many disjointed thoughts flying around in my head. I feel like I spent all night in a fantasy novel and now I'm having trouble figuring out what year it is and what land I'm in." She opened the door and jumped down.

Trevor came around the front of the truck. "You're in the land of Lincoln."

Paige laughed. "Right. Illinois."

"Come on in," he said, taking her hand cautiously. "I am warning you—there is still a lot of work to be done. Promise you won't judge too harshly."

"Promise," she replied, following him to the back door. "You have an enormous yard."

"Yes. Plenty of room for my nephews to zip around on their battery-operated cars. Come in." He walked into the house first, holding the door open for her.

They walked into a large kitchen. It would be a perfect movie set for a 1980s sitcom. The cabinets were white with oak trim. The countertop had white ceramic tile whose grout had seen better days. There was a wallpaper border above the cabinets and all around the kitchen in a green ivy pattern.

"Wow. I take it you haven't done a lot of work in here," Paige said with a teasing lilt to her voice.

"I know it's hideous, but it actually functions well. I've focused on the things that don't work first, like knob and tube wiring and corroded pipes."

"Knob and tube what?"

"Wiring," he answered. "Early twentieth century technology. The house was built in 1910 and the wiring and pipes were original. Unfortunately, the kitchen is not original. I think they remodeled in the seventies or eighties. Remember, no harsh judging."

Trevor led her through the dining and living rooms on the first floor. He didn't brag to Paige, but he was proud of the work he'd completed in them–the newly stained woodwork and freshly painted walls. A smaller room, next to the living room, that he was using as a home gym had free weights, a bench, and a treadmill. Paige murmured her admiration in each room.

Upstairs, Trevor showed her three bedrooms and one shared bathroom.

"The bedrooms are big," she observed. "I'm surprised at all the guest beds. Do your nephews stay with you a lot?"

"Not yet. It's not safe enough. But I'll be prepared when they do."

Trevor led the way back down the stairs and into the kitchen. "I hope you're hungry," he said, gesturing Paige to take a seat at the small table.

"I could eat," she said.

"All right." He grabbed a loaf of crusty Italian bread from its wrapper. "I have a lasagna warming in the oven. Let me slice up some bread and I'll plate up dinner."

"Lasagna? Did you make it?"

"No, I ordered it. Brought it home after work and put it in the oven before I came to pick you up."

Trevor dished up the lasagna and set the plates on the table. "Smells delicious," Paige said.

"I hope you like it. Trevor's Treehouse could use a positive Yelp review." Trevor's eyes scrunched at the corners as he smiled. "Let's eat."

They ate dinner while Trevor talked about his plans for the house. He knew there was a serious conversation coming, but he didn't want to ruin their appetites by jumping into what needed to be said too soon.

After dinner, Trevor put the leftovers away and washed their dishes. He enjoyed talking to Paige while he worked. It made the cleanup fun. As he put the last fork in the dish drainer, he turned to Paige and asked if she'd like to sit outside to talk.

Outside, with the sun sinking down and the temperature cooling, they sat on a two-person bench swing hanging from a giant oak tree in the backyard.

"First," he said, shifting in the swing to where one leg was on the bench, and he could face Paige while pushing the swing with one foot on the ground, "I want to apologize for Friday night. It must have been a shock for you when Tricia opened the door."

"Yes, it was a shock," Paige agreed, looking down at her hands. "But it wasn't only her. You'd said you had a farmhouse, and that was a brick ranch. I thought you'd lied to me about the house. If you lied about that, what else would you lie about?"

"I didn't even think about that. I have to get the letterhead changed on my invoices. But anyway, is that why you went home over the weekend? To get away from me?"

"Partially," Paige said slowly. "I went to clear my head. After the party at Anna Lee's, I didn't think you wanted to have anything to do with me."

"Well, if you were shocked to see Tricia on Friday, I was shocked walking into your party on Thursday." He stopped pushing the swing, and they stopped moving. "You had talked about the internship, but I'd hoped that you'd change your mind about going. It was wrong of me to presume that. I should have brought it up before Thursday. I really, really like you Paige and I thought you had feelings for me too."

"I do have feelings for you. And," she stressed the word, "I want to do this internship. I'm interested in publishing. I don't think it has to be one or the other."

"Why an internship in New York? Can't you work in publishing from here? Can't you continue the freelance work that you've done?"

Paige paused before answering. "Freelancing scares me. I don't like the uncertainty of it. It's better to have a steady job with a steady paycheck and benefits. I'm going to go to New York because I already accepted the offer, and I won't go back on my word."

"Okay. Okay," he said. He paused. "I understand keeping your word. Admire it even. Tell me more about your fear of freelancing."

"I told you my parents never had steady incomes. We had a lot of tough times, financially. My brothers and I started doing whatever odd jobs we could to have our own spending money for the clothes we wanted, books, other stuff as soon as we were old enough. I think it's why we're all driven. Why we seem to be all geared towards corporate-type careers. Though with Logan, who knows?" She laughed softly.

Trevor noticed Paige was twisting the ring on her right hand again. He wondered if she even knew she was doing it. He needed to ask the next question, though he didn't want to. "Are you concerned with me being a plumber?" Did she look down on him for being a laborer and not a corporate worker?

She paused before answering. "Well, I don't actually know how steady the work is. I know plumbing is important and tough work. I don't know if you have long dry spells…" her voice trailed off.

Trevor was relieved to hear her words. "Paige, I work hard, I do a good job, ensure my reputation stays stellar so I don't have dry spells. However, that doesn't mean there won't be in the future. But I know how to hustle. I watched my dad hustle. He was a single father, and he ensured we had food on the table and whatever we needed."

"We had food, we had what we *needed*, don't get me wrong. Mom gardened and canned food. She always said, if we work with nature, nature will take care of us. I don't mean to make it sound worse than it was, but there were lean times. And I started working young to have my own spending money. I just," she paused and looked up, locking eyes with Trevor, "I want to have control. Power over the situation."

Trevor nodded and reached for her hand, the one with the ring. He pulled the hand closer so he could grab it with both of his hands. "Hey, I get it. Thanks for explaining it. I won't stand in your way, Paige. Ever. You want to go to New York for the internship, I'm here rooting for you. If you needed to go to South America for work–wait, for a work trip, not a relocation!" He smiled. "I'm for it. I want you to do what you want to do, and I hope there is a place for me there too. Plumbing is a relocatable skill. If it comes to that."

"Wow. You'd consider that?" she paused. "For me?"

"Yes, I would. It would require a conversation first. I happen to love Central Illinois. My sister and nephews are here. This is home. But I love you too, Paige." There, he said it. No turning back now.

"You do?"

Trevor smiled. "For a smart girl, you ask a lot of questions. Yes, I do."

"Why?"

"Didn't I just say you ask a lot of questions?" he teased.

"You said a lot, not too many. Besides, how do you think I got so smart?" she said with a teasing lilt.

"You got me there," he responded, shifting closer to her on the swing. "Well, you're kind, smart, and interesting. And it doesn't hurt that you're beautiful."

He wanted to say more but didn't have the right words. How do you say I love you to someone who's probably read all the great love stories, written by lovers of words? He was only a plumber, after all.

"Where did you go?" she asked softly.

"What?"

"Just now. You went somewhere. In your mind."

"See," he said, "another thing I love about you. You can read me. Like a book."

"And?" She wasn't letting him evade the question.

"I was thinking that you've read a lot of books. You probably have great expectations about how a man should confess his love to a woman. And I'm sure I'm falling short."

"Ah," she sighed. "Dickens."

"What?"

"Nothing," she said, letting out a long breath. Trevor did not want to hear what she had to say next. "I don't need pretty, romantic words—"

"What do you need?" he interrupted.

"Time," she paused. "Time to think. I'm sort of shocked at how tonight has played out. It's sudden. We haven't known each other that long."

"Three weeks. To the day."

She shrugged with her free hand. "I can't decide on a new used car in three weeks."

"I get it. Take whatever time you need. But know that I'm in this for the long-haul, Paige. When you go to New York in the spring, we'll make it work. I can come for a couple of visits. I've always wanted to see New York. Visit," he stressed.

"That would be nice. I mean. If—"

"Don't say it."

"Are *you* reading *me* like a book now?" She smiled. "How did you know what I was going to say?"

"In this situation, no *if* was going to be followed by anything good."

"Well, you may be right."

"I'm right."

"Fine. I won't say it. Let's leave it, as that would be nice." Paige hesitated; she knew she needed to say this next part but wasn't sure if it would be enough. "And I need to apologize to you for not responding to your text Monday night. I wanted to talk to you face-to-face ever since you walked out of In Bloom. That's why I went to your dad's house and it's why I didn't respond to the text. Things are so often misunderstood over the phone–texting or talking–and I knew we had a lot to talk about. But that's no excuse. I should have called you over the weekend, instead of hiding away at home." She looked down at her ring, hoping for strength.

"Hey, Paige. It's okay. I shouldn't have run out on you. Let's call it even and we'll both do better communicating going forward, okay?"

"Yes, I agree. We can communicate better." She yawned and covered it quickly with her hand. "Sorry, I should get home. I have an early shift at Max's and then I work at In Bloom. I'm trying to pick up extra shifts this week since I was home for a few days."

"Sure, sure. I'll take you back. Speaking of home, how was your visit? Did you spend a lot of time with your parents?" Trevor hoped the answer would be a simple yes.

"Yeah. I spent time with them."

He heard a hesitation in her voice but didn't want to probe too hard. "I'd love to meet them sometime." He pulled her to her feet and started walking towards the house.

"Trevor," Paige took a step but halted. "Since we're clearing the air. I have a couple things to share." She pushed her hair back over her ear. "I saw you at High Jinks Thursday night. I was there with Nica and Izzy. Nica mentioned it at the apartment." She paused and he nodded. "Anyway, I saw you at the bar, drinking. Looked like you were pounding a few shots, so I didn't want to approach you. I didn't think it was a good idea."

Trevor clenched his free hand. "That was probably best. My head was not in a great place then. I needed some time to think and a little tough love from my sister."

Paige gave him a half smile. "Tough love, huh?"

"My sister can tell it to me straight," he said. "She can put me in my place when I need it. And she did."

"Siblings are great for that." Paige hesitated. "I hope you're not mad that I didn't approach you."

"No, not at all. Don't worry about it."

"Good." She sighed. "I have one more confession."

Trevor tensed, he dreaded hearing what she had to say.

"When I was home," she continued, "I ran into an old friend. An old boyfriend, actually. We hung out a bit."

"Your ex-fiancé?"

"No, not him!" Paige shook her head. "A guy I dated before him. The first guy I ever dated actually. His name is Rick. Like I said, we hung out a couple times, but I'm not interested in him, not romantically. It was just fun connecting with an old friend."

Trevor felt a pang of jealously, but looking into her eyes, he felt he saw her heart. There was no deception there, he trusted her saying that it was just an old friend. He smiled. "Thanks for being honest with me. I'm not happy that you hung out with an old boyfriend, but after the way I took off Thursday, I can understand it. If you're sure you don't have feelings for him."

Paige replied quickly. "I don't."

"Good. And like I said before, I would really like to meet your parents." He tugged on her hand lightly and started walking.

Paige looked up at the house as they walked towards it. "That would be nice. I'd like to meet your sister, officially. And your nephews, too."

"Right! I forgot to tell you. I'm planning a cookout on Father's Day. They'll be here. I hope you can come."

"I plan to go home to spend time with my family."

"I assumed that. The cookout will be in the evening. Seven-ish. Could you drive back in the late afternoon and come?"

"Yes, we eat brunch together. My brothers, Jack and Brian, will want to get home Sunday afternoon too. Evening will work. I look forward to meeting your family."

"Good. Now," he stopped walking and turned to her, putting his hands on her shoulders. "Paige, I know I was a jerk running out of Anna Lee's last week. I'm sorry about that. Seeing that celebration, seeing the joy in your eyes, it took my breath away. Which surprised me. I didn't know I was falling in love with you until the thought of you leaving rocked me to the core. It was an overreaction. I rarely run when times get tough. My dad taught me to be a better man than that. But," he took a deep breath and looked at the ground, "sometimes, that little boy whose mom left him rears up and takes control."

Paige gasped and threw her arms around him. She started rocking slightly, squeezing him. Trevor rested his cheek on the top of her head and held on to her, taking all the strength she was giving him.

CHAPTER THIRTY-SIX

IT SURPRISED PAIGE to wake before her alarm Friday morning. With a sigh, she turned off the alarm. It was only ten minutes early and it would be helpful to have an extra cup of coffee before she left.

She got in the shower and replayed the evening with Trevor in her mind. She wasn't ready to declare her love, but she had strong feelings for him. He took his job seriously and did quality work. He was attentive to her in a way that even Caleb hadn't been, and he helped to take care of his sister and nephews. Paige was looking forward to meeting his family. And every time she was around him, she felt the lure of her attraction to him. She wanted to lose herself in his gaze and run her hands through his slightly shaggy hair. Don't even get her started thinking about the rest of his body.

Tiptoeing into the kitchen, she looked at the flowers in the center of the table again and sighed. She leaned over the table to breathe in the sweet smells from the bouquet. When she saw the flowers yesterday, she thought they were from Rick. Frowning, she knew she'd need to deal with him soon, but probably not today. Today she had a full workday.

She moved to the counter to make coffee, glancing at her watch. She heard a door open and chided herself for making noise.

Nica walked through the living room, towards the kitchen. "Morning, Paige."

"Sorry to wake you. I was trying to be quiet."

"It's all right. I'm a light sleeper. This is good. I can go for a long run this morning. Need to move my legs. Make a full pot of coffee, okay? And I want to hear about last night. What happened with Trevor?" Her eyes shifted to the flowers on the table.

"It was amazing. He took me to his house for dinner."

"He made dinner?"

"No, he ordered dinner. But he showed me his house. And explained that the house I went to on Friday had belonged to his dad, but his sister lives there now. That's the beautiful woman who answered the door." Paige looked away from Nica, feeling sheepish while admitting her mistake.

"See? I told you not to jump to conclusions! So, what happened? Did you kiss and make up? Did you do more than kiss?"

"No! We talked. We cleared up some things. Shared some things. It was very eye-opening. I'm still processing it. Not ready to share more yet. And I have another problem to deal with."

"What, *Chica*?" Nica got a coffee mug from the cabinet and handed Paige her to go mug.

"Well, when I was home, I ran into an old friend. An old boyfriend and we hung out a few times." Paige took the creamer from the refrigerator and put it on the counter by the coffeepot. "I thought it was simply two old friends catching up, but he thought it was more. I need to make it clear to him I'm not interested in rekindling anything."

"Oh. That's a wrinkle. Did you tell Trevor?"

"Yes, I want to be completely honest with him." Paige was glad she told Trevor about Rick, if they were going to get better at communicating, they had to be honest about everything. "Rick, he's the one I saw at home, texted me three times last night. I need to talk to him."

"Yes," Nica chuckled, "yes you do."

"Well, it's going to have to wait. Two shifts today. I'll see you at In Bloom."

Paige filled her travel mug and grabbed her purse, leaning over the table to smell the flowers one more time.

PAIGE PUT HER laptop and a notebook in her tote bag and sat on her bed to pull on a pair of sandals. After her four-hour shift at Max's Coffee Shop that morning, and a full afternoon at In Bloom, it was a relief to have her feet out of tennis shoes. She tossed a hoodie in her tote bag in case the air conditioning was cranked up in the library. She wanted to spend some time there working on the latest freelance assignment.

She glanced at her planner on the bed beside her and reviewed the day's to-do list. "Call Rick" was on the list and as much as she didn't want to, it would be better to get it over with before going to the library so she could concentrate on the assignment for Garland Wilson Publishing.

Rick answered on the second ring, "What's up, Buttercup?"

Paige groaned, "When did you get so cheesy?"

"I think I've always been. You just didn't notice before."

"That may be true."

"I texted last night-" he said.

"I know," she cut him off. "Look, I've thought about what you said the other day. About continuing to see each other and seeing where things go."

"And?"

"Rick, I like you. You are an amazing guy. You're funny, driven and have your head on your shoulders. All things I appreciate."

"But..."

"But I don't have the sparks for you, and I want you to find someone who does." She paused.

"Wow, that's not what I wanted to hear."

"I know. I'm sorry."

"Don't be sorry. I know it probably seemed impulsive."

"Well, yes, it did. But even if we'd spent the week together, it wouldn't have changed things for me."

"Is it this other guy?" he asked. "The one that didn't contact you last weekend?"

Ouch, that stung. Rick had a few similarities with Trevor. Both were funny, confident, outgoing. But her feelings for each man couldn't be more different. She saw Rick as a friend. Someone she dated back in high school.

She thought about Trevor. He was the one she had sparks for. Sparks and more. She could see a future with him. She could daydream about marrying him someday, having children with him someday, growing old together someday. He was the one that made her think about life outside of a career.

"Yes, that's part of it. But not the main reason, the main reason is…" she began.

"You don't have the sparks for me." He laughed softly. "You know most people say, 'don't have the hots for you'. You're so dang cute, Paige. I hope this other guy knows how special you are."

"I don't know about that," Paige muttered, though it was clear Trevor acted like he thought she was special.

"Hey, friends?"

"Yes, friends," she agreed, relieved.

"Great. Take care, Paige. I'll see you around."

Paige hung up the phone and scratched "call Rick" off her to-do list.

CHAPTER THIRTY-SEVEN

PAIGE PICKED UP all the shifts she could for the next nine days. Luckily, another server at Max's was on vacation and she picked up several shifts throughout the week.

On Father's Day, she drove home for brunch with the family. It was wonderful to be with all three of her brothers in the same place at the same time. She got to talk to Jack and Becca about the expansion of their family, and she told them she had a list of baby names from literature if they were interested.

Brian's fiancée, Lily, confirmed that Caleb would be at their wedding. Paige didn't hide her groan. Lily promised that she would do everything she could to minimize their interactions. Lily asked Paige if she'd have a date for the wedding and Paige knew that she'd have a date, even if she had to hire one. No way was she going to be at a wedding where her ex was without a date.

It comforted her when Lily told her that Caleb and Moria were having a "rough patch". She wouldn't provide any details, but it amused Paige slightly and she admonished herself for the feeling.

Leaving her parents' house late in the afternoon, her mom followed her to her car carrying a homemade apple pie. "Take this to Trevor's party with you."

"Thanks, Mom. You didn't need to do that. Trevor told me not to bring anything. He knew I was out of town today."

"You don't show up at a party empty-handed. I raised you better than that." Sue put the pie on the floor in front of the passenger seat of Paige's car.

"I have soda in the trunk!" Paige exclaimed. "I wasn't going empty-handed. You *did* raise me better than that."

"Good girl. Now, go and have a great time. Trevor was very thoughtful to have a party late in the evening to allow you to spend time at home with your family and then time with him too."

"He didn't do it just for me. He said several friends would be with their dads today."

"Tell yourself what you want, hon. I love you. Drive safely."

PAIGE PULLED UP to Trevor's house a little early, but it still surprised her to only see Trevor's truck in the drive. There was going to be a party, with other people, right?

She grabbed the pie and a case of soda from the trunk and walked to Trevor's backyard. Trevor was arranging chairs around a fire pit.

"Hello!" he called, setting a chair down and rushing towards her.

"Hi," she said. "Mom baked a pie. I brought soda."

Trevor took the case of soda from her hand and sat it on the picnic table. "What kind of pie?"

"Apple."

"I love your mom already."

Paige laughed. "She's pretty cool."

They could hear a car coming down the driveway. Paige set the pie on the picnic table and turned back to her car. "I have more soda in the trunk."

"Let me get it," Trevor said, walking beside her. "Oh, that's

Tricia and the boys. I'm shocked they're early. They're never early." He laughed softly.

"I bet it's hard getting two young boys ready," Paige replied.

They walked to Tricia's sedan and waited for her to climb out. "Hello again," she said, looking at Paige. "I'm Tricia."

"Great to meet you *formally*. I'm Paige," Paige held out her hand.

"Girl, we're not formal like that." Tricia stepped forward to hug Paige. She then turned and lifted the older boy out of the backseat. Once he was on the ground, Tricia nudged him. "Waylon, say hello to Miss Paige, Uncle Trevor's friend." She drawled out the word with a raised eyebrow.

"Hi, Miss Paige," the adorable boy held out a hand.

Paige laughed. "Well, hello Waylon. It's very nice to meet you." She shook his hand.

"And this is Willie," Tricia said, lifting the two-year-old out of his car seat. "Willie, can you say hello to Miss Paige?"

Willie didn't answer. He leaned forward and held out his arms for Paige. Paige reached for him and brought him to her. "Hi, Willie. I'm Paige."

"Now, that's adorable. You're a natural," Trevor said, looking at her with a heat in his eyes that Paige wanted to bottle.

Two more cars pulled into the driveway, and they made their way to the back of the house, boys, bags, and soda in tow.

It wasn't long before Paige wished name tags had been issued. After meeting Hank and his wife Jennifer, Aria and her husband Devonte, Louisa and her girlfriend Kelsey, and the singles–Hawk, Rob, Natalie, and Chase–she was having a hard time keeping Trevor's friends' names straight. She kept calling Hawk, Hank and vice versa.

Hawk was Trevor's oldest friend. They met in fifth grade when Hawk and his family had moved in next door. Paige liked him immediately; he had a laugh that could be heard above the noisy din of the group no matter where he was in the yard. He was a software programmer at State Farm and volunteered at a youth crisis center. Paige asked him about his work there.

"It is the most rewarding experience I've ever been a part of," Hawk said, swatting at a mosquito on his wrist, nearly spilling the beer in his hand. "It can be absolutely heartbreaking at times though."

"Why did you decide to volunteer?" she asked.

"They saved my life," his light blue eyes clouded with pain, "and I wanted to give back."

"How do you mean?"

"My parents divorced when I was thirteen and I was lost. I was angry and bitter. I didn't see the divorce coming. I thought things were fine. Then one day my dad announced at dinner that he was leaving. He packed a couple bags after dinner and left. My mom was shocked, we were shocked. She went into a deep, deep depression. She seemed to forget we, my brother and I, existed. It was bad."

"Wow, that's terrible. I'm so sorry that happened to you." Paige thought about Lauren. If she came back from Europe without finding love, Paige would consider trying to set her up with Hawk. He was handsome, smart, and full of compassion.

"Hey, thanks. It sucked." He looked over to where Tricia's boys were squirting each other with water guns. "I started getting into fights at school, had a few run-ins with the police that I'm not proud of. It could have turned ugly quickly but one of the cops that caught me out *way* past curfew one night saw the chip on my shoulder and took the time to intervene. After taking me home and talking to my mom, he started coming by in his free time to take me to the center and hang out, play basketball, introduce me to other kids my age going through similar things. He was a godsend. If it wasn't for him and the center, I believe I could have ended up in jail or dead."

"Where was Trevor in all this?" Paige looked around for Trevor as she asked.

"We had lost touch. After my dad left, mom couldn't afford the house we lived in next to Trevor's. So, we moved to subsidized housing and I was in a different school district. We reconnected a couple years later. It helped when we got our driver's licenses and cars. Speaking of cars, did Trevor tell you about the time we took a school bus for a joyride?"

He said this as Trevor walked up to Paige with a fresh glass of iced tea. "No," Paige responded, looking at Trevor with a raised eyebrow. "Please go on."

"No, not today, my friend," Trevor interjected. "You've been monopolizing Paige's time long enough. Its time she mingled with the others."

Trevor led her over to Louisa, Kelsey and Chase who were setting up to play a game of cornhole. "Have you played bags, Paige? Chase is looking for a partner."

"Yes, I have."

Paige stood by Louisa during the game and enjoyed getting to know her. Louisa owned a bakery in uptown Normal and had met Trevor in high school when they were chemistry lab partners. Trevor was the first person Louisa confided in when she decided to come out. They double-dated to prom, both wearing tuxedos.

After the game of bags, Paige spent time commiserating with Chase about their defeat. Natalie strolled over and Paige could see the attraction between the two. She speculated that it wouldn't be long before Chase asked her out. She made a mental note to ask Trevor about helping move that potential relationship along.

Paige sat with newly married couple Devonte and Aria, who held hands and couldn't stop smiling at each other. They shared their wedding stories and highlights of their Hawaiian honeymoon. Trevor was a groomsman and Devonte recounted how Trevor had instigated a surprise after-party in a hotel conference room after the reception. Trevor asked permission to use the room and proceeded to bring in a giant cooler filled with drinks and a portable karaoke machine. Aria said that the after-party was a blast and she appreciated Trevor's foresight to set it up.

When the party finally wound down, Paige offered to help Trevor clean up. Tricia had left an hour before to get the boys in bed. Running around the yard chasing fireflies had worn them out.

Trevor protested lightly, but Paige insisted. He had friends pick up cans from the yard before they left. In the kitchen, they fell into a comfortable rhythm, putting food away and wiping down the counters.

"What a fun night. Thank you for inviting me. It was great to meet your family and your friends. This was a very enlightening evening," Paige teased.

"You have to take those stories that my friends shared with a grain of salt. They were trying to see how far they could push their luck."

"With me or you?"

"Definitely you. They know how far they can go with me. I hope no one was too annoying."

"No, but I would like to hear more about that joyriding incident."

Trevor grabbed her around her waist and leaned on her back. "I love watching you work in my kitchen."

"Because this is where a woman belongs?" Paige asked with an edge to her voice.

"No!" he said, lifting his arms and backing up. "No, ma'am!"

Paige turned and smiled. "Right answer."

Trevor smiled at her. "Hey, I would love to see you watching TV in my living room, and eating in my dining room, and—"

"Whoa. Hold that thought Mister."

"And reading on my front porch! I swear that's what I was going to say!"

Paige laughed. "That's more like it. But you don't have any furniture on your front porch."

"I'll work on that." He pulled her to him in a tight hug. "I'm very glad you were here tonight. What's your schedule like this week? Can I take you out?"

"My schedule is pretty full. When do you want to go out?"

"Every night?"

"Every night?" she repeated.

"Am I being pushy?"

"Maybe. I don't *not* like it."

"For being so well read, you talk in riddles sometimes."

Paige laughed. "I need to go. Early shift tomorrow."

"Max's?"

"Yes."

"I'll try to make it in for breakfast. If I don't see you, I'll text you later in the day."

"Sounds good." She tried to step out of his embrace, but he held her tighter. "Um, Trevor."

"Mm-hmm," he said, resting his head on top of hers.

"Are you falling asleep on me?"

"No, trying to memorize this moment." He pulled back and looked down at her. "I love you."

Paige wanted to say it back to him, but she couldn't. She wasn't ready. Instead, she stretched her neck and put her lips on his and kissed him with all the passion she contained. Would her physical attraction to him to be enough until her heart was ready to attach itself to him? When it was ready to be vulnerable enough again.

IN HER BEDROOM after Trevor's party, Paige called Macey to talk, but got her voicemail right away. Excited to share her growing feelings for Trevor with someone, she texted Lauren.

> **PAIGE:** Morning (your time)! Had a great night meeting Trevor's friends and had to share. I think I could fall for this man!

Paige put the phone down on the bed and looked over her planner for the week, not expecting a quick reply from Lauren. Even if she was awake, she was probably doing something amazing.

Coming up this week she had five shifts at Max's and four shifts at In Bloom. Trevor wanted to take her out Friday and Saturday night and Tricia planned a picnic for them on Sunday. Her calendar was full and so was her heart.

Her phone beeped.

> **LAUREN:** Marvelous! Happy for u!

> **PAIGE:** How's the travel? Meet Mr. Right yet?

> **LAUREN:** No. But I'm going to Spain today. Perhaps love will find me there!

Paige thought about Hawk again and hoped Lauren would come home single.

> **PAIGE:** remember our bet, if you're still single, I set u up

> **LAUREN:** we shall see, gotta run

> **PAIGE:** safe travels

CHAPTER THIRTY-EIGHT

SUE'S KITCHEN WAS bustling on the 4th of July. She was overseeing and participating in an assembly line decorating three hundred sugar cookies with red, white, and blue icing. They had started at ten a.m. and were rushing to finish on time to leave for the county park, where Sue would sell them to the holiday fair attendees.

Jack, Becca, Brian, Logan, and Paige were regulated to "backgrounds," meaning they were only allowed to cover cookies with a solid layer of a single color. Lily, Trevor, Sue, and Frank would then decorative them with lines, stars, and other finer details to make them 4th of July festive. All the helpers were "auditioned" by Frank to see who had artistic flair and who needed to stick to the simple spatula work. Paige was proud when Trevor took his place among the decorators. She and her brothers had never been allowed to don the "decorator" hat.

The room smelled like vanilla and sugar. Oh, the sugar. Between the cookies and the icing, there were calories for days wafting from the open windows. The noise level in the kitchen was intense, and the laughs were constant. It didn't take long for the family to warm to Trevor and he was fair game when it came time to dishing taunts and light-hearted insults. Trevor held back for the first couple of hours but pulled off his figurative gloves and let loose on Paige's brothers as good as he got.

Trevor showed off his creative chops to Frank and Sue's delight. He drew a squirrel holding a sparkler on one cookie and showed it to the group.

"Oh Trevor, that's great! I hate squirrels, but I love that cookie. Too cute!" Sue said as she grabbed his arm.

"You've got talent, kid," Frank said, looking over the details.

"You hate squirrels?" Trevor asked.

"Yes," Sue replied, brushing her bangs back from her forehead, "they dig in my flower beds hiding their nuts or looking for nuts or just being nuts."

Paige's cell phone vibrated in her back pocket, and she stepped back from the table and peeled off her plastic food gloves to answer it. It was Macey asking if they needed help. "Yes, please come!" Paige answered. "You can join the decoration team. We are out-pacing them two to one and there's no way we'll finish on time at this pace."

Macey promised to be there in twenty minutes and hung up.

"The cavalry is on the way," Paige announced to the room.

"If by cavalry, you mean a team of twelve decorators, we should be fine," Frank responded.

"Sorry, no. I think it's only Macey."

"Dang, Paige, you may have to step over to our side of the table and help us," Frank declared.

"No. Not. Can't. Won't," she protested. "I tried that two years ago, and you yelled at me the entire time."

"I have a solution!" Sue chimed in. "I have red and blue star sprinkles. If it comes down to it, you can shake them on the cookies, Paige!"

"Are you sure, Ma?" asked Brian. "Won't that devalue your cookies if Paige goes anywhere near the decorating side?"

Trevor laughed but jumped to Paige's defense. "Hold on now. I'd pay double for a Paige-sprinkled cookie."

"Aww," Sue said. "That's sweet, Trevor. How much cash do you have on you? We'll figure out how many cookies Paige can decorate right now."

The others laughed, and Paige rolled her eyes. She was thrilled that Trevor was quick to stick up for her. She appreciated the way the family had accepted him into their group so fast. She knew if they were laughing and joking with him; they liked him.

The conversation turned towards Brian and Lily's upcoming wedding plans. Paige was pleased that they had nailed down the date–October 24th. She was thankful it was in the fall. She wouldn't need to come home from New York to attend. Lily told the group that her brother, Philip, would be the D.J. for the party and that she wanted everyone to send her the songs they wanted to hear at the reception.

Frank rattled off several songs with "love" in the title. "I've got songs for you! 'Let Your Love Flow' by The Bellamy Brothers. Or 'Love Train' by The O'Jays. Or my favorite, 'Love Will Keep Us Together' by Captain and Tennille."

"Dad!" Brian said. "No one wants to hear your sappy 70s songs at our wedding."

Sue laughed. "There will be older people there that would love those songs. And I think the idea of songs with love in them is adorable. We could move into the 80s and go with 'Love Shack' or 'Modern Love' or 'Higher Love'. Those are all great."

"Whoa. Whoa. Whoa." Brian threw up his hands. "For the love of everything holy, do not, and I repeat, do *not* let Philip play 'Love Shack' at my wedding. I beg you! I hate that song. Hate it like it kicked my butt on the first day of school."

Macey entered the kitchen through the back door. "I brought reinforcements!" Her mother, Judy, and sister-in-law, Lisa, walked in behind her.

"Hallelujah, we may make it in time," Sue said, as she rushed to greet the newcomers.

"Judy and Macey, you are on the decorating team. Lisa, do you have the skills to decorate, or do we put you on the prep team?" Frank asked as he sized up the newcomer. Judy and Macey had pitched in several years in a row, so he was confident in their skills.

"I decorate Christmas cookies and do pretty well," she answered.

"All right," he replied. "we'll start you on our team. If you can't cut it in the finer details, you get bounced to the dark side."

Ninety minutes later, they had all the cookies decorated and packaged. Everyone took a box to the van and watched Frank and Sue leave for the park. Macey's mother and her sister-in-law followed behind. Macey stayed back to ride with Trevor and Paige.

Paige checked that her brothers had the picnic baskets, blankets, and chairs loaded. They would meet up to watch the live music and fireworks together. Paige and Trevor were responsible for the wheeled cooler of soft drinks and bottled waters, which was already loaded in his truck.

Climbing into the truck, Paige slid into the middle seat and moved the bag of suckers to the floor.

When Macey got in behind her, she grabbed a sucker and said, "Suckers? This is like going to the bank. Can you cash a check, Trevor?"

"Naw, Mace. Sorry. I'm saving all my cash for Sue's cookies. I have to take some home to my sister and nephews–they'll never believe I helped decorate them."

"Oh, I took lots of pictures," Paige said. "I have all the proof you need."

"Awesome! They'll get a kick out of that. So, Macey, what dirt do you have on Paige that I need to know?"

Macey laughed. "She's been my best friend since *forever*. I have tons of dirt, but I'm a faithful friend and I'll never tell."

"That's fair. I respect your integrity. Tell me, what do you like most about Paige?"

Macey paused for a moment. "I love her creativity. She was always the one to instigate our playtime and she would come up with the most elaborate scenarios–we would be swashbucklers one day, princesses the next, and firefighters the day after. Paige could weave the most intricate story lines and set-ups. I always pictured her becoming a screenwriter, theater director or novelist."

"Huh. A side of Paige I haven't seen a lot of. I see the kindness and the driven hard-worker. Would love to see that creative side." he responded.

Paige shifted in her seat. "I create but I don't show many people."

"Yeah?" Trevor asked. "What do you create?"

"Stories. I write when I can."

"That's awesome! I'd love to read something." He squeezed her knee.

"Back up and get in line buddy," Macey replied. She tilted her head back, her blond curls resting on the headrest, and let out a beep-beep noise, like a truck backing up.

Paige changed the subject by asking Macey about her remaining summer break plans.

After the fireworks, Paige and Trevor helped her family gather their belongings and load them in the red wagon that Frank used to carry the cookies across the fairgrounds. After saying goodbye to everyone, they climbed into Trevor's truck for the drive back to Bloomington. Though Sue offered for them to stay at the house, Paige needed to get back to work at the coffee shop the next morning.

On the drive home, Trevor talked about how much he enjoyed the day with her family. Having grown up with only a sister, he loved the natural teasing and competitiveness between her brothers.

"With your brother Brian getting married and Becca having a baby, your family is growing. It's great to see."

"Yes, it is. I love Becca and Lily like sisters already. And I can't wait to be an aunt."

"Does it make you sad knowing you'll be in New York when the baby is born?"

"Yes, indeed," Paige yawned as she answered. "But I'll come back to visit as soon as I can. And we'll be able to video call. Technology helps close the gap when we're away."

"Sure, sure. But you don't get that new baby smell through your phone."

"True." Paige was sad that she would likely be in New York when her first niece or nephew was born, but there would be more in the future. And maybe she would find a career that would keep her in the industry but not require her to live in New York. Coming back home was sounding better and better each passing day. The more her family grew and the more her relationship with Trevor blossomed, the more she regretted leaving.

CHAPTER THIRTY-NINE

P AIGE BLINKED AND it was August tenth. Dates with Trevor, three jobs, several trips home to help with Brian and Lily's wedding plans and the days were flying by. She was thankful to have things under control for the moment.

Fall semester was starting in two short weeks. Her final semester of college classes. The heavier schedule was daunting, but she was confident she'd pull it off. It was Friday and a day she had been looking forward to for two months–Lauren had flown home from Europe two days ago and was expected to come into In Bloom for a visit and to talk to Anna Lee about her fall work schedule. Paige was baking both chocolate chip and oatmeal raisin cookies to take to the welcome home party for Lauren.

Nica walked into the kitchen in her jogging attire–light gray tank top, black shorts, and tennis shoes. "Oh my, those cookies smell fabulous! Thankfully, I'm going for a run!"

Paige removed a cookie sheet from the oven and sat it on top of the stove. "The cookies are going to In Bloom for Lauren's party. Are you planning to stop in?"

"Yes! I should be there before Lauren, around two. Since you're bringing cookies and we know Anna Lee will bake her famous chocolate cake, I'm going to bring a veggie tray. It will be super to see Lauren again. I hope to get to know her better now that she's back."

"I can't wait to hear about her travels. And to find out if she met a guy on her trip. If not, I met a friend of Trevor's that I think will be perfect for her."

"Look at Paige–the matchmaker." Nica stretched her hamstrings, holding on to a kitchen chair. "Why is it everyone in love wants to play matchmaker to everyone else?"

"I wouldn't say that. But speaking of matches, any one new on your radar?"

Nica laughed and threw her head back. "Way to prove my point. And nope. Happy and single. I'll leave the love drama to you and Izzy."

"Hmm, maybe I'll keep scouting Trevor's friends for another match." She winked at Nica. "Speaking of Izzy, when does she get home this weekend? I thought we could plan a shopping trip. Stock up on a few things before things get crazy with classes."

"She'll be back tomorrow morning and she works tomorrow night. Maybe Sunday we can shop."

"Sounds great." Paige began moving cookies to the cooling rack. "See you at Anna Lee's."

"Later, *Chica*."

ANNA LEE HAD the workroom mostly decorated before Paige arrived. She asked Paige to spot her on the ladder to hang the "Welcome Home Lauren" banner from the ceiling. Paige thought the rickety, wooden ladder was as old as the building, but it did the job and Anna Lee safely hung the banner.

Paige asked Anna Lee if anything else needed to be done for the party before she took her place in the retail shop.

"No. Everything is as right as rain here. I hope we have a lull in the store when Lauren gets here so you can join the party. Tilly is coming in at noon to help me with arrangements for a retirement party tomorrow morning. We should have those whipped up in no time."

"Where's the retirement party?"

"A new venue on Market Street. I forgot the name of it. Gotta look in my book. It's a retirement party for a bigwig at State Farm. Expecting one hundred and fifty guests on a Saturday morning, can you imagine? When I retire, I'm just going to lock the door and hang up a sign–'out to pasture'." Anna Lee cackled at her own joke.

"You're not retiring anytime soon, are you?"

"No! As long as I can physically do what I do and the cops don't take my driver's license, I'll be here."

"People love you, Anna Lee, they love your store, they love your artistry with flowers. I'm glad you don't have plans to retire."

"Maybe I'll even get to do the flowers for your wedding one day," Anna Lee's eyes sparkled.

"Ha! That will be a long time down the road, but if I ever get married, I would feel blessed to have you design and provide the flowers." Paige tossed the bag that she brought the cookie trays in over her shoulder and hugged Anna Lee tightly.

"It would be my honor to support your wedding day any way I can. Especially if that wedding involved a certain plumber I know."

"Anna Lee! Don't rush things and don't jinx it."

"Things are going well with the young man I take it?" Anna Lee walked towards the retail shop and Paige followed.

"Yes, they are. We see each other frequently. He's fun and energetic. I love spending time with this sister and nephews. He's met my family and they like him. I don't know what our future holds, but I'm excited to see what happens. I'm pretty confident that we'll manage the time apart with the internship. I'll come back a couple times; my brother's wife is having a baby in February. I'll be home shortly after that. I probably won't make it down to Bloomington then, they'll have the baby in Chicago, but if I do, I'll stop by for a visit."

"You'd better." Anna Lee pulled her order book out from under the register and flipped it open. "Ah, that new venue is called Darrell's. Now, let's get this box of candles and those new teddy bears on the shelves before we open for business.

NICA ARRIVED FIVE minutes before Lauren, veggie tray in hand. She chatted with Paige and Anna Lee in the retail store as they all watched for Lauren to pull into the parking lot which she did a few minutes after two, driving to the employee parking area in the back.

Paige rushed out the back door and hugged Lauren as soon as she got out of her car. "I missed you! I'm glad you are back. We have so much to catch up on. What are you doing tonight?"

Lauren laughed. "Oh my, Paige! You are about to burst. I missed you too!"

"No, you didn't! You were seeing all those amazing places; you didn't have time to miss anyone. But the real question is, did you meet a man? Did you fall in love?"

"No," she paused. "I can't remember. Does this mean I lost a bet?"

"Not a bet per se, but I get to set you up on a blind date and I have a great guy in mind. Now, come on in before everyone has a fit."

Lauren grabbed a tote bag and her purse from the backseat. "Right, now I remember. And since you are seeing Trevor, I can't send you on a blind date. Bummer. Oh well. Hey, I have gifts for everyone. Did anyone new start over the summer?"

"No, not since Nica. You met her before you left."

"Right. Great. I brought a couple extra gifts to ensure I had enough. Tilly's still here, right?"

"Yes and she's in today too."

"Marvelous!"

Inside, they gathered around the worktable and snacked while catching up. Lauren gave each of the young ladies a beautiful makeup bag from Italy, and for Anna Lee, she had a framed watercolor print showing flower vendors in Paris. She thrilled them with stories of her travels and promised to bring in a photo album to show Anna Lee once it was ready. Anna Lee said she had no patience to look at pictures on a phone.

CHAPTER FORTY

PAIGE LAUGHED AT the dance moves her brother Brian was making with his new bride. Trevor walked up to her with a drink in each hand and Paige gladly took the glass of white wine that he offered.

"Thank you. Are you ready to bust a move?" she teased.

"Say the word and my dancing shoes go into overdrive," he replied. He lifted the cup of draft beer to his lips. "Let me get my go-go juice down and I'll be ready to pop and lock."

"What are you talking about? I didn't know you were a fancy dancer, besides being handy and handsome! Is there anything you can't do?" Paige beamed at Trevor and knew what love meant. Sure, the wedding and the vows and the flowers and the music all helped set the mood, but standing in front of Trevor, taking in the way his eyes shone just for her, made the night magical.

The wedding party and happy guests filled the outdoor event tent. Paige saw Caleb and Moria during the ceremony and was surprised that she didn't feel any anger or hurt at the sight of them together. The breakup with Caleb felt like a distant memory. Having Trevor sitting at her side, with his arm draped across her shoulders and leaning into her, had something to do with it. She silently wished Caleb and Moria a happy future together.

The song that Brian was making a fool of himself to ended and Dierks Bentley's "Say You Do" came on. Trevor put his drink down, grabbed her hand, and led her to the dance floor. "Do you know this song?" he asked as he pulled her in close, one arm around her, the other folding her hand in between them.

"No, I'm not familiar with it, but he has a smooth voice," she responded. She was more aware of the feel of Trevor's body against hers than the song that she barely heard over her heartbeat.

"I'll tell ya what else is smooth," he said, using the hand behind her back to sweep her hair aside. His fingers lightly stroked across her upper back, exposed due to her strapless dress, sending a chill down her spine.

"I know you're a smooth talker," she retorted, her cheeks blushing.

"And you like me, you like me a lot." He kissed her lightly on the cheek. "Tell me about your dream wedding. Do you want something like this, a destination wedding, a big event or small and intimate? A three-carat diamond? What?"

"Would you believe me if I said I never thought about it?"

"No," he shook his head. "You were engaged once. Didn't you have some of your plans in place before you broke up?"

"Not exactly. We wanted to focus on finishing school first. We weren't in a hurry."

"Now, the diamond. Tell me what I'm competing with."

Paige took a deep breath. He's going there? It wasn't unreasonable for a wedding to prompt the conversation, but she wasn't expecting it from Trevor, even though things were going well.

"Want to know a secret? I'm not a big fan of diamonds. Sure, they're beautiful, but maybe I've read too many classic novels. I love the Victorian age tradition of giving the bride her birthstone as an engagement ring. Or some other stone that has meaning."

"And your birthstone is a..." he started.

"Well, it depends on what country and historical calendar you're using. For instance, in old Roman traditions, agate was the May stone. And in the old Tibetan calendar, it was sapphire. The modern tradition is an emerald." She smiled. "More than you wanted to know, right?"

"Several options there. But what is your favorite?"

"I'm partial to the emerald myself."

"Well, you never cease to amaze me." He tightened his hold on her and gave her a dip as the song ended.

A fast song came on next. "Is it all right if we mingle for a while?" she asked. "I want to talk to my parents and brothers, and I suppose I should congratulate Brian."

He smiled. "Sure, sure."

Her parents were fulfilling their role as parents-of-the-groom by making sure guests were having a great time. People were congratulating Jack and Becca for their upcoming new family addition. Becca's baby bump was on display and Paige smiled every time she looked at her sister-in-law. She said a silent prayer of gratitude. While she didn't grow up with sisters; she was grateful for the two she had gained by marriage.

Paige led Trevor to her family, who were all gathered near the DJ table. "Uh oh," she said, "this looks like trouble. No telling what they are up to."

"Paige!" Sue said, grabbing Paige's hand and pulling her into the circle. "Remind us what song Brian said could NOT be played at his wedding. Remember, we were talking about it on the 4th of July."

Paige frowned.

Trevor leaned in. "'Love Shack'!"

Sue's eyes lit up. "That's it!" She turned to the DJ and requested that he play The B-52s hit. To Trevor she said, "Look at the big brain on you!" She squeezed his arm playfully.

Paige watched the exchange between her mom and Trevor with a smile. She was excited that they had hit it off so well and pleased when she found out they texted back and forth, sending memes about squirrels and other silliness to each other.

Macey and her date, Ben, joined the group. They met recently at an informational Teach For America meeting on campus. Paige was thrilled to see how happy Macey looked; she was glowing. Macey and Ben returned to the dance floor when Rick approached the group and asked Paige for a dance.

She introduced the two men, then looked at Trevor and raised an eyebrow. He nodded slightly.

Rick put his hand on her lower back and followed her to the dance floor. Paige turned towards him and put both hands up, making it obvious there would be a proper amount of space between their bodies while they danced.

"Your brother's wedding was good," Rick said, leaning close to Paige's ear.

"Yes, it was. He cleans up pretty nice." Paige chuckled softly.

"You clean up nice," Rick said, pulling her closer.

Paige ignored his comment, not wanting to make a scene at her brother's wedding, so she hoped the slow song would end quickly so she could make her way back to her family circle and to Trevor.

Rick plowed on. "I don't understand why you continue to be with that plumber," he said the last word like it was filthy. "You know I'll have my own car dealership in a few years. And I'm growing my rental holdings. I have three houses already. I'll take care of you, and you won't be required to work. You can read and write all day, every day."

Paige smelled the alcohol on his breath. He must have been downing the booze quickly, it was still early.

"Rick, please don't make trouble. It is my brother's wedding. And I'm pretty crazy about Trevor. He treats me well, and he does fine as a plumber. It's a respectable trade. You don't think about it until you need it and then you appreciate his skills." She smiled, trying to keep things light.

"I'll show you skills," he said, pulling her tightly against him.

Paige flushed and squirmed. "Loosen your grip," she spat.

"I'm cutting in now," Trevor said, laying his hand on Rick's arm.

"No, you're not, the song's not over," Rick slurred.

"Maybe not, but it is for you, buddy." Trevor pulled Rick back. "I'm dancing with *my* girlfriend now and will be for the rest of the night."

Paige let out a breath when Rick stalked off.

"Thank you for rescuing me," she said as Trevor pulled her into his arms.

"I didn't rescue you, sweetie. You could handle him. I just made sure he knows your dance card is now full."

"Well, whatever you call it, I appreciate it." She leaned her head on his shoulder and closed her eyes. "I love you, Trevor," she whispered, feeling a tear slip from her eye. The encounter with Rick shook her up more than she realized.

"What did you say?" he asked, lifting her chin to look her in the eye.

She smiled. "I love you."

"That's what I thought you said. It's about time." He beamed. "Didn't think it would take that jerk to bring that out of you. Oh well," he shrugged. "I'll take it. I love you too, Paige. I have for a long time."

Paige sighed, feeling the release of tension. Nothing like a near fight and a wedding to bring the romantic out of even the most guarded hearts.

CHAPTER FORTY-ONE

NEW YEAR'S EVE always excited Paige. She loved making New Year's resolutions and goals. She loved the start of a fresh year, a chance to make improvements and changes in her life. But this year, it meant she was leaving for her internship in ten days, and she was not looking forward to being away from Trevor for four months. Yes, he said he'd visit, he said he'd call, but it was four months. Would he feel the same way when she was out of sight and out of mind?

She put on her lipstick and looked in the mirror. She smiled at her reflection. Fake it until you make it, she thought.

Nica yelled from the kitchen, "Paige, Trevor's here!"

In the kitchen, she found Trevor and Nica talking about refinishing the floors in Trevor's house. He was planning to tackle the worn oak floors soon, and Nica was eager to help. Any chance she could get to help Trevor with rehabbing his old house, she was taking it.

Trevor whistled when he saw Paige and her little black dress. "Wow. You said you had a special dress. I had no idea."

"Twirl for him, *Chica*!" Nica exclaimed, her beautiful smile beaming.

Paige twirled and a shiver run down her exposed back when Trevor whistled again.

"Well, that dress is the reason we need more than one New Year's Eve each year." He stepped to her and rubbed her arm. "I hope you have a heavy coat; it is freezing tonight."

"I do. I have lived in Illinois all my life, you know." She walked to the coat closet and took out her heaviest winter coat. Trevor took it from her and held it up so she could slip into it easily.

"Hey," he said, "I shifted our dinner reservations back. I have to run to the house first. I hope you don't mind."

"I'm surprised you could move a reservation on New Year's Eve." Paige picked up her evening purse. "Not a problem. Izzy made a late lunch. Good night, Nica. Have fun, be safe. I'll be home late, as I imagine you will be."

"Same."

In Trevor's truck, Paige wondered why he was so quiet. She tried to talk about their plans for New Year's Day with his sister and nephews, but he wasn't holding up his side of the conversation. Paige worried that he was having second thoughts about their upcoming long-distance relationship. She thought about Caleb and how she thought things had been going well with them minutes before he broke things off. She shook her head to dispel that thought.

"Hey, what's going on over there?" Trevor asked, reaching for her hand across the seat.

"Nothing. Lost in thought. Sorry."

"Don't apologize. I haven't been helping with the dialogue. Guess my mind was roaming too." He turned into his driveway.

"Did you forget something?" Paige asked, looking up at the house.

"Yes. I did. Would you mind coming in with me?"

Paige thought that was strange. If he needed to grab something, why would she need to get out into the cold?

"No," she responded as the truck came to a halt.

In the kitchen, Trevor took his coat off, suggesting she do the same. "This will take a few minutes," he explained.

Paige shook off her coat and put it on the back of a chair. Trevor took her hand and pulled gently. They passed through the dining room, towards a closed door. The room where he kept his workout equipment. Paige thought it strange that they were heading towards this room.

Trevor opened the door; the room was dark. He pulled her hand for her to step in front of him.

"Trevor?" she murmured, as he turned on the light.

She blinked at the bright light, but even more so, she blinked as she looked about the room. The workout bench, the free weights, the treadmill. They were all gone. Around the room, on three of the walls, stood floor to ceiling bookcases. Beautiful wooden bookcases. In the middle of the floor was a square area rug with muted colors of green and yellow. Next to the door was an easy chair. A chair that was made for curling up and reading. On it lay a beautiful woolen throw blanket. Next to the chair was a side table with a vase filled with the most beautiful peonies she had ever seen, spotlighted by an over-sized floor lamp that Trevor had turned on while she moved into the room.

Paige gasped. "Trevor. What is this? Where is your workout equipment?"

"The equipment has a new home in the basement. This room is for you. Your reading room. I hope that someday these bookshelves are filled with the books you work on in your career. Besides those that you already have and love. And maybe, someday, books that you write."

A buzz of excitement tingled over Paige's skin at the thought of writing. She had been warming to the idea since falling in love with Trevor. He brought out her creativity and curiosity.

She noticed one shelf with several books held in place by a book end. She walked over to investigate. *Fahrenheit 451* was displayed on an iron book holder, the kind you would use in a kitchen for a cookbook.

Paige smiled seeing the book Trevor read on their reading date. "Trevor. This is "amazingly amazing"!" She knew he wouldn't understand *The Hitchhiker's Guide to the Galaxy* reference, yet, but she hoped he would someday.

She sighed; this was the sweetest gesture. Trevor really cared. She was still excited about going to New York, but she was going to miss him.

"I hope you don't think I did this to manipulate you to coming back."

"I didn't-" she started.

"These are bookshelves. Wood and nails. They can be built anywhere. If you decide you love New York, love the work you're doing there, and you want to stay there, we'll make it work. I will lease or sell this house, I will find work there, and we'll make it work. If you decide you want to come back here or go to Chicago where you brothers are, we'll make that work too. It doesn't matter to me where we are as long as we're together."

She turned to look at him, noting he'd been quiet for several seconds. When she turned, he was kneeling on the floor. She felt her heart skip a beat.

"Paige, I will be waiting for you. I want you to have a great time in New York. Learn everything you want to learn at the internship. But remember this. Remember me. I'll be waiting for you. And," he reached into the pocket of his suit jacket, "so you don't forget me. I want to give you this." He opened and held up a ring box. She could see a twinkle of the gem from where she stood.

"I love you, Paige. And, when you are ready, whether that is in six months, a year, two years, will you marry me?"

"Betelgeuse!" she exclaimed. Her head was hitchhiking around the galaxy.

"Is that a yes?" he asked, the creases on his forehead forming a map.

"Yes," she said, "yes". She stepped forward, and Trevor jumped to his feet, wrapping his arms around her.

"You had me worried there for a second, Paige. Why are you yelling out the name of an old Michael Keaton movie?"

"It's not that. I'll explain another time." Tears spilled from her eyes. "I'm shocked. I was worried that you were breaking up with me. Because I'm leaving."

"No sweetie, no. I love you. I want to be with you forever. Here," he pulled back to show her the ring again.

Paige looked at it. It was a green stone, not a diamond. "You remembered."

"Of course. I listen to everything you say, Paige. It's an emerald. It's what you said you wanted."

Paige sighed. "Trevor, you are everything I ever wanted. I love you."

He slipped the ring on her finger. The warmth of his hands on hers spread throughout her body despite her exposed back. "I love you, Paige. Ready to go to dinner?"

Paige laughed. "Um, can I count the number of bookshelves first? Can I move my books in here tomorrow?"

"Yes! Let's overeat tonight, so we have the strength to move all your books tomorrow."

The End

There is a Bonus Epilogue with a very special event for Paige and Trevor five years after *Peonies for Paige*. If you're curious about their lives in the future, please join my newsletter and receive the epilogue by going here: https://dl.bookfunnel.com/ov9hj8py2n

Up next, creative Nica is pursuing a teaching degree to appease her parents, but she dreams of flipping houses. When she meets her handsome, but grumpy, landlord, Grady, they clash over Nica's "fix-it-herself" nature.

Grady must spruce up a flailing apartment rental building or risk losing investors' support. Desperate for a fast and cheap solution, he asks Nica for help. She wants to refuse, but needs a date to a family celebration.

Maybe they'll get everyone off their backs and then go their separate ways, or maybe, sparks will ignite into something neither sees coming.

order *Dahlias for Dominica* today.

WHAT'S NEXT

I hope you enjoyed *Peonies for Paige*! Your honest review will help future readers decide if they want to take a chance on a new-to-them author. Please consider leaving an honest review on Amazon or Goodreads or wherever you normally leave reviews.

Coming up next, Nica's story will be told in *Dahlias for Dominica*. If you like multicultural characters, workplace chemistry, and stories that tackle modern issues, then you'll adore this magical makeover!

Paige was excited to meet Trevor's friend, Hawk, the software developer that volunteers at a youth crisis center. She thinks he'll be a great match for her smart and driven friend Lauren! Be on the lookout for *Lilies for Lauren*.

Tilly's the bubbly one who's trying to get it all together, but a gaping hole in her family tree has her questioning who she is and who she's meant to be. When her big brother's best friend moves in down the block, his nearness brings sparks new questions. Will those sparks bring the answers she's looking for? Find out in *Tulips for Tilly*.

ACKNOWLEDGEMENTS

First, I want to thank my husband, Tim, for supporting my writing dream. Thank you for being my sounding board, my inspiration, and my champion. I don't know what I would do without you. I love you!

A huge shout out to the friends and family members that took the time to beta read and provide criticism and feedback—Uncle Norman, Heidi E., David S., Michelle G., Kathi C., Betty B., Lynn F., Rebecca E., Eva W., Jackie C. and Heather C.—thank you for your kind words, constructive feedback, and brilliant ideas.

Thank you to my cousin Mark for the chat about all things plumbing.

Family is everything and I owe a sincere thank you to my siblings, siblings-in-law, aunts, uncles, cousins, nieces, and nephews for all the encouragement. I love you infinity!

Thank you to the professionals that supported this journey—Jo, Emily, Dr. Jeff, and Rebecca H. for editing services; Renea for proofreading; and Stephanie at Alt 19 Creative for the interior formatting and gorgeous book cover!

Special thanks to Alexa Bigwarfe at Write | Publish | Sell for creating and providing the Women in Publishing Summit, Women in Publishing School, and Book Launch in a Box program. You and your team have been a wealth of knowledge in my indie publishing journey.

And a heartfelt thank you to you, dear reader, for taking a chance on this story from a debut author.

ABOUT THE AUTHOR

Kasey Kennedy is an Illinois gal through and through. She grew up in Central Illinois, graduated college at Southern Illinois University Carbondale and soon after, moved north to Chicago. She's been in Chicago or the surrounding suburbs ever since. 

Kasey is very happily married to her husband Tim and loves nothing more than spending time with him–especially when that involves live music! If not attending a live show, they are usually enjoying evenings on the deck, listening to music; visiting their large families; watching movies; or planning their next trip.

When not dreaming up new characters and new stories, Kasey is reading or planning what to read next. Occasionally, she pulls out the guitar that she has been trying to learn for 30+ years and strums enough to annoy her cat, Pepper.

Keep in touch:

FACEBOOK:

https://www.facebook.com/kaseykennedy8/

INSTAGRAM:

https://www.instagram.com/kaseykennedy8/

WEBSITE:

https://www.kasey-kennedy.com